Avril Cavell is the pen name of a psychologist who began writing in 1983 and published three non-fiction books, with Anne Wollett, about twins and their families. She has published several novels and the two most recent, TWO FOR JOY and THE YELLOW SILK ROBE, are also available from Headline Review.

Also by Avril Cavell from Headline Review

Two for Joy
The Yellow Silk Robe

The Birthday Party

Avril Cavell

First published in 1996
by HEADLINE BOOK PUBLISHING

First published in paperback in 1997
by HEADLINE BOOK PUBLISHING

A REVIEW paperback

10 9 8 7 6 5 4 3 2

ISBN 0 7472 4932 6

Printed and bound in Great Britain

HEADLINE BOOK PUBLISHING
A division of Hodder Headline PLC
338 Euston Road
London NW1 3BH

For my husband, who in equal measure made writing this book possible and impossible, with love.

Chapter One

My wife, who normally won't swallow so much as an aspirin and believes standing on her head doing Yoga is the answer to everything, has a pot of Valium hidden in the airing cupboard and thinks I can't see she's having a nervous breakdown.

Tom Morrissey, financial director of Garcia Goddard International Ltd, lay on his back in the dark and stared at the ceiling, cold, tired and worried to death, his thoughts bringing him out in a sweat as he lay wide awake and alone, at half past five in the morning. Every time he moved, the springs in the brass bed seemed to creak. The squeaking and creaking were creating a problem.

'I don't care what the neighbours think we're doing! Do you think they don't do it too?' he would yelp when Janey retreated further and further away from him, to the edge of the bed.

'We *squeak*,' she whispered, pushing him away. 'They can hear. There's nothing between us and downstairs except floorboards. We can hear them cough and plug the telly in, so they can hear us . . .'

She grew anxious and inhibited, so they squeaked less and less often.

He tried the psychological approach. 'What's *really* the matter?'

'You *know* what's the matter,' she answered. 'We need a new bed.'

He pored over his bank statements, searching for money to buy a good quality divan base, but found nothing in the wasteland of his overdraft. He looked at his Barclaycard. He was overdrawn and over the limit.

'We haven't got any money,' he told her.

Gusts of icy rain spattered against the window, draughts stirring the curtains. At half past five in the morning, in the cold and dark, traffic was already busy along the main road a hundred yards away. A Spanish superlorry with sixteen wheels splashed past, shaking the walls of the rambling, converted Edwardian house in which he lay, as it took a short cut through back streets where it wasn't allowed for the A4, the motorway and the frozen North.

The North, as usual, was paralysed by the fall of a few inches of snow, high winds, deep drifts, black ice on the roads and chaos. The television showed pictures of cars and lorries littering the countryside and motorways, sheep dying on hillsides; farmers, drivers, motoring organisations and British Rail, all taken by surprise, blamed each other and screamed they couldn't cope. Later in the year, it would be leaves on the lines, but autumn was a long way off as he listened to raw February winds howling round West London, flattening snowdrops and crocuses and taking loose tiles off rooftops as he lay trying to blot out facts as grim and unpleasant as the weather.

'Asses,' he muttered from underneath the duvet, meaning Spanish drivers who broke the rules and disturbed people trying to sleep in residential streets where they were forbidden. He peered out with one eye. The digital clock flashed a quarter to six. Tom groaned, turned over, covered his head with his pillow, tried to count dying sheep on snow-covered hillsides and go back to sleep. The more he tried, the more facts unreeled across his mind, a mental loop with a life of its own and no stop button.

Nineteen ninety-four. The country is bumping along the bottom – I am bumping along the bottom and sinking fast – in a recession which is to all intents and purposes a slump, whatever the bloody government likes to pretend. The hell the High Street is picking up. I'm financial director of a company whose business is keeping a finger on the pulse of the retail trade, and I know they're lying. Consumers have no confidence, the housing market is dead and buried six feet under. They're going to reduce MIRAS tax relief and our flat is worth thirty grand less than the joint mortgage we took out seven years ago. We are stuck, stuck, stuck.

Seven years ago, when property was booming, the bank had fallen over itself to lend them money. *Them,* he reflected gloomily, being the operative word. Janey had been in regular work with the Royal Ballet Corps; back row thumpety-thump stuff but she loved dancing and was good enough for the chorus of a major company. Then she got pregnant and that was the end of *that*. By three months she was too big for a tutu and wobbling on her pointes; they were still learning to manage on one salary, to make the money stretch.

He threw the pillow off his head, rolled on to his back and stared resentfully at the ceiling in the half dark from the streetlight below. Negative equity and making money stretch wasn't *living*, it was merely managing. He hated it.

Fierce nostalgia flooded through him, a childish longing for the old days, for when they bought the top-floor converted flat and played at house like children. Besides two small bedrooms under the eaves and the TARDIS, a bright red bathroom just large enough for one person at a time, it had a square kitchen with two big windows, an uneven wooden floor and solid, built-in original oak cupboards that had been used to store apples and pears in winter.

The woman from the estate agency who showed them round was vast-hipped, with a smoker's cough and damp patches under her cardigan from her struggle with half a dozen flights of stairs.

'Look at *this*,' Janey called, ecstatic, opening doors, poking her head into other rooms as he jostled with the estate agent, trying to dodge getting close-coupled between her and the brand new lavatory, itself close-coupled with a midget-sized bath. 'Oh, *Tom*, we have to buy it.'

He found her in the living room, a vast, low-ceilinged, converted attic, light pouring in from four floor-length dormer windows. The attic spanned the width and length of the huge old house, overlooked a jumble of grey slate roofs, chimney pots and television aerials. She flew, enchanted, arms outstretched, to show him, pirouetted with lean, narrow, contained grace, dark hair flying.

'It's perfect. I can practise.'

Tom wandered around, pretending he knew how to spot beetle, damp, dodgy plumbing and other reasons not to buy.

'Needs redecorating and it's more than we want to pay,' he said, talking to himself, running his finger down paint already flaking off new plaster. 'Ten per cent of the asking price is more deposit than we've got.'

'We can paint it magnolia. Soft but bright.'

'Insipid and middle-class.'

'OK, we'll paint it communist red. And we'll ask my parents.'

'I don't want to ask your parents what colour I should paint my walls.'

'Money, Thomas.'

'I want to borrow from them even less.'

'Then I will. I'll call Daddy right now. Darling, it's *perfect.*' She held out her hand.

Daddy rarely refused Janey anything, would see it as a good investment. Which it was. Silently, Tom handed her his mobile phone.

The estate agent cursed herself for not putting a couple of thousand on the price; she couldn't have guessed they'd be so keen. Clutching the mobile, they vanished into one of the bedrooms, to talk loans with Daddy. By the time they emerged, to offer the asking price, she was dying for a cigarette, and wished small, fine-boned, elegantly muscular Mrs Morrissey with her classically even features and flying dark hair would stop getting overexcited, stop showing off and doing the splits, before her jeans did. Denied a cigarette by professional niceties, she told them some of the history of the house instead.

Until early 1986 it had been an Anglican convent, its warren of rooms monastic cells in which a hearty little group of nursing sisters had lived since before the war. Midwives by vocation and profession, they ministered to the pregnant women of Acton and lived, as it were, over the shop, until they woke up one day to a delicious smell and found the youngest baking herself a cake, 'Happy Retirement, Sister Columba' piped painstakingly on its top in pink icing.

'Sixty years old today,' the dark little nun from Havana chirped triumphantly. 'I'm an OAP with a bus pass waiting and not a worry in the world except those stairs and how long it will be before one of us falls down them. Praise the Lord.'

They sang 'Happy Birthday To you' in clear, mellifluous voices, well oiled from years and years of daily practice, then trooped down the main stairs, curved and highly polished with a threadbare narrow carpet in the middle of the treads, for matins in the ground-floor front room which served as a private chapel.

'Very well, ladies.' Seventy-six-year-old Mother Matilda made her announcement at elevenses, popping sponge cake daintily into her mouth with twisted, arthritic fingers that had delivered a thousand babies. 'I know how to take a hint. Time for us to be put out to pasture. I don't know about you, but if the good Lord intends that I should live to his praise and glory until I go senile, then I think He can provide somewhere a lot more comfy than this. With no stairs and proper central heating.' She paused. 'He can provide a lift.'

'Amen,' the ladies chorused, and finished the cake.

Confronted with thirteen selectively deaf, wordly-wise nuns in close touch with their local Pensioners' Rights Group, the Order consulted its most senior management who consulted its solicitor who consulted Savills the estate agents. Astonished by the value put on the old convent, it hurriedly sold the great draughty mansion and large garden to a developer for a price at the top of the market, and relocated its elderly little flock to a modern, purpose-built condominium of sheltered accommodation in Acton, with a lift, central heating, smart kitchens and place of worship accessible to wheelchairs.

In short order, the developer developed luxury flats and sold them at an enormous profit.

The allotments that had kept the sisters' kitchen self-sufficient, and flourished in the care of the Order's two ancient hermits, were first churned by bulldozers and cement mixers, then built upon. The rest became a token garden, a bland expanse of thinly planted flowerbeds and lawn.

Not interested in gardening, Tom and Janey didn't care about the mean flower borders and weedy lawn.

Their attic faced east and west through the four windows that caught the sun and flooded the room with light that shone dully on stripped and polished wooden floors.

Plants, an old leather chesterfield inherited from Tom's grand-parents, Janey's grand piano, a deep red Indian carpet, two armchairs occupied by two Siamese cats and a rocking chair was all the furniture they had, other than a scarred oak dining table from an antique shop in Brighton and the desk that held Tom's computer. Over to the west, at night, they watched lights forming a Jacob's ladder; planes landing into and climbing out of Heathrow.

One west-facing window opened on to a small roof garden. Herbs, green tomatoes and sweet peas flourished in a corner sheltered by a brick wall and wrought-iron railings until the 1987 hurricane blew them all away. They woke to the roaring scream of the wind, stood terrified, watching their garden table and chairs go whirling away, whipped across the rooftops in a hail of chimneys and slates, scattered by the violence of the storm. It was around the time of the storm that Janey got broody.

'I'm twenty-five and fed up with bleeding toes,' she announced one evening, lying with her back to him, his arm round her thin, hard waist, in the brass bed. 'I'm never going to be a prima ballerina. I want to stop dancing and have a baby.' She turned towards him. 'What do you think about a baby?'

'I think babies cost,' he said truthfully.

'You can't turn having a baby into a financial calculation.'

'Babies *are* a financial calculation. A huge one.'

She had dropped the matter at that, gone very quiet.

Then one night she burst out, 'I want a baby so much, I don't know how to keep on saying *no*.'

They had talked and talked, always coming back to the same point, until they agreed to try. He couldn't blame Janey, he thought, lying there in the dark, struggling with the truth. Half of him, despite the dire arithmetic of what a child would cost, and against all common sense, had been broody too.

Janey's parents took out a school fees policy the day Janey found she was pregnant, put Francesca down for Benenden the day she was born.

'I did OK at a comprehensive,' Tom protested when nobody asked his opinion. 'I don't want my daughter at Princess Anne's *alma mater*. Look where it got Princess Anne. *Horses*.'

'It's more academic than it used to be and their results are good. And Princess Anne is into Save the Children and the Olympics, as well as horses,' Janey argued stubbornly, who since she was nine years old had boarded at ballet school. 'She gets to travel all over the world *and* she's the hardest worker in the royal family. What's wrong with that? It's more exciting than being an accountant.'

They glared at each other.

'Being the Queen's daughter might have something to do with it,' Tom snapped.

'I'm sorry *you* haven't got any parents who are over the moon about having a grandchild.'

It was a raw nerve: painful jealousy of the indulgent parents he had never had. His parents had divorced when he was very young, he had been brought up by his mother in bitter, embittered, poverty until the day he had qualified and moved out.

Mrs Morrissey senior lived in Southend-on-Sea, did not know he had a child, and he would not tell her. Everyone else was happy. His wife was happy being a mother, her parents were happy at becoming a grandparents, Benenden was happy with one-week-old Francesca Morrissey on its waiting list. He wrenched his mind into positive mode: *he* was happy being a father, provider and family man, everything under control.

Control. What a joke.

Tom hiked the duvet under his chin to keep out the cold. They had been innocent about babies, naive and unprepared as babes themselves.

Francesca was a sleepy cherub for the first few weeks, Janey a serene and engrossed mother. Immediately her doting grandparents went home, his perfect daughter turned into a fretful monster and screamed with colic. Janey, walking the floor night after night, exhausted and depressed, lost her temper and fell out with the neighbours.

'They complain we're keeping them awake.'

'We do.'

'So what am I supposed to do?' she yelled above the baby's wails.

'Keep her quiet,' Tom answered evenly.

'She won't. She won't bloody *shut up.*' Suppressing a fleeting longing to beat Francesca's head against the wall, she clutched the baby to her, covered her with kisses and went to sleep in the nursery instead, a light, wary sleep, no rest at all, alert in her dreams for the moment Francesca would twitch, startle awake, so that she could pick her up, comfort or feed her, before she started to howl.

'There is a nasty atmosphere in this house,' she said flatly when Francesca was six months old, sitting cross-legged on the floor in leggings and one of Tom's shirts, an empty feeding bottle in her hand, the sleeping child curled like a kitten in her lap.

Tom was watching the Nine O'Clock News.

'They hate me.'

'They don't hate you.'

'While you are at work, I have to carry her and half Boots and Sainsbury's up and down half a dozen flights of stairs. They watch me but no one ever helps. You should try having people watch you from the cracks in their doors, wishing you'd drop dead.'

'They don't wish you'd drop dead,' he said, gazing at Gerry Adams mouthing words being repeated by an actor. 'Why do the government bother with all that nonsense?'

She wasn't interested in IRA censorship. 'I have something else to tell you,' she said, holding the baby like a shield, looking at him over Francesca's head. 'I think the atmosphere here is about to get worse. *Tom.*'

Tom was absorbed in the question of Gerry Adams.

'The pram got stolen from the hall this morning and . . .'

Something in her voice distracted him from Sinn Fein.

'And I'm pregnant.'

He turned. She put her cheek on the baby's soft downy hair, tears sliding from her eyes at the devastation on his face.

'I swear to God, Tom, please, I've been taking the pill.'

'No.'

'But I went back on it too late. I never thought,' she looked him straight in the eye, 'that I could conceive. Not while I was breastfeeding. I swear to you, that's the truth.'

'Twelve weeks and a healthy baby,' a doctor told them in the antenatal clinic, concentrating on the scanner. 'Congratulations.' He beamed with professional pleasure, expecting them to beam back, but Janey closed her eyes, lying on the narrow couch.

Two children under a year. Tom hardly heard the doctor's words through the pounding in his head.

The scan had been two weeks ago.

Three and a half months pregnant and Janey sick as a dog and getting worse. Her doctor put it down to stress.

We have to move, he thought, looking at the flashing clock again. It's time to get up.

His mind circled the problems, obsessed. Twenty thousand short of his mortgage, no money, an overdraft, two children in six months' time, in a fifth-floor flat, and not a chance the bank would lend.

'*I* am going to have a nervous breakdown,' he snarled at the sleet flinging itself at his window. 'Sod Janey's nerves. Equal opportunities in the brilliant nineties means having nerves isn't just a woman's right!'

Sarcasm didn't help; his mental mousewheel flew round and round.

She'd been in the TARDIS for ages. Tunnelling out of the warm duvet, throwing aside his pillow, he could hear her retching. The lavatory flushed, the tap ran briefly and the light clicked out. A door opened and closed quietly as she looked in on Francesca, then she climbed into bed, smelling of toothpaste, and lay very still.

'Stop holding your breath.'

She didn't move.

'Cup of tea?'

'No.'

He yawned hugely. By six fifteen he had to be up, out by seven, fighting the wind and ice clawing at his bedroom window with a sound like scrabbling fingernails that set his teeth on edge.

'Vampires can only come in if you invite them,' he remarked suddenly with black humour. 'Can't they? I was just thinking, the undead have got better manners than babies, haven't they?' Into her stony silence he went on recklessly, 'Babies come swanning along without so much as a do-you-mind or a by-your-leave. Don't wait to be asked. And while we're on the subject of do-you-mind, I want you to know I do mind.'

'I know.'

'No, you don't. I mind because I happen to know you're taking Valium.'

'Imagine this,' she began as though she was on stage about to tell a fairy tale. 'Two babies. Screaming in the same bedroom, the neighbours going mad. Only one room for you to work in and them to play in. No fresh air unless we put bars on the windows and make them so the children can't fall out.'

'Children don't fall out of windows.'

'Yes, they do. Eric Clapton's son fell out of a window. Ours reach right to the floor so they're easy. Five storeys to fall down and five flights of stairs to climb up. Won't I get fit?'

In the silence he could hear himself breathing very slowly.

'Then there's the little matter of a main road right outside the front door. All those fumes and lead.' Janey stopped, then went on,

'No garden to park the pram in, nowhere to dry all the washing. Downstairs will be queuing up to organise a lynching party even more than they are already. We can't afford another baby. We'll end up divorced. I don't want to be go mad *or* be divorced. Tom?'

That they couldn't afford it was true.

'So,' she began again, brightly, 'I asked Mr Singh for an abortion. I did when I first found I was pregnant but he told me to get lost.'

'*What?*'

'I said, I want you to rethink my case. I'm asking you how *your* wife would manage with no money, two babies in an attic flat and people being hostile. It didn't get me anywhere. His wife's probably got six children in Southall and a whole tribe of grandmothers and aunts to help her look after them.'

'You can't have an abortion.'

'Old Singh agrees with you. He looked down his nose at his notes so he didn't have to look at me and pronounced. Playing God. "There are many women who would give anything to have two healthy . . ."' She mimicked the doctor's adenoidal Wolverhampton accent, crossed with a dialect from Delhi learned from first-generation immigrant parents. '"I can't recommend an abortion, Mrs Morrissey, but I'll refer you to our social worker."'

Janey was half laughing with rage.

'When I told him where to stuff his bloody social worker, he went all snotty and said perhaps I would prefer to see his registrar in future. Then he gave me a Valium prescription. I'm fourteen weeks going on fifteen. Soon it'll be too late for a termination.'

Francesca stirred and cried in the next room.

'Here we go.'

Janey got out of bed, shivering. On her way past the airing cupboard she stopped, reached in for a nappy and clothes for Francesca, felt the warm shape of the Valium bottle inside a pile of sheets.

'You're not having a termination,' he called furiously.

She wondered, since he never made beds or changed nappies, how he had found the Valium.

'You're having a baby,' he muttered as she disappeared into Francesca's room. 'I'm going to do something about this mess,' he added to himself, getting out of bed, already late. 'Even if I have to go and rob a bank.'

Chapter Two

Garcia Goddard International Ltd had their head office in Islington, home to the London design trade. An elegant, double-fronted white Georgian house with a discreet brass plate, not far from the Angel but in a quiet side street away from the traffic, it made highly suitable premises for a company that led the industry in international design and retail consultancy.

From his office window under the eaves of the top floor, where there had once been housemaids' bedrooms, Tom Morrissey overlooked a row of long, narrow, leafless North London gardens. By the time the row of clocks on the wall behind the reception desk showed the time in cities where they had offices, London 8 a.m., New York 3 a.m., Tokyo 4 p.m., the building was already busy. On all four floors below him, GGIL hummed with people.

In the room below Tom's, a young Japanese trainee with a smooth, flat, exquisite oriental face sat in careful, silent concentration, rapidly drawing ideograms, translating faxes to Tokyo into his own language. In the basement studio a score of freelance designers were at work, boxes of fabric samples piled around them. Photocopiers hummed, telephones rang, and the smell of fresh coffee drifted from a small kitchen. Someone, arrived from an early flight into Heathrow, whistled and sang in the shower next to the kitchen, and above it all Garcia Goddard's hearty laugh burst from his secretary's office on the first floor.

For a company directly affected by global recession in retailing, they appeared to be doing well. For the first time in several years, the order book looked good, with presentations in four countries due for urgent completion and more contracts coming in.

By mid-morning a white winter sun diffused its heatless rays in a hazy sky, thin ice crackled on puddles formed in gutters by the overnight rain and a dog barked, shivering miserably, from a corner of the pitted Tarmac behind an Islington council tenement across the way, banished by its owner to relieve and exercise itself in the flats' parking lot.

Tom, his jacket slung on the back of his grey executive chair, irritated by the frantic barking, briefly contemplated calling the RSPCA. Keeping dogs in flats should be banned. He forced his attention back to the figures on the computer screen in front of him, groped for the second half of the cheese sandwich he was chewing. Through the open door behind him he could hear Garcia, from his office below, drowning out the wretched Alsatian by shouting at his American business partner, Millie.

'Can't hear you,' he yelled as her car phone crackled, faded, went out, then recovered the connection. She slowed, pulled the BMW into the right-hand lane of the freeway as traffic bunched approaching roadworks chaos, and tried to stay composed.

'Is that any better?'

The hour it took her to drive from her candy-coloured townhouse in Connecticut to their offices in Manhattan was generally a good time for them to talk. This morning, they did – until Garcia's voice rose in frustration to a bellow, followed by abrupt silence, which generally meant he had thrown the receiver down.

'Paranoid bloody woman,' came floating up the stairs.

'Fighting again,' observed Garcia's secretary, Emily. She grinned cheerfully from the landing outside Tom's door, peering over the top of a pile of files and loose typing. She wore oversized, rimless spectacles on the very tip of a short, slightly splayed nose, emphasising plump round cheeks and a prettily childlike face. The glasses slipped.

'Push my specs up, I've got both hands full.'

He reached over and jammed them on her nose. Emily's glasses made Tom edgy, constantly on the alert for the moment they would fall off. She giggled, a hoarse, mocking, Australian chuckle.

'It's happened again, and her who must be obeyed can't stand it.'

'The Japanese.'

When it came to signatures on contracts, the Japanese had an upsetting tendency to reject Millie's because she was a woman. It drove her wild.

'They want to talk to Garcia. They reckon Millie should stay in her rightful place,' Emily chuckled. 'Which is nowhere. She's been yelling and screaming down the line that she's chief executive around here, and if the Nips won't accept the signature she just put on a deal, it's because *he's* a male chauvinist pig. As company chairman and her boss, what's he going to do about it?'

Tom fiddled with his keyboard, jumping the cursor through his figures. 'Nothing. He'll leave her to fight her own battles. If she wants knights in shining armour, forget it. She's got the wrong man.'

'This is true,' Emily agreed solemnly.

'What does she expect? He and the Tokyo Mafia were bosom buddies while she was in tunics and short socks.'

Emily tried to imagine Millie in short socks and school shoes, tunic, blazer and plaits instead of Armani suits, Gucci loafers, and a sleek, shoulder-length blonde bob. She couldn't.

'They don't have school uniform in America,' she said accusingly, resting her files against the door jamb to ease her arms as the spectacles slid down her nose again. She rammed them up with the edge of a file. 'Millie wouldn't wear short socks.'

'Preppies wear socks and loafers.'

Tom harboured sympathy for Millie, a fellow underdog, who had bothered in her own time to learn the Nips' impossible language, could drink them under the table at business dinners and had the bottle to go belting out the karaoke afterwards in Tokyo drinking clubs. She was invited to their homes and was entertained *en famille* by wives who taught her to cook, wear a kimono and one year gave her an exquisite formal one which hung in a glass frame in her house. For the Japanese, who *never* invited *gaijin* to their homes, this quite extraordinary personal respect failed to change the fact that they didn't like her signing contracts. She was a woman.

'They'd rather talk business with Garcia through a translator and he doesn't care. He *is* GGIL,' said Emily placidly.

'He would say he cares.'

'Sure. Mr Goddard, New Man. Any day. You watch.' The idea amused her. She laughed, jammed her glasses back up her nose and ambled off. Tom glanced at his watch, pushed away the curling remains of his sandwich, pushed his own, tortoiseshell-rimmed glasses up his nose and concentrated on his work.

Tom loved accountancy, loved figures, loved playing with them, their flexibility, their orderliness, the satisfaction of recording, checking, balancing, the way they could mean different things depending on how they were arranged. He enjoyed real beauty, aesthetic and intellectual, in numbers, loved long, tidy columns of currency, pounds, pence, dollars, yen, just as he liked good, well-cut, dark blue or grey suits, good shirts – good *style*.

In his mid-thirties, shortsighted and of medium height, he had an earnest expression, was already losing his waist, and his hair, dark brown, piebald with grey and cut well by an expensive barber, was thinning. A certain lack of humour was sometimes offset by a serious boyishness, a look very much like Clark Kent before he changed into Superman.

Not having much of a sense of humour, Janey would say when she wanted to be hurtful, was his main shortcoming.

Where was *her* sense of humour, he retorted, when it came to the hours he worked?

Long hours, on the stage and in the office, once a shared commitment, after Francesca was born became a sore point.

'I'm going to send Garcia Goddard a bill for all the babysitting I do while you're still there until eleven at night,' she threatened when he worked late every night for a fortnight. 'Why don't you take a camp bed and just move in?'

Instead of laughing, going along with the tease, he took her seriously, felt criticised and defended himself, a mistake that led to an all-out row.

'It's a global business,' he said pedantically. 'You have to take time differences into account. Quite often I stay late to talk to New York and Garcia often works an eighteen-hour day, then goes to a hotel because it's too late to go home. Goes with the job, Janey. I can't afford hotels, though.'

'Ah,' Janey leaped in. 'You'd be staying in hotels if you could *afford* to, would you?'

Tom, a plodding individual incapable of fancy emotional footwork, went straight ahead and made things worse. 'You haven't got so much to complain about. Not if you think what a hard time Josephine Goddard must have. Garcia's out of the country more than he's here, and she puts up with more than you do. I may come home late, but at least I come home.'

Janey's eyes narrowed dangerously but he couldn't help himself.

'If I was overseas nine months of the year clocking up time out of the UK so the Inland Revenue couldn't tax me, think how lonely you'd get.'

Janey was temporarily speechless, then managed to get across to him that she couldn't care less what wealthy Josephine Goddard might endure in her big South London house with its big corner garden and pretty view over rows of parked Saabs and BMWs to the common and duck pond on the other side of the road. In March and April daffodils massed the bright grass, geese squabbled at the water's edge and ducklings paddled frenziedly after their mothers in long nursery crocodiles, bobbing bundles of fluff. 'The only things bobbing along in *our* street,' she finished furiously, 'are lorries and buses, and the nearest *I've* got to a common is a bit of grass up the road on the corner where the council have put a sign saying it's a *temporary open space. I* don't have a house in Bermuda or an apartment in New York or a farmhouse in the South of France, do I? Huh? I'm so *sorry* for Garcia Goddard's poor neglected wife.'

Tom blinked at her, solid, stolid and unperturbed about the inequality of their different lives. Normally a rational, stable woman, Janey could have hit him.

By late afternoon, the figures that eventually showed on the screen drove all thought of Janey, babies and abortion from Tom's mind. Despite the air of confidence in the company, new contracts coming in and a general feeling that business was picking up, what he saw was worrying.

The company suffered not just from recession like everyone else, but from absentee management. Garcia and Millie were away too much, out of day-to-day touch, without their fingers sufficiently on the pulse of a business in subtle but increasing distress. For five years they had relied on Tom, his assistant and an accountant in Bermuda for day-to-day financial management.

Tom tapped some keys, studied the result, leaned back in his chair, pushed his glasses to the top of his head, closed his eyes and considered.

Garcia and Millie do not know how bad things look and are used to my protecting them.

He began mentally to go through the options.

Involve them or make my own decisions? I could make them sit down and listen while I explain the facts of life. One: a company needs its top management to be more than occasionally on hand.

Two: the yen is too strong and getting stronger, so Tokyo costs are through the roof.

Three: New York. Our offices are half empty, under-used and a waste of money but we can't get out of the lease.

Four: Britain. The retail trade is a disaster. Along with America and Japan, we are still in recession and full of consumers who can't or won't consume. Who buys new clothes and fancy housewares when they are either too scared to spend or haven't any money?

Facing harsh realities would lead to rationalisation, redundancies and closures, not to mention explanations and recriminations. *Why didn't you tell us sooner?*

Tom dragged his glasses back on to his nose and shuddered; he hated confrontations. Garcia would be like a bloodhound in full chase, mercilessly questioning; why, how, when, where and, worst of all, *who* would fire at him like bullets sprayed from a machine gun. Under the pressure, he would waffle and fluff, cowed by the impossibility of saying, 'It is partly your own fault.'

Sometimes, just listening to the rows on the telephone brought the whole office to a petrified halt, but to be on the receiving end of those two terrible tongues, Millie's cutting, sarcastic New York drawl – the prospect terrified him.

It'd bring the roof down around my ears, he thought dismally. Farewell, job, when I need you most. Or, he brightened up, I can go on putting a little touch here and a little touch there. Massage the figures. In the larger picture no one will notice I've tidied up.

Studying the figures carefully, he became convinced he could ride it out; no recession lasted for ever. He did it regularly in any event, smoothed things out, moved money around, tidied up. Nothing of any great importance, just achieving the balance and symmetry that were irresistible, and for an accountant as good as he was it wouldn't be difficult, the little adjustments here and there that kept things looking on course to meet projections, avoided trouble. The auditors audited, never noted anything wrong, gave them an annual clean bill of health.

Tom sat staring at the dead gardens below, expressionless,

contemplating possibilities. The sky had clouded and a dull, liverish tinge meant snow was on the way.

He handled accounts from four different offices in four different continents, dealt in any number of different currencies. Garcia's staff travelled constantly and Tom shared with Emily the job of handling hotel and airline expenses in fluctuating exchange rates. There were also air-mile accounts, entertaining expenses, client expenses such as gift buying, everything down to taxis, tips and petty cash. In his safe were bundles of Hong Kong dollars, US dollars, Australian dollars, Japanese yen, Deutsche Marks, francs and more. The complexity helped mask the losses they were making, which could be buried further. Money could vanish in a hundred ways even the Fraud Squad would find difficult to trace.

Negative equity, a second child and nowhere to put it, a distraught wife.

The possibilities such thoughts opened up passed uneasily through his mind and he sat, thinking things through in his methodical manner until Emily climbing the stairs to his door jolted him out of it.

'Cuppa,' she announced in her Australian twang, slopping a mug down on his desk, shaking a tin under his nose. 'Ginger bix or plain digestive. Pigs in marketing ate all the chocs.' Her glasses slid to the tip of her nose. He eyed the smear of chocolate at the edge of her mouth and helped himself.

'I'm more than good enough,' he muttered as Emily went to the room next door and rattled biscuits at his secretary.

'What the hell are you doing working for me if you aren't?'

Tom jumped, spinning in his chair to find Garcia looming over him with no warning at all. 'I wish you wouldn't do that.'

Garcia grinned. He had his Spanish ancestors' features, dark, narrow and haughty, coarse, sallow skin, and his English father's height, love of practical jokes and cricket. Two deep concentration lines drew flat black brows together over restless, slightly protuberant black eyes and a long, thin, conquistadorial nose. At forty-six, with a vanishing waistline and a lot of grey hair, he still possessed the splendind, arrogant conviction of the Spanish Inquisition, whose blood ran through the Spanish half of the Goddard family tree in rivers, that he was always in the right.

'You make me nervous, creeping around,' Tom snapped.

When Garcia laughed, you could see that almost all his teeth were capped with gold.

He had an orange folder tucked under one arm. 'Have a look at this.'

As it slid across his desk, Tom pulled it round by a corner and opened the flap. It held a thin sheaf of letters with the black horse logo, a bundle of bills and a couple of cheque books.

'Sixty thousand sterling in a Lloyd's personal account,' Garcia explained, scratching strong five o'clock shadow with one long finger still sunburned from a board meeting in Melbourne that had included a couple of days of cricket. 'For you to pay my builders. I've told Richard Adams to contact you when he needs cash.'

'You're moving house?'

Garcia looked grim. 'No. Building a granny annexe. The cheques can be drawn on my signature or yours.'

Tom gaped. Paying Garcia's private bills had never been part of the job.

'I'll be in the Far East for a month and I can't keep track of builders and plumbers and what have you. Everything's in the folder. Any problems, fax me or talk to Josephine. Sorry to add to your workload, but it shouldn't be complicated. Except I want you to claim the VAT.'

'Granny annexe? What granny annexe?' Tom demanded, astounded.

'Emilia's granny annexe,' explained Garcia, wandering to the window, standing with his hands in his pockets and looking out. It was already dark, and in the light from the window he could see specks of frozen ice trying to turn into proper snow dancing in the freezing air. 'My wife and my mother have decided they'd be happier in separate establishments, so to keep the peace I'm building a self-contained annexe on to the side of the house. Planning permission came through four weeks ago. *That* cost me a social arm and a leg.' He was clearly pained at the thought.

'Good Lord, whatever brought that on?' asked Tom, looking at the orange folder like a mongoose at a snake. He cleared his thoat and coughed to cover the violent turmoil of his thoughts.

'Half a dozen mind-numbing drinks parties and a personal intervention at the Golf Club,' Garcia complained. 'We had to fix the handicap. Got it as a fax from the Mid Ocean in Bermuda. They'll never check.'

'I meant the annexe, not the planning permission. I thought the Goddards were one big happy family,' Tom croaked, nudging the edge of the file with the tip of his finger as though it was red-hot and radioactive.

'Arabs brought it on,' said Garcia gloomily, darker faced than ever.

'Sixty thousand quid is one hell of a granny annexe. You could buy her a house.'

'Not in Barnes. In any event, she doesn't want a house. My mother is Spanish and in Spain sons are expected to look after their mothers. If you read the folder you'll see it also covers some work to the main house. I've allowed for pulling down a couple of walls and extending Josie's study into what she is pleased to call a proper office. Then there's redecorating and refurnishing. On the annexe it'll be a question of professional fees, construction costs, fitting a bathroom and kitchen, drains. In the end, no matter how much I budget, they'll try their damndest to double it. They're already buzzing like wasps round my back yard, starting to dig holes and make a mess.' Garcia looked gloomy. 'And it is a mess. When they've done, they've got to clear up the mess and replant the garden.'

'Ah,' said Tom, wishing he could manage something more intelligent.

'Jo and Emilia haven't been speaking but I banged their heads together,' Garcia growled. 'Jo will do the interior and since neither of them have any notion of budgets they will enjoy themselves spending my money, once they've buried the hatchet. A few trips to Harrods should grease the wheels. All this fuss just because my mother's damned dogs lost Jo a contract. I'd shoot those bloody animals if it weren't for the RSPCA.'

'Emilia's dogs did what?'

'Rambo or Barney Darling bit someone,' said Garcia without a trace of his normal humour. 'One of 'em got excited. The mistress of one of Jo's clients came to inspect my mother's bedroom because she wanted one like it.' He frowned. 'Strikes me as highly improbable. My mother goes in for Portuguese tiles in the bathroom and Liberty quilts covered in poodle hairs whereas Arabs generally go for orange marble brothels in Knightsbridge. Beats me what some Arab mistress was doing in Emilia's room.'

Tom, who only knew about Arabs from watching Peter O'Toole in *Lawrence of Arabia*, peeped into the cheque books.

'I *loathe* builders,' Garcia confided, showing no inclination to go away, which Tom desperately wished he would so he could open the orange folder properly. 'I've a friend in Johannesburg,' Garcia ruminated stubbornly, sitting down on the edge of the desk, taking a linen handkerchief out of his pocket and blowing his nose noisily. He had, Tom thought irritably, a Mediterranean attitude to bodily functions, and never mind a friend in Johannesburg, Garcia's friends practically peopled the globe.

'Yes?'

'Used to live in Wiltshire and buy up rundown properties, to do up, then sell on. His wife did the overseeing and they made a lot of money. Five years ago he bought a rundown estate, handed the job over to her as usual, only she was pregnant and her mind wasn't on it. Halfway through the renovations they found the builders had gone three hundred per cent over budget and the bastards sued. Bankrupted him. Can't be a stockbroker and a bankrupt, so he got struck off.'

'I wouldn't have wanted to go and live in South Africa five years ago.' He sounded pedestrian compared to Garcia, positively *lumpen*. For the first time, Tom realised he resented it.

'Neither would I, but it was the only place with a decent climate that would have him. Builders and anything to do with them bring me out in hives. Look after the money as though it's your own and *watch them*,' ordered his boss.

Garcia's feet thumped down the squeaky stairs on the way back to his office. Tom opened the orange folder, his heart thumping like his boss's footsteps with nervous excitment, tight against the tight wall of his chest.

Sixty thousand pounds. *Look after it as though it's your own.*

He could transfer money back and forth until the auditors went giddy trying to see what was what. The thought filled his mind, uncontrollable and terrifying; Garcia's personal bank account could be manipulated and siphoned off, to cover the loss on the flat. Accountancy was not a problem. The problem would be Janey.

'Bonus plus share options,' he muttered, taking his glasses off and burying his face in his hands. 'I got a productivity bonus and cashed in executive share options.'

No good. She'd wonder. She'd want to know why he'd let her worry all this time if he had money in shares.

'OK. I got a productivity bonus and *just* got executive share options as part of a promotion, and I'm cashing them in at once.'

Janey was a dancer, not a businesswoman, and probably didn't know what executive share options were or how they worked. In any case, she was anxious about babies, desperate to move, and unlikely to press for answers to questions she probably didn't understand enough to ask.

He'd play Janey by ear.

Tom reached behind him to close his door, got *The Times* out of his briefcase and spread the job pages out on his desk, then paused to calculate.

The baby was due in August. He had six months, could not stay at GGIL longer than that. Since he could not get another job without a reference, he needed to have a job and hand in his resignation *before* Garcia and Millie found a black hole in their accounts and started asking questions. Which would paralyse them because they would have neither his help in unravelling the mess nor the money to prosecute him.

As he pushed his glasses up his nose and concentrated on reading the financial jobs, Garcia's voice floated from downstairs, passing Emily's little office where the sound of typing momentarily stopped. '. . . mistakes cost a *fortune,*' he roared.

Garcia and Millie were brilliant, the best, but impossibly emotional, impulsive to the point where they made unnecessary mistakes. He was tired of being poorly paid to disguise Garcia's mistakes, which were *wholly* his own fault, unlike negative equity and Janey accidentally getting pregnant.

Tom knew details of the Bermuda trusts that held all Garcia's assets, had helped Emmanuel Gilmour and the Bermudian lawyer set them up. Garcia Goddard was ring-fenced. Safe. Under international law, no government could take his property away from him and put him into negative equity. He didn't even pay tax. Nor did Millie. Garcia and Millie would be just fine, and so would Garcia's family.

Tom read through the jobs columns and circled one or two advertisements that might be possibilities, in red.

Chapter Three

The atmosphere here, Garcia thought, arriving home, is *awful*.

Given to flamboyance and exaggeration, for once, in telling Tom he had domestic problems, he had not inflated the seriousness of the facts. It was impossible to exaggerate the seriousness of his wife and his mother falling out; it reduced his home life to conflict and discomfort and gave his mother every excuse to be full of inconvenient reproach.

'Josephine,' she murmured later that evening, her devious black eyes half closed, about to launch into new tales of neglect and abuse. 'She—'

'You've rubbed along for *years*,' he said, exasperated. 'Why can't you go on doing so?'

'Your mother is *impossible*,' his wife complained half an hour later.

'Is this some kind of conspiracy?' Garcia demanded.

He didn't believe a word of it, but his mother was his mother, had lived with them for years, so if she and Josephine had really fallen out, desperate measures were called for. Like the building of an annexe.

Cordial relationships of mutual interest with his neighbours, favours owed and influential membership of the same prestigious golf club that the Planning Committee's chairman had been trying to join for six years had brought his planning permission through in record time. He had told his architects to present it at the Town Hall as a very urgent matter.

'It *is* urgent,' he said acidly when Richard Adams, his surveyor, pulled a long face and pointed out that they might have to be patient. It could be at least Easter before the Planning Committee finished mulling over the prospect of building on to the end of a fine Victorian terrace overlooking Barnes Common. Garcia shouted and wouldn't have it.

'But it is a highly sensitive proposal,' Richard protested patiently. 'If we don't get it right first time, we stand very little chance on any subsequent appeal. Getting it right takes very careful planning and that takes *time*.'

Garcia was unimpressed. 'I've got three women in my house barely speaking to each other and none of them speaking to me. At Christmas. What could be more sensitive than that? Eh?'

Richard was shocked. 'Josephine and Emma and Emilia aren't speaking?'

'Why the hell do you think I'm doing all this?'

Richard, who had known and worked for Garcia for twenty years and more, started to inquire why suddenly no one in the Goddard household was getting along with anyone else, then thought better of it. Stroking a toothbrush moustache on a lugubrious long face, he wisely decided that with that volatile family, it was probably better not to know.

'How's Josephine's business going?' he asked diplomatically, changing the senstitive subject.

'Hurrrumph.'

Richard deduced from the thunderous frown on Garcia's swarthy face that either it was going too well and he was feeling threatened by wifely success, or it was going badly enough to cost him money.

Either way, moving Emilia out of the family bosom into a place of her own was an unprecedented and drastic measure, so something *most* peculiar must have happened.

There was never any consensus about whose fault it all was. Josephine blamed Emilia for being drunk in charge of Emma in the middle of the afternoon and not controlling her dogs, Emilia blamed Josephine for coming home when she wasn't expected, and Emma, misunderstood and betrayed, blamed everyone.

'Oh, Lord, would you look at that.'

Peering from a window to see whether it was still raining, Josephine watched her client climb out of a taxi and stand in the downpour paying the driver.

Sherrine, youngest mistress to Sheik Abdul of Saudi Arabia, Josephine's first serious client, tottered and splashed in soaking stilettoes through pouring rain and December darkness, slipped on wet cobbles, trailed the long coat in a puddle and stood peering up to see which was the right house.

Josephine ran for the door. 'Let me take that and put you by the Aga to dry.'

The smell of wet wool and musky perfume filled the hall as Josephine held out her hand for the long black cashmere coat and two very black, cynical young eyes surveyed the inside of Josephine's home and came to rest curiously on Emma's mountain bike, left lying, shedding mud and scraping paint, against the dining room door.

'My daughter's,' Josephine said, following her gaze. 'She's not supposed to bring it inside.'

The little Saudi who, underneath expensive cashmere and high-heeled shoes, was not much older than Emma, gazed with great sheep's eyes of longing, then handed Josephine her coat haughtily, to disguise the fact that she would kill to chase around Hyde Park on a bike like that.

It wasn't going to happen. She picked her nose regretfully as they went down the hall to the kitchen; the sheik's minder, who had only allowed her out alone this afternoon because it was a visit to a private home for professional reasons, would never let her do what she wanted, go racing round the Serpentine.

'You sit there and warm up and dry out. Would you like a cup of tea?'

Sherrine nodded, two thin brown hands, their small oval nails painted scarlet, curled like sparrow's feet over the big blue Aga's shiny rail. Slight and slender as a reed, not quite five feet tall, with thin, childish, slightly bowed legs, her ankles were tiny, her waist-length hair glossy and black. A full, pouting, determined mouth gave her the look of a demanding child. It pouted now as, stork-like, she folded herself on to the chair and watched Josephine put on the kettle.

At five foot six, Josephine towered over the little Arab. Feeling tall was not a sensation she was used to, she didn't like it, it made her awkward, as if she had suddenly turned mannish, overpowering, acutely aware of the pounds she had put on recently, of her own middle ageing, thickening waistline compared to the exotic, fragile child in her kitchen.

Josephine's looks had been preying on her mind as her fortieth birthday loomed. Not naturally vain, she caught herself looking in mirrors and windows, studying her reflection with a newly critical eye, not liking what she saw.

A natural blonde, her hair had begun to fade, to need careful highlights to disguise traces of grey and an upsetting tendency for it to look a trifle pepper and salty but tinged with *green*. 'That's age,' her hairdresser had said matter-of-factly, holding it up in both hands. 'Shall we cut it nice and short? Like so?' Nice and short like so. The cut for the older woman.

Josephine had leaned forward and inspected herself in the salon's flattering light that minimised the laughter lines by her mouth, the soft hint of a sag at the jaw, the crow's feet that stomped themselves all over her eyes when she smiled. There was nothing to laugh about when it came to the downward spiral into middle age; she hated and resented ageing.

'No,' she'd said firmly. 'Not yet.'

'Earl Grey, English Breakfast or Lapsang Souchong?' she asked brightly, getting packets out of a cupboard.

'Earl Grey,' Sherrine answered, busy studying Josephine's kitchen.

Josephine opened the hotplate cover and wondered briefly whether she could fit an Aga or Rayburn into Sherrine's Knightsbridge flat, regretfully dismissed the idea; twenty-five per cent on an Aga was juicy commission but in an Arab love nest – in any love nest, come to that – the kitchen wasn't generally much of a consideration.

Her own, which was preoccupying Sherrine who had never seen anything like it, was very large, over thirty-five feet long and twenty wide, knocked into one room from what had once been a maze of pantries, sculleries, passageways, an outside lavatory and a big square morning room. Josephine had had all the internal walls pulled down and spent six months creating a stunning kitchen that had made a major feature in *Homes and Gardens* and was photographed in the German manufacturer's brochure.

At the far end an uncurtained window, dark and running with rain, was half obscured by a profusion of plants, at one side of which a collection of old-fashioned wicker picnic baskets was piled, one on top of another in a display of carefully arranged casual disorder.

A scrubbed oak table, purpose made to fit the dimensions of the room, seated a dozen people comfortably on oak carvers. Down one long wall, maple shelves were crammed with cookery books and exquisite, white and yellow, blue-rimmed Limoges porcelain from Monet's house in Giverny, too beautiful, too delicate to use. Propped against the cookery books a copy of *Homes and Gardens* lay open at the relevant page.

The only other traditional aspect of a room only Germans could have designed was the Aga. Around it were clean, sharp lines of modern, state-of-the-art kitchen furniture, fusing midnight blue with pale, honey-coloured maple. Deep blue chorion worktops were backed by a seamless sheet of brushed steel that glowed dully in the light of two dozen halogen lights set into the ceiling.

Dull, brushed steel ovens with shiny black glass doors, a steel hob, a great oblong steel extractor unit, white sinks and the deep blood-orange gleam of polished terracotta tiles added to a design in which beauty and technology combined to create facilities close to professional standards. An American fridge with a blue door, almost big enough to walk into, hummed to one side, clunked the internal workings of its ice dispenser, then fell silent.

'Do you have milk in your tea?' Josephine opened a second, smaller fridge, with a box of Mars Bars tucked into its door next to a glass container of milk.

Sherrine's eyes widened.

'Would you like one?'

The childlike pout became a greedy, beaming smile. 'And just sugar in my tea.'

Must be overwhelmed, Josephine thought, seeing her gazing round. Too impressed to comment.

The Saudi licked chocolate off her teeth, full of wonder and amazement that anyone could prepare anything so sensual, comforting, sociable, voluptuous and sexy as food in a place as hard and gleaming as this, more like a laboratory than a place where women would work and talk and live together, and cook. An aristocrat from a nomadic tribe, she understood neither the British nor their way of life, nor their kitchens, but she knew about Raleigh bikes.

'You sell bike?' she asked, ready to bargain and barter. Even if the minder wouldn't let her ride it in Hyde Park, to have it would be a minor triumph, and you never knew . . .

'Good heavens, whatever for? I would have thought the sheik could have bought you a dozen bikes with gold-plated handlebars,' Josephine exclaimed. 'What do you want Emma's second-hand for? In any case, I doubt she'd want to give it to you.' Josephine didn't understand.

The little Arab shook out her drying skirt, scowled and drank a great many small cups of her favourite drink; half a box of brown sugar lumps dissolved in boiling trickles of Twinings Earl Grey tea.

'We go and see the ottoman?' she suggested when she had had enough.

'It's upstairs in my mother's room.'

Now the moment had come, the client here, Josephine knew uneasily that showing Sherrine into Emilia's room without asking was taking liberties that Emilia would resent, but the client needed to see a rising ottoman, and with the Christmas crowds making the shops unbearable and turning Harrods into a zoo, showing her Emilia's, in the comfort of home, had seemed the logical thing to do.

'I'll show you round the rest of the house, as we go,' she offered.

It might give Sherrine ideas for interior decor that would come in useful later on.

Upstairs, there was panic.

Emma, standing in the middle of her room on the very top floor, wearing one of Garcia's old sweat suits, sleeves rolled up, waist tied with an old school tie and a dripping paintbrush in her hand, froze when she heard the front door bang and her mother coming in.

They had moved all the furniture out on to the landing, leaving Emilia tucked up in a tartan travelling rug in Emma's armchair with Rambo and Barney Darling snoozing and grunting in her lap, marooned in a sea of newspaper put down to protect the carpet. She paused, her glass halfway to her lips.

'Mum,' Emma hissed, panic-stricken.

'She might not come up.'

'What's she doing here? She said she'd be on site all afternoon.'

The two poodles raised their muzzles and listened intently to barely audible sounds of someone moving around three floors below.

'It's Josephine. Lie down and be quiet,' Emilia ordered. 'And don't make me spill this. More?'

Emma shook her head as her grandmother parked her bottle down the side of her chair.

'I should just lock the door and pretend we're not at home,' Emilia suggested airily. 'Then she won't see this until you're finished.' She waved a languid, supervisory hand at the open pot of black emulsion by Emma's feet and caught the ear of a plastic, life-sized blow-up Father Christmas with bushy cottonwool beard and eyebrows and a bucolic leer, which had been leaning on the side of her chair. He toppled tipsily into the freshly filled tray of black paint that Emma was spreading over her walls. He lay, his woolly beard slowly soaking paint and turning black as Barney Darling, sensing agitation and alarm, snickered, growled and cocked his ears.

'*Now* look what you've done.'

'Santa's had an overdose of Lady Grecian Two Thousand,' Emilia remarked, giggling and eyeing the damage.

Emma swore, jammed her brush in the paint pot, leaving a slash of black across the newspapers, and looked up at the wall. Half of it was black, like the rest of the room, black over its original duck-egg green which her mother considered a suitable and tasteful colour for an adolescent's bedroom.

'Your mother's going to have a fit when she *does* see it,' her grandmother warned complacently. 'Don't say I didn't tell you.'

'I would have had it finished. She can't see it before because she'll go apeshit, but it'll look brilliant finished,' Emma wailed. 'She *said* she'd be out all day.'

'Whether four black walls and an American flag with hellfire licking around it painted on the ceiling next to a portrait of Salvador Dali sliding over the cornice in the style of one of his own paintings looks brilliant is a matter of taste,' Emilia observed, tilting her head back to have another look. 'You have done it rather well, I must say, but taste is something your mother thinks she knows about, and she may not agree with you.'

'You bought it,' Emma yelped, shot in the back by a two-timing, cowardly partner in crime.

'All I said, Emma darling, was that if black, white, red, orange, maroon and blue paint was what you wanted for Christmas, then black, white, red, orange, maroon and blue paint was what you'd get. I never said it was a good idea,' Emilia pointed out calmly. She fished down Barney Darling's flank and found her bottle.

'Good Lord, have you really got through all that?' Emma's jaw dropped.

'When your mother arrives up here, Emma darling,' her grandmother added, pouring the dregs, 'which I have a feeling she will do any minute, don't try and pin the blame on me.'

Downstairs, Josephine, praying that Hosannah the cleaner had for once done some cleaning, bought them time by giving Sherrine a guided tour.

'Drawing room,' she said, leading the way.

Also photographed for *Homes and Gardens*, the room, lamps turned low, a Christmas tree winking with silver and gold baubles in one corner, heavy curtains pulled against the dreary evening outside, was elegance and comfort in perfect harmony. In summer, the long windows overlooked a swimming pool surrounded by paving and shrubs. At the far end a weeping willow half hid a mirror set into a wall, to deceive the eye that on the far side lay a secret garden, waiting to be explored . . .

Sherrine's voice rattled, hoarse and dry as if desiccated by desert winds.

'The ottoman, Mrs Goddard?'

Josephine suppressed a sigh. Rising ottomans didn't feature in nomadic life, and when she had first brought up the suggestion, Sherrine had been clearly and impatiently baffled. 'It's to put the telly in,' Josephine had explained.

In between bouts of lovemaking, Sheik Abdul liked to catch the news on CNN and watch old movies on satellite. In between bouts of Sheik Abdul, Sherrine needed something to do other than going to Harrods, Chanel and Harvey Nicks to help spend her lover's billions. It wasn't that Saudi mistresses couldn't get out of bed, more that they didn't need to or weren't allowed to. The answer was technology, but rising ottomans, outside

Sherrine's experience, needed to be demonstrated as she could not commission something she couldn't imagine. Twenty five per cent on a top-of-the-range ottoman was not to be sneezed at. Hence the impulsive invitation.

Sherrine gave a backward, longing glance at the bike in the hall.

'Sell bike?' she murmured hopefully.

'For goodness *sake,*' Josephine began, reined herself in. The client is always right. 'I tell you what, when we've looked at the ottoman, I'll go up and see if Emma's in. Then you can ask her yourself.' Emma will say, no, and that will be that.

Sherrine followed her towards the stairs and as they climbed, Josephine prayed silently. Please God, let Hosannah have penetrated up here with Hoover and duster. Let Emilia have put her clothes away and made her bed. Let all the loos and baths be clean. Above all, let Emilia forgive my trespassing, if ever she finds out.

Please, don't let her find out.

Amen.

'Don't come in.'

Crossing the small top landing, which had Emma's bed dragged against the wall and everything from her room thrown in a higgledy-piggledy heap, Josephine opened her daughter's door, recoiled, stepped back hard on to Sherrine's foot.

'Sorry,' she said automatically as the little Saudi hopped and squealed. 'But you can't go in.'

Sherrine's black eyes sparked, the mountain bike in their sights, its owner the other side of the door.

'Sell bike?' she called imperiously, pushed past and flung the door wide.

Josephine moaned in a stifled kind of way and tried to take in a sight that looked a cross between the Black Hole of Calcutta and an opium den.

Emma, gawky, startled, innocent as Charlie Chaplin in a fix, stood in one of her father's tracksuits, the bottoms rolled up, spattered with black emulsion. A cigarette smoked in the lid of a paint tin and Emilia, forbidden like everyone else to smoke in the house, sat centre stage like royalty, wine glass in one languid hand, the rest of her draped with dogs and rugs.

'Shouldn't come snooping in other people's private rooms,' Emma mumbled, scarlet with resentment. 'Who's she?'

Grandmother, mother and daughter faced each other and except for Sherrine's fussing and rubbing her foot where Josephine had stood on it, there was a brief, electric silence.

A marked family resemblance ran through all the women in Garcia's family. Even Emma, with more English than Spanish blood in her, looked like her grandmother, dark-eyed, oval-faced with high forehead and heavy brows. Only her hair showed the mixing of blood, long and tawny as a tabby cat instead of pure Spanish black. But one day, like Emilia, Emma would have an olive moustache on her narrow, curved upper lip.

Pale-skinned, austerely beautiful, Emilia, nearly seventy, still had the pure oval face, carved, curving, elegant mouth and supercilious bearing of a marble saint in a Spanish church, only a little blurred by age. All three of them, Emilia, Garcia and Emma, had the same heavy-lidded, deep brown, rather protuberant eyes. Longsighted with milky rings round the irises, Emilia's were nonetheless usually sharp and alert as a ferret's, not detached and dreamy as an opium addict's. Josephine recognised that look: it meant Emilia was more than slightly drunk.

'Is she a customer, or what?' Emma demanded rudely.

'Client,' Josephine corrected. 'Sherrine is a *client*.' She looked up and caught Salvaldor Dali's leering orange eye. 'Just *what* do you think you're doing?'

'We're decorating,' Emma answered sullenly.

'*You* are decorating, Emma darling,' her grandmother murmured.

Sherrine stopped hopping up and down and looked around her with interest. Mrs Goddard's daughter's room was comforting and familiar, like the inside of a tent in the midday sun. Dark and colourful.

'Why is your *client* in my bedroom?'

Josephine, guilty, couldn't meet Emilia's wandery eye. After the rising ottoman had risen and sunk enough times to wreck the mechanism and the remote-controlled curtains had opened and shut countless times with manic speed, she had wrenched the red-hot control unit from Sherrine's hands.

'Let's go,' she cried desperately, 'and see if we can find Emma.'

Sherrine reached for the remote control.

'*Bike*,' Josephine bleated, reduced to lunacy.

And here they were.

'We've had lunch,' Emilia said with dignity.

Bending down, Josephine fished out an empty wine bottle, a half of gin and a barely touched bottle of tonic water from underneath a pile of crumpled newspaper.

'Liquid lunch?' she asked sarcastically. 'Really, Emilia, you're worse than Sophia. I suppose you've been encouraging Emma to drink.'

Sherrine clutched Emma's arm. 'You sell me your bike and I keep it here?' she asked desperately. 'I ride here?'

'Why is she going on about my bike?' Emma demanded.

'No one makes her do anything,' Emilia snorted, appearing to wake up and take notice. 'No one straps her to her bed and forces Pinot Noir down her, do they, Emma, darling?'

Sherrine shook Emma's arm like a fretful child.

'She wants you to barter,' Josephine said hopelessly. 'Over your bike. I've tried to tell her you don't want to sell it to anyone.'

'You came on a bike?' Emilia looked Sherrine over carefully. 'In this weather, and dressed like that? How shocking. Josephine should call you a cab.'

'Be quiet, Emilia. You are drunk.' For Josephine, the American flag was bringing on the beginning of a migraine, tightening a band round her head.

'Black cab,' Emilia drawled, hanging on to Barney Darling who was straining against his collar until his eyes stood out. 'Room as black as a cab was what she wanted for Christmas. I told her you'd be mad.'

'You offered,' Emma wailed.

'This was *your* idea?' Josephine rounded on her mother-in-law.

'Me? She designed the flag in Art at school,' Emilia retorted slyly. 'Got an A plus for it, didn't you, darling?'

Josephine ran her hands through her hair in desperation. 'Now people will think I've got the taste of a rave artist and no control over my daughter,' she muttered. 'I could wring your necks, both of you. Word gets out. It'll be your fault if I can never bring clients home again.'

Emilia struggled upright in her armchair, took her dogs by their collars and began murmuring into Rambo's floppy poodle ear as Barney Darling scrambled to his feet, eyes rolling with all the tension.

'Vandalism,' Josephine was saying in a voice that sounded on the edge of tears. 'Look at this.' She stared with her head back as if hypnotised by hellfire licking the edges of the American flag.

Emma burst into tears and fought back. 'You *said*, Nanna, you *said* it was a brill idea.'

Scared and angry at bad feelings, raised voices, and the way Sherrine was hanging on to Emma's arm, Barney Darling flew to everybody's rescue, barked furiously, slipped his collar and vented his fright on the nearest unfamiliar object. Rambo leaped to join him and Sherrine leaped into the tray of black paint, shrieking like a banshee because Barney Darling had just sunk his teeth into her thin, black-stockinged ankle.

Chapter Four

Josephine came back from taking her client – now her former client – to the sheik's private doctor in Harley Street for a tetanus jab and a single stitch.

'Dog bites, Mrs Goddard?' the doctor had said in a tone that labelled her criminally irresponsible and Barney Darling fit only to be shot.

Josephine knew he had asked Sherrine if she wanted to report the assault to the police.

She parked on the road opposite her house and got out of the Saab to find carol singers in the courtyard, collecting for the Samaritans. As she crossed the road, traffic splashed past, spattering her skirt and legs, deepening her black and angry mood.

'Away in a manager, no crib for a bed, the little Lord Jesus lay down his sweet head. The stars in the bright sky looked down where he lay . . .' There were no stars looking down from the dark and murky London sky which had been black with rain all day. The singers' voices rose from under a cluster of umbrellas, as mournfully sweet as the words of the carol. Josephine tried to throw off her sudden flush of misery by searching her purse for change. As she threaded coins into their tin, she saw that Garcia might be home. His study overlooked the road and behind his drawn curtains his light was on, someone was in his room.

'Happy Christmas,' the singers cried.

Halfway up her steps, she turned back and stuffed a five-pound note into the tin.

'Thank you!' the tin-holder cried, surprised.

'Not generosity. Insurance. I might be needing you.'

Fumbling for her key, she thought angrily: minus a client, minus a contract, minus the commission on a rising ottoman and a lot of other things besides. She had left the clinic with the vague but alarming threat of a law suit for negligence and assault hanging over her head. Wondering how she stood vis-à-vis her professional insurance, she found her key and let herself into the house.

Hosannah's television was blaring up in her room, turned up annoyingly loud. It always was. Serb guns and mortars had sent Hosannah rather deaf and she claimed she couldn't hear it otherwise. When she chose to, she seemed to hear quite well . . .

Josephine's mood lifted. Hosannah's Christmas present should scotch any nonsense and was ready to wrap – a pair of very good, very comfortable earphones to plug into the box. That would silence her for good.

Garcia's study was the only room in the house which Josephine had not designed herself. He had done it and the effect was like its owner: dramatic. Unlike its owner, he had also managed to make it restful; dark greens, dark blues and tartans created a soothingly cave-like effect.

In a *cave,* his wife thought acidly, as she often did when she went in there, was where Garcia sometimes behaved as though he belonged, complete with bearskin and club. It was, though, the decorator in her admitted, perfect for him.

A gas fire pretending very convincingly to be a log fire burned brightly at one end, drawing the eye into the room, lit only by a Chinese porcelain lamp with a green silk shade and a green glass shaded banker's light on Garcia's crowded desk. Two of the deep green walls were covered with paintings and framed photographs, a third with bookshelves. The rest of the room was chaos. Piles of papers littered the lichen-coloured carpet, scattered the Black Watch sofa. Three telephones and a fax machine filled a table beside the desk.

'You're early.'

He stopped unpacking an ancient green briefcase covered with British Airways stickers and a Concorde cabin luggage tag to kiss her. 'They upgraded me and put me on the fast one. Three hours twenty minutes. I've been looking forward to seeing you for every minute of it.'

She pulled away. 'I just got back from Harley Street.'

'You're sick?'

She shook her head.

'My mother?'

'No one here is sick. But I'm sick *of* things.' She cleared a space on the Black Watch, sat down and fiddled with her hair in a way she did when she was determined. 'Garcia, remind me about your domestic commitments and your tax arrangements.'

'Why?' he asked, going back to his unpacking. 'You know them.'

'Repeat it to me, as if I am an idiot.'

'If I stay out of the country at least forty weeks of the year and I have an address in Bermuda, from the Inland Revenue's point of view I don't live in the UK and I don't pay income tax.'

'Or VAT. Or council tax.'

'Correct.'

'You have to stay away two hundred and seventy-five days every year to save tax.'

'It's a *hell* of a lot of dough.'

It was.

'It's the reason we can live as we do.' He finished spreading papers over every square inch of desk and carpet and threw the empty case in a corner. 'Let's have a glass of wine and you can tell me what you wanted to talk about, sweetie.'

'Living as we do.'

He looked up sharply. At the same moment, paper began to slither out of the fax machine on the table in the corner.

She tried to keep her tone light and easy. 'Emma needs you. Or at least she needs a firm hand and some discipline. So does your mother who is getting out of control. The damn dogs are biting people. And *I* need you. Some things are more important than not paying tax.'

He was examining the incoming fax. 'I disapprove of giving forty per cent of my income to a government I didn't elect and don't trust.' Garcia, shocked at the notion of voluntarily funding John Major's limping government – or any government – went into automatic counter-attack. 'Travel *with* me, Jo. It's not just you who gets lonely.'

'And sit in a hotel room with nothing to do in Tokyo or Taiwan or Indonesia? Why?'

'You could at least come to New York where you have a home and friends.'

'And do what? Shop till I drop in Saks and Bloomingdale's and Barney's?'

Garcia liked to find solutions. The irritable way he handled the fax meant he was already losing interest.

'You can help me make a life of my own so your being away doesn't matter so much. Your mother is making it impossible.'

'Aha. It turns out that this *is* about my mother. How would you like me to discipline my mother?' he asked, cheering up, scenting the true purpose of the argument as the business line on his desk began to ring.

'Don't tempt me,' Josephine choked. 'She egged Emma on to paint her room black. She's got an American flag on the ceiling. Go up and look.'

Garcia reached for the telephone, chuckling.

'*And* she lets Emma drink. They were both bouncing off the walls when I took a client up there, and the reason I've been to Harley Street is that your mother's bloody poodle bit her.'

Garcia tried to stop laughing, only laughed harder.

'That was my first major contract, Garcia. I have lost *money*.'

That sobered him up.

'Stitches and tetanus jab in an hysterical Arab. They had to give her a Valium injection to calm her down. They should have given me one. I only hope Sheik Abdul doesn't sue for damages. I might have just waved my career goodbye before it even started, thanks to your mother. How do you think I feel?'

'Understandably upset.' He grabbed the telephone. 'Hullo, love,' he cried, delighted to escape the looming confrontation. 'Donald *Trump*?' he cried derisively. He put his hand over the receiver, grinning from ear to ear. 'Millie went to a power breakfast in the Waldorf and got stuck with the mayor. He left her sitting between the president of Wonderbra and *Donald Trump*.'

'I don't care if she had to sit next to Hitler. I'm fed up with running a bed and breakfast. I want you to be here more, and your mother and those wretched dogs to live somewhere else.'

But he didn't hear because he was roaring with laughter, telling Millie about Emilia's dog biting Jo's client, and Emma's American flag.

'Painted her room *black*,' he guffawed, delighted.

'*You haven't even seen it*.' Josephine, beside herself with frustration, yelled the words as hot tears of fury stung her eyes.

Chapter Five

'What's that?' demanded Emilia suspiciously, sniffing steam as the dogs sniffed hopefully around her ankles in the kitchen, getting in Hosannah's way. Hosannah had offered to cook.

'Croatian cooking,' Garcia said gloomily. 'Why do we let her do it?'

'It makes her feel at home,' Josephine answered.

'It makes me feel like leaving home.'

'Little bit cabbage, little bit onion, little bit garlic, little bit tomato, little bit kidney bean,' Hosannah intoned happily, stirring a saucepan vigorously on top of the Aga. 'And deleeecious polenta.'

'God, you sound like a witch with a shopping list,' Emma said critically, plugging into Elvis on her Walkman before Hosannah could reply. 'That stuff's *disgusting*. Worse than school.'

'I will *not* eat *polenta,*' Emilia threatened mutinously.

Busy stirring her yellow goo on the Aga, her back to them, Hosannah licked her lips and smirked triumphantly.

'Why do you let her make this ghastly stuff?' Garcia hissed half an hour later, pushing his uneaten food away.

'*Are you lonely toniiiight*' squeaked tinnily out of his daughter's musical fallout shelter.

'Not at the table, *please,*' Josephine begged, drowned out by Elvis and ignored.

Hosannah munched happily, mopped up the last smears of polenta and offered seconds.

They gazed at the barely touched contents of their plates.

'Thank you, Hosannah, but I ate on the plane,' Garcia said, pushing away Croatian bean and cabbage broth with distaste and pouring himself another glass of wine.

'It's very slimming,' Emma said, too loudly because she couldn't hear herself. 'Gives you diarrhoea.'

Garcia sniggered.

'There's nothing to do on planes except eat and drink, and in any case his stomach thinks it's teatime, so he isn't hungry,' Josephine explained hastily, kicking Emma under the table, but Hosannah looked sideways at the floor, stubborn, which meant she was upset.

'Got any cigarettes?' Emilia inquired, shorthand for 'Go away, Hosannah, and have a smoke.'

Hosannah scraped her chair noisily and went outside.

'I know she smokes indoors when she thinks no one knows,' Garcia remarked. 'Why is it that someone I employ is the only person who doesn't obey the smoking rules in this house?'

Emma glanced at him incredulously, dropped her eyes hastily.

Josephine said, 'Your mother—'

'For God's sake, Jo,' Garcia protested loudly, 'can't you *ban* that woman from the kitchen?'

'*Someone* has to do the cooking,' she retorted but she went and fetched some cheese and biscuits.

The meal ended in a stiff and unsatisfactory silence.

'I'm going next door,' Emma announced.

'You're grounded,' her mother snapped. 'And it's too late.'

Emma wheedled her father from under her lashes.

'You're grounded,' he agreed.

He sounded half-hearted, amused, not cross at all. Emma chewed her lip and Emilia smiled a small smile, signalling, 'poor you.'

There was complicity even in their fighting, Josephine thought, left out in the cold.

'You deserve grounding until you go back to school for what you've done.' She carefully kept her voice reasonable, so no one could accuse her of overreaction. 'As I said earlier, word will go out that I have the taste of a rave artist and keep rabid dogs, thanks to you two. *Won't it,* Emilia?'

Emilia looked into her empty glass hopefully and Garcia, picking up the order with subliminal ease, obediently filled it up.

'You'll survive, Jo.' He scrubbed at his eyes, which felt full of grit, he was so tired. 'Where's your sense of humour? It's not as though we need the money.'

Aiming to pour oil on troubled waters, he seriously miscalculated. Josephine was beside herself.

'I—'

'The artwork is actually very good,' he went on, pushing Emma's Doc Martens off the chair next to him. 'Excellent graphics. What else do they teach them at that school?'

'I—'

'Dali is particularly clever. She's caught that manic, loony, lizard-eyed look. Perhaps she should come and work for me.' He leaned forwards and shouted over Elvis. 'Thought of going to Art School, Ems?'

Josephine suddenly shouted, 'Talking of manic and loony—'

Hosannah came back indoors, marched past the table and began banging pots into the dishwasher.

'Shut *up*,' Josephine rounded on her.

Hosannah froze.

'I want your mother and her wretched dogs to move somewhere else. Sheltered flat or something. I've had enough. Can't cope any more.' Josephine picked up her glass and swallowed half her wine. The unsayable was out.

There was an appalled and pregnant silence.

'I'm his mother,' Emilia said haughtily, as if that ended the matter.

'I'm his *wife*.'

'And you get on fine,' said Garcia. 'All of you. Don't you?'

Emma took her earphones out and announced she *was* going next door.

'Sheltered flat, indeed,' Emilia added, making it sound like gas chamber.

'An unsheltered flat, then,' her daughter-in-law snapped. 'Or a dear little cottage with roses round the door. So long as it's not here, I couldn't care less.'

Emma coughed with laughter, got up and disappeared.

'You just gave her an excuse to disobey you,' Emilia remarked.

'A lot of the time, *you* are her excuse for disobeying me,' Josephine snapped back.

Garcia began to sense a rift that would not easily be healed. 'My mother is not going into a flat.'

'Then *I'll* go into a flat. So long as I can get on with my work without being plagued by self-indulgent *women*.'

Hosannah, listening, caught the reference to herself, crashed a pile of pans into the sink and left them there.

'Now look what you've done,' Emilia sniffed. 'Help doesn't grow on trees.'

Josephine shrugged dismissively.

Pale as a plaster saint with rage, Emilia got up, scooped up Barney Darling, called Rambo to her with a piercing shriek and departed upstairs.

'Oh, Lord. Maria Callas on a bad day,' Josephine muttered.

'If I lived in America, I'd divorce you and put myself in care,' Emma said righteously, coming back. 'Nanna should divorce you because you're being mean.'

'Good idea,' Josephine answered. 'Why doesn't she?'

'I think I'll go and live in a caravan,' Emma threatened.

'Clacton-on-Sea or Southend,' Josephine suggested as Emma sidled towards the back door, to go through the hole in the wall to next door. 'Caravans galore. I'll even drive you down there, take you to the shops to stock up, lend you pocket money and pay the first quarter's rent. Just so long as you take your grandmother with you.'

'You're so *sad*,' Emma sighed, and disappeared.

'You can't mean it, Jo.'

'I mean it.'

He'd only been home a couple of hours, and his home was falling apart. Garcia got up and opened another bottle. Towards the bottom of it, he proposed a compromise.

'Tell you what, we'll build on a granny flat. Solves the problem and puts the value of the house up.'

'You'll never get planning permission.'

'Negative, negative, negative.' Garcia wasn't in a mood to argue any further.

Ron and Sophia next door were working late and the paying guests were mostly out, so Emma wandered home again.

'What you up to?' demanded Hosannah, coming out to the back step for a Marlboro last thing. There was an old wooden pew in the glass-roofed lobby leading to the garden, where smokers roosted. Emma was sitting there, listening to Elvis, sheltered from the rain.

'Waiting for you to come out and lend me a fag and hoping Dad will forget I'm grounded,' she answered, pulling her earphones out. 'Sophia and Ron are having a Christmas drinks party.'

Hosannah pulled out a crumpled pack of cigarettes.

'Paul Scheinfeld'll be there,' Emma said, blowing smoke through her nostrils.

'You too young, like Irma.'

'Too young for what?' Emma asked scornfully.

Hosannah puffed and didn't answer.

'Irma's *twenty*. I'm nearly sixteen and I'm practically the last virgin in my class. Why do you think I put an American flag on my ceiling? It's a symbol of America, licked and devoured by the flames of passion!'

'*Mon Dieu*,' Hosannah said, impressed.

'I got the idea when I was reading Blake,' Emma explained casually, flicking ash. 'Innocence and Experience. That kind of stuff. *You* know.'

'Sure.'

They leaned against each other to keep warm. It was hard to imagine Hosannah knowing about romance and sex and being in love, though she must be quite experienced and not at all innocent since she had a filthy sense of humour, an ex-husband who had run away from the fighting in Bosnia to Germany, and a daughter, Irma, who worked for two doctors in Manchester and was trying to get political asylum.

Sometimes Emma wondered doubtfully if Hosannah was really a woman at all. She had the strong, sturdy build of a man, broad shoulders, a short neck and big, squashy chest. She walked with a man's aggressive stride and had narrow hips with no bottom, never wore skirts, just trousers and baggy, shapeless jumpers from the Oxfam shop. Emma was *positive* she shaved her upper lip.

A gust of wind from the darkness blew rain into the porch and lifted Hosannah's ragged hair. Cold weather whipped high colour into her cheeks, chapped and red like a child's, made her deepset brown eyes water. Hidden behind heavy spectacles and lowering brows, the eyes were clever and sad and scared.

Hosannah was no fool, knew what was what.

Once, she had told Emma she should have been a man. 'With

the soul of a woman,' she added, cackling, after a lecture in her deep, hoarse voice and much consultation of a dictionary about the consequences of too much testosterone in the system.

'He makes you horny,' she explained, then added regretfully, 'but when you ugly like me, no pussy.'

Emma considered that dreadful dilemma at length, and thereafter regarded anything to do with hormones with exaggerated respect.

Huddling closer, because of the cold, she asked, 'Why are you called Hosannah?'

'Religious mother,' Hosannah cackled derisively. 'When I am born she so excited, she start praying and crying like crazy woman and my father and everyone think she want to call me Hosannah. After, he got stuck.'

'It,' corrected Emma automatically. 'A name is *it*.'

They sat in silence, smoking a last cigarette, lost in fantasy.

Hosannah thought about Irma, spending another Christmas in Manchester, that a letter from the Home Office giving her asylum would be the best Christmas present, and that no amount of prayers or letters to Santa would bring it.

Emma thought about Paul Scheinfeld, one of Sophia's paying guests, doing Europe while waiting to go to Yale. Six feet five inches tall, an all-American boy with blindingly capped orthodontically correct teeth, a JFK smile and a fantastic talent for laconic one-liners that would one day help him become a wealthy barrister like his father. Paul Scheinfeld had shown her photographs of himself in the High School football team, strong, long thighs pumping. He was athletic, smart, and from New York, and the coolest dude in town.

Paul would leave on New Year's Eve, for Paris, and she was grounded.

She threw her cigarette stub after the others, into the garden where her mother would find them and shout at her. She sighed.

'Paul, eh? Hah. You learn,' Hosannah teased, her voice like tearing sacking. She dug Emma painfully and good-naturedly in the ribs, and grinned.

'Mum and Dad have gone, at least,' Emma said, listening to silence in the enormous kitchen. 'D'you think Mum would really make Nanna go away? It wasn't her fault Barney Darling bit that stupid woman.'

Hosannah was only hired help and wouldn't be drawn, so they went into the house, turned off the lights and went to bed.

Chapter Six

When her predecessor left to have a baby, Hosannah Zorvat arrived in Josephine's house as a daily cleaner, sent by Mrs Bee of the Busy Bee South London Cleaning Agency. She came from the Balkans, via Manchester, Sophia's Paying Guest service and Willy Flynn's bedsit in Surbiton. It was obvious from the very start how much she hated cleaning.

'You've either got to stop sulking about it and get on with the job or find something else to do,' Josephine told her crossly, coming upon her smoking furiously in the kitchen lobby when she should have been Hoovering. 'You're puffing smoke in the kitchen, and if Garcia smells it, he'll sack you. What's the matter with you?'

Boredom. Humiliation. Rage and fear. Hosannah spat words in Croatian that made it clear being sacked from *cleanings* didn't count as a real sack at all.

In a country where Serbs and Croats were busy slaughtering each other with commitment and enthusiasm, Hosannah had the worst of all possible misfortunes: a Serbian mother, Croatian father. An economics graduate from Zagreb University, she bought locomotives and other rolling stock for the Yugoslav Railways. When Yugoslavia ceased to exist, so did Hosannah's job, without warning or explanation.

'I've been working here for fifteen years. What are you going to do about this?' she shouted, going into her old office and confronting the Serb in charge, who in the days of Yugoslav Railways had trained and promoted her steadily for twelve of the fifteen years. She planted the brief letter terminating her services on his desk with a loud slap. 'Give me back my job.'

'I can't. You are Croat,' he said, his expression wary and bleak and angry. 'Go away, Hosannah.'

She stormed down the corridor.

'Who knows as much about buying and managing rolling stock as I do?' she demanded, nose to nose with Goran, her former assistant. 'Help me tell those idiots in there, they need me back.'

'You are Serb,' Goran answered quietly, as if to say, 'Isn't it obvious?'

'And what the hell are you these days?' she retorted. 'Apart from just a yob?'

An economics graduate from the same university, he had been bright, polite and eager. Now, he lounged, a leery, shifty-eyed fanatic, looking for trouble and fingering a gun in his belt. A filthy handkerchief tied round his head held back greasy hair.

'Goran?'

'It is the war.' He had several days' growth of beard and exhausted eyes, empty and shiny and flat like glass.

'This war is crazy children and bureaucrats playing at shooting. We're all *mad*,' shouted Hosannah, unimpressed and stamping out.

'*Now* what?' She looked at her clock. Eleven o'clock at night and someone banging at her door.

She fished her slippers on to her feet and slopped down her small entranceway, peered through the spyhole. The bulbous figure on the other side was leaning with his hands against her door, head down, waiting. She recognised the magnified top of that head.

'Go away, Goran,' she shouted, putting the chain on. 'Enough, for one day.'

He lifted his head in surprise. Then there was a tremendous blow right in front of her face, the unmistakable sound of a gun barrel splintering wood.

'Goran, *stop that!*'

The hammering stopped. She put her eye cautiously back to the peephole, made out Goran's magnified face, distorted by the glass, bandanna awry and tongue hanging out with effort. As he raised his rifle butt to her door again, she slid the chain off, stood to one side, wrenched her door open, and listened with satisfaction to his grunt of surprise and pain as he catapulted into her tiny hall with his gun barrel narrowly missing one hairy nostril.

'Shoot yourself, why don't you?' she suggested. 'Go on. Don't worry about the mess.'

He sat up, put the Kalashnikov in the crook of a knee and swore at her worse than she had heard from trackmen in all her years on the railroads.

'I suppose you can't blow your brains out if you haven't got any. What do you want?' she demanded, cutting him short.

He wiped his nose on his hand, went exaggeratedly cross-eyed to check if it was knocked sideways and said sullenly, 'Your flat.'

'Well, you can bugger off, then. You can't have my flat.'

He stood up, fumbled in his pocket and took out a handkerchief. 'I need a flat.'

'Go find one somewhere else. Go filch someone else's flat.'

He shook his head. 'You got no job. You'll end up in the camps. You don't need your flat.'

She stared at the gun lying beside him, on her floor, and turned away contemptuously.

'They wouldn't give either,' he said, unrolling the handkerchief. He peered up at her, cunning, and thrust the palm of his hand up flat, to show her what lay in it. Two human ears nestled in the stained cotton folds, waxy and bloodless, one containing an earring, a little gold and coral stud. 'Croats.'

Hosannah pulled her short, sparse hair back, dry and dull from lack of food, vitamins and luxuries like shampoo. 'Oh, my. An *ear* collection,' she cried sarcastically. 'Go ahead, asshole, if you want two more. God knows why – my hearing isn't so good since the mortars and I haven't washed them out in weeks because the water's off and I've got no soap. But if you've got better use for them than me, Goran, take 'em. You're welcome. My flat is all I got left for me and Irma since I divorced my husband. Ears or no ears, you took my job and you're not getting my flat to go with it.'

She held her damaged door wide as he shuffled out.

After that nothing frightened her except hunger and losing Irma. Irma, eighteen years old, was starving. Goran was right, with no job and no hope of a new one, she had no money and no food and would soon end up in a camp. The camps would feed anyone who came and begged, but no one went there except as a last resort.

'We have to go eat with the refugees,' Hosannah announced,

her stomach aching with hunger, her head in her fridge in order to make an inventory of their rations and finding nothing except some old ice cubes in it.

Irma, who had her grandmother's dark Hungarian looks, pulled a bad face and turned her back. 'No *way*. It's humiliating.'

Hosannah grabbed her arm and rounded on her. 'For an oh-so-clever university student about to go into the mathematics faculty, you are stupid. You can be humiliated or you can be dead of starvation,' she shouted. 'When you're starved to death, humiliation won't matter. Nor will mathematics. So you better choose now.'

Refusing to look behind her to see if Irma was coming, Hosannah marched to the refugee camp on the outskirts of Zagreb, stood in line like an animal waiting for feed, eyes blank and her nose in the air. White with rage and hunger, Irma scuffed after her like an angry child, heavy legs like her mother's in broken boots, her painful thinness disguised by an oversized blue overcoat. When she shuffled up to her mother in the queue, Irma had a bit of blanket wrapped round her head.

'Nice hat,' Hosannah said sarcastically.

Irma scowled. 'It's so that no one will recognise me.'

'You think anyone *here* could care?' Hosannah looked around at the patient, starving people, so afraid and depressed by what they were becoming that her scornful words died away on her lips.

The next part of her plan to save Irma required money, and was much more difficult.

'You are going to put off going to university,' Hosannah announced, fingering her ear, which had recently become a habit.

'Why would I put it off?'

'You are going away. Year out, as they say.'

'No, I'm not,' Irma said, astonished.

'Yes, you are.' Hosannah watched her daughter's deep brown eyes turn mutinous and her heart sank. Irma was stubborn as a mule – and her mother. 'You have to. I don't want you growing up thinking this country is *normal*,' she pleaded, frightened to death that if Irma dug her heels in she wouldn't be able to force her to go. 'You think people in other countries are all murderers? Ethnic cleansing.' She spat the words. 'You think the British put people in concentration camps?'

'The British,' Irma answered, 'invented concentration camps.'

'Not for their *own*,' her mother dismissed the problem. 'Most people do not think it is all right to bomb hospitals and shoot women waiting for bread. Or children, playing in the street. Do you think the English or the Americans eat in refugee camps?'

Irma began to argue, but Hosannah hurried on, 'Former Yugoslavia needs a psychiatrist. You stay here, *you* will need a psychiatrist. It isn't individuals any more, it's the country. In a psychotic country, everyone is crazy. I can't bear to see *you* go crazy, and you are *leaving*.'

Postage to England was so expensive, it took weeks to find the money. Hosannah bartered food from the camp until she had enough to send for a copy of *The Lady* which she'd heard about.

'Mothers' helps and *au pairs*. Translate them for me.'

'I won't leave you,' Irma said.

Hosannah banged the table, frustrated, as guns went *pop, pop, pop*, like toys, away in the distance.

Irma read the columns sulkily.

'Good,' said Hosannah, circling probables and possibles with a pencil. 'Now, you write the letters.'

Bitter winds blew outside, winter on its way. Later that evening she broke up the table for firewood.

'England is the right place,' she said as the fire sparked. 'The English sent their children away in the war, so they understand. The English are decent.'

'I won't go without you.'

'I'll come later. When there's the money.'

'How?'

Hosannah rolled her eyes in exasperation and threw a table leg on to the fire. When the woman from the ground floor flat went out to buy bread the next morning and walked into a mortar lobbed from the hills, Irma and Hosannah visited her in the hospital. Irma took a good look round and went very quiet. Then she agreed to go.

When Irma had been away one and a half years, Hosannah sold her washing machine, dishwasher, her heavy gold neck chain, her engagement and wedding rings to buy an airline ticket to go and see her.

The surgeons whose child Irma looked after lived in Manchester. Manchester had no guns, no soldiers, no mortars, a huge amount of rain, mushy peas and boredom. There was also a lot of bad news on the television about Bosnia where even Paddy Ashdown, the Blue Berets and the glamorous and charismatic General Rose together couldn't stop the war from escalating.

'We are going to ask for political asylum,' Hosannah told Irma when the six months she was allowed to stay were up.

Genocide at home was giving her the shakes. Severed ears she could manage; Irma back home, raped, starved, killed, she could not. Terror drove her, heart pounding, sick with fear, to wander the wet and dingy streets of Manchester, unable to come out of her panic until she made up her mind. 'We will go to London and ask at the Home Office for asylum.'

'All we'll get is time.'

'And money. Income support and a work permit,' her mother said. 'I've been finding out.'

'Only until our papers and our applications reach the top of the in-tray and then they'll send us home. It's usually about two years and it's policy,' Irma warned. 'In Britain, even when they sound as though they come from Lancashire, like we do, people from former Yugoslavia don't get political asylum.'

Willy Flynn, whom Hosannah had met in the Tottenham Court Road McDonalds shortly after she arrived in London, and from whom she rented a room, had said The Angel, Islington, for free advice. Shortly before she started working for the Goddards, Hosannah took the piece of paper on which he had written his number and an Islington address, got on the Tube, and after a good deal of wandering around (in the course of which she unknowingly passed the offices of Garcia Goddard International), found the Islington Law Centre.

'Why have you waited so long?' the dapper Pakistani lawyer asked irritably, looking over the notes he had taken. 'You and your daughter should have applied for the right to reside in this country when you got here. By waiting until now, you have greatly weakned your case and made our job a lot more difficult.'

She stared at him for a long time, willing herself not to shout at him or cry. She waited until she could put the awkward English words together without emotion.

'I wait for peace. He have peace plans – Dr Owen and UN. I look at TV and I read newspapers. Plans, plans, plans. I wait. Perhaps plans *work* and I go home. Hah. I go home . . .' She laughed, put two fingers to her forehead, pulled a trigger.

His face was expressionless.

'Or I go in camp and I starve. Is important how I die?' her hoarse, masculine voice grated sarcastically. 'I know, I am one *leetle* person. I am not important.'

'Whether you are important or not is not the issue. The issue is convincing the Home Office that you are likely to die if you return to Croatia. That's a very different matter to convincing me,' he said, thin, well-manicured brown hands lying on top of his sheaf of notes. 'But we'll have a go. Tell me, out of interest, are you homesick?'

She answered without hesitation. 'No, I am not homesick for my country who doesn't exist any more. The country that is now is not my home.'

He nodded as if satisfied. 'We will have to put a case together, an argument.'

'I speak bad English,' Hosannah warned.

'I have no Croatian interpreter. We'll take it slowly.'

For what seemed like a very long time, he sat writing down more details. Then they began to piece together her story.

Over two visits, she told Mr Nishawawi everything he wanted to know. On her second visit, she told him about Goran and the ears, about the camps, and about Irma's schoolfriends who had been raped, and her terror that had made her send Irma away.

That night she slept fitfully, plagued by nightmares in which mortars screamed down upon a busload of people, all of whom she knew. They stared at her reproachfully, as though it was all her fault, dead faces, living eyes.

Her ears had been damaged by an exploding shell fired by a nest of bored, frustrated Serbs at the bus she was in late one afternoon, travelling back to Zagreb from a meeting. It was a long time since she had thought about that.

She got up just before dawn, with a pounding headache, sat in Willy Flynn's big bedsit, listening to fat raindrops drumming on the corrugated roof of the unused garage outside her window. Mentally, she drew up a credit and debit list of how she stood.

Despite the impenetrable mixture of Yugoslav and Lancashire accents, her English was good enough for her to argue her case with dapper little Pakistani Nish who specialised in asylum applications from refugee clients with no money, status or passports; the more indigent and dispossessed, professionally speaking, the more he relished the challenge. Unofficial Home Office policy was to refuse citizens of the former Yugoslavia the right to reside in Britian. Even refugees fleeing the slaughter in the safe haven at Bihac were grudgingly being given the right to stay for one year only. Serbo-Croatian Hosannah, whom no one wanted, was a particular challenge. Nish was a crusader. Each needed the other, which gave him enormous professional satisfaction, while his client suffered migraines of resentment.

Hosannah was also fluent in Soap, knew precisely who was doing what to whom in the Rover's Return, the Queen Vic and the Water Hole. Watching repeats of *The Good Life*, she found herself recognising Surbiton, where it was made, and laughing aloud at the jokes. Knowing a bunch of characters on television was a poor substitute for knowing real people.

Pain stabbed in her head. With real people, except for fat and kindly Willy Flynn who didn't care about her moods, her record wasn't good. She had snubbed a man who approached her one evening in the local pub, was on nodding terms with the divorced alcoholic from Kingston in the room next door, swapped insults with malevolent intensity with the middle-aged drug addict from a women's refuge who lurked in the room at the top of the stairs, watching out in case her husband came.

Hosannah slid her feet into the old slippers she had worn when Goran came to call, rummaged in a battered leather holdall for the flimsy buff booklet Nish had got her from the Home Office and looked at it with disgust. It gave her the right to claim income support and a work permit while they considered her case, just as Irma had said.

She smoothed out the work permit and studied it.

I eat humble pie, she thought. Hah. So what?

Sidling out into the cold hall, she darted at the dog-eared *Yellow Pages* wedged underneath the communal payphone and shot back into her room before the drug addict could catch her and demand to know what she was doing. Hosannah made a cup of tea, then, sitting on the floor with the steaming mug in front of her, she rifled through C until she came to Cleaning. Later that day she signed on with Mrs Bee.

'You know, the fighting isn't in Zagreb,' Garcia said on her second day. He had come into the kitchen to make himself some tea and found her busy ironing his shirts. 'I shouldn't think the Home Office think you're that much at risk.'

'No job,' Hosannah said tersely. 'Can't work. Starve.'

'Doesn't that make you an economic refugee?'

Hosannah, on a short fuse, raised her voice to her new employer in a paroxysm of frustration. 'I tell Nish, in former Yugoslavia is not psychotic *persons*, is psychotic *nation*. Former Yugoslavia need psychiatrist. *Crazy*. I don't want to live in crazy nation.'

Garcia recoiled, astounded.

'Serbs looking like crazy for excuse to kill Croats and your papers say Serbs are monsters. Aggressors. Hah. Where were Croats in the war?'

'OK, OK.' Garcia could see what was coming.

'With Hitler,' Hosannah yelled. 'Nazi fascists. Serbs don't forget.' She peered round from her ironing, leery, her tongue hanging out, breathing hard, black eyes sliding from side to side. 'Peace plan, *hah*. They don't want peace. They want to get even. They look all round, like this, panting like dogs to be first to shoot each other. Serbs, Croats, Muslims. Long memories and any excuse. *Crazeeee*.'

'Are you sure about that woman?' Garcia asked Josephine later.

'Don't you go upsetting her,' his wife answered. 'I'm desperate for someone since Lydia went off to have her baby, and Hosannah's all Mrs Bee could get.'

Chapter Seven

The magnificent Victorian terrace in which the Goddards owned one of the double-fronted houses was made up of three large dwellings. Ron and Sophia Larkin lived in the middle house which was distinguished by a neat, shiny, illegal brass plate. The plate was illegal because they ran businesses in what was strictly a domestic residence. Knowing it would never be given, they had not applied to the council for a change of use, just gone ahead, gung-ho and never mind the consequences.

Ron's business was Larkin Recruitment Consultants whose London office was newly and even more illegally housed in the recently semi-converted attic at the very top of the four-storey house, breaking every building regulation and a potential fire hazard.

'It's discreet,' Ron argued when the Goddards, outraged, protested and threatened to report him because of the risk. 'Private. In my line of business, that's everything.'

Garcia, furious, sat down to write and shop them to the council.

'You can't take their living away from them,' Josephine cried. 'It's not their fault they're stuck. You write that letter and you'll break them. You've upset them, too, with Emilia's annexe. In fact, you've upset the whole terrace.'

Garcia dropped his pen. It wasn't the Larkins' fault they had no money and were stuck. And, although he didn't care two pins, he *had* upset the terrace.

Well set back from the road, the three houses fronted on to the cobbled courtyard in which Sherrine had slipped in last December's rainstorm. Enclosed by high, wrought-iron railings, at present, in summer, covered by honeysuckle, the courtyard had double gates opening inwards from the pavement, facing the duck pond on the fashionable village green of Barnes Common. For several months, throughout spring and early summer, communal peace had been rudely disturbed by scaffolding, cement mixers, piles of bricks, builders and builders' chaos for the building-on of Emilia Goddard's granny annexe.

The Larkins' house, like the third, was slightly shabby, rundown, in need of a coat of paint, a sure and universal sign of depressed and worrying times. The Goddards' house stood out in contrast, immaculate. Their black front door and elegant white windows were recently painted, their brass door furniture was polished like mirrors, two canary-yellow burglar alarms were prominent on the front and side walls.

Tasteful and exquisite furnishings lay beyond its swagged and tailed windows, every room a testimony to Josephine and good taste. Garcia's constant travel was evident. Fine, unusual, beautiful things, antiques, many from China and the Far East, were in every room. Sunning herself on its front steps this fine August morning was Hosannah, who now looked after it all.

When she had first arrived, Mrs Bee's note of introduction in her fist, she had walked up and down the pavement, too gobsmacked and disbelieving to go inside the courtyard gate, checking and rechecking the address on the paper. It was next to where she had once stayed and the coincidence took her breath away. Once inside the Goddards' house, she was speechless. Nothing in Zagreb had prepared her for capitalist wealth on Garcia Goddard's scale.

Six months later, she was languidly poking spiders from under front door steps with her brush handle, a bucket of water beside her, pretending to scrub. It seemed a lifetime since she had stayed in the tenement next door. Early morning sun beat on her back. Sleepy as a cat, Hosannah parked herself on the baking concrete of the top step, got out a packet of Marlboros and settled down with her back against the front door, thick legs splayed comfortably. Through the curl of cigarette smoke, she gazed through the wrought-iron gate at the world drifting by on the other side.

The Paying Guest Service was the Larkins' second illegal business. Sophia had lived in 23 Byron Terrace all her life until at twenty-two she had left home to get married to an artist who painted pictures that hung in the Royal Academy. When he wasn't painting, he drank. Prodigiously.

When she tired of hiding from bailiffs, putting out fires started by his cigarettes and being frightened, she divorced him and came back home just after she turned thirty-five, with nothing. Insecure, convinced she was unattractive, she was bowled over by Ron's single-minded pursuit of her body. Shortly after they started sleeping together, he moved in. After two divorces, from wealthy women, and two children, he owned even less than Sophia. He looked carefully around the house.

'This'll be yours when the old guy pops his clogs?'

Sophia winced, but he was hers, and she loved him. 'Yes.'

As soon as his decree absolute came through, they were married. Sophia's father also married twice, the second time to Sophia's Australian stepmother. Egged on by Ron, Sophia inquired diffidently about her future expectations.

'Wills. Back to back. If I die first, she gets the property. If she goes, I get it. Whichever, you inherit eventually.'

Sophia thought about it, and frowned.

'We have a clear understanding,' her father said stiffly, reading her expression.

Wills were a personal affair. Even when one's husband didn't get on with an inheriting stepmother-in-law, it wasn't the kind of thing one could argue about.

Her father died of a stroke. Four years later, her stepmother died of cancer.

'She's left it to her son in Sydney, whom I've never met, to live in or to sell *once I leave*!' Sophia came out from hearing the will read white with shock.

The burden of keeping up such a large house was enormous, and they had no money. Unable to sell, or move, all she had was the right to live in her stepbrother's house, without the right to sell.

'She always thought you were on the make,' Sophia said bleakly.

'Detested me,' Ron muttered.

'She swore you'd never benefit from her death but I never thought she'd go this far.'

'Well, she did, didn't she? Evil old bat.'

The will left them well and truly snookered. Ron retreated inside his shell and acted very bitter.

While Hosannah lounged outside, just starting work for the day, he was reading the *Financial Times* over breakfast in their shabby kitchen.

'Prime central London property is still at a premium,' he snarled, scanning a report from Savills, the estate agents. 'If we could only sell this place we'd be laughing.'

'Don't start that again.'

Sophia was folding sheets. The paying guests helped make ends meet. Legions of English language students and backpackers passed through her rooms. They stuck photographs of home, posters of Greek islands and Australian beaches with drawing pins on to faded silk wallpaper and sent her postcards when they went away. They played *Eric Clapton Unplugged* and Tina Turner very loudly, then descended locustlike into her kitchen to devour her very basic, penny-pinching cooking. Her other attempts to find a way out of her stepmother's trap had come to nothing. She'd tried.

Sophia liked everything just so; she folded her sheets precisely and, spurred by Ron's remark about the Savills article, thought back.

'It's not *fair*,' she had screamed in the lawyer's office. 'I want you to appeal. She hated my husband. She knew what the bills would be, and that we can't afford them.'

'It's perfectly valid,' the lawyer said.

Sophia screeched, jabbed at the photocopy on his desk. 'And written out of pure malice.'

'Unfortunately, malice is not grounds for appeal against an otherwise perfectly legal will.'

'Spite and wickedness. I want you to contest it. Who nursed her, those last months? *Me*.'

He spread his hands sympathetically. 'An appeal would cost money you can ill afford to spend, and you would lose, I guarantee.'

He had a paperweight containing a gnome in a snowstorm. He turned it upside down and waited for the snow to settle. Its vulgarity generally caught the client's attention and gave them a chance to compose themselves. As the gnome grinned out of his artificial blizzard, Sophia folded her small arms stubbornly and looked as though she would never go.

'Sophia, people often make wills with the express intention of upsetting everyone as much as possible from a point of vantage where they can never be got at themselves, since by the time the will is read they are well out of it. In my view you cannot possibly overturn this one. Why don't you try putting it to your stepbrother that this isn't a very fair way of distributing your family's wordly goods? You might find him very reasonable.'

Her stepbrother was his mother's son; he had already had the house valued, from Australia.

'*Never.*'

His appointments were running late. He shook the gnome again and decided to get his clerk to come in with urgent business if she didn't look like leaving.

'She *can't* get away with this.'

At getting on for two hundred pounds an hour, she erupted into the most expensive tantrum and crying jag of her life. After it was over, disregarding his glances at his watch, she fixed her make-up over his office fireplace.

'I hate favouritism,' she said through clenched teeth, slapping liner and mascara on reddened eyes, the effect being a cross between a rat and a panda. 'What that wicked old bat wanted was to *hurt* me. And she has succeeded. But I'll *never* leave that house.'

He shrank into his leather executive chair, peered over a Manhattan skyline of piled up papers and reached for his telephone. 'As you wish.'

'I'll take lodgers,' she snarled, looking at the ceiling. 'Are you listening up there? I'll turn it into a tenement and do bed and breakfast.' She looked down at him as he dialled next door for rescue. 'She'll hate that so much she'll come back and haunt me. Let her. I'll have her exorcised. Straight down to hell.'

'Could you come and see Mrs Larkin out?' he said to his clerk. 'Offer her a cup of tea before she goes. She's had a most upsetting time.'

Sophia dismissed the embarrassing memory of that horrible interview, put the sheets away and followed Ron up to the very top of the house, to his office. Four Velux windows set into the roof stood open. Sophia could hear the geese on the common, honking in a frenzy. Standing on tiptoe, she could see out. 'It's that tramp again, giving them crusts out of someone's dustbin,' she said, looking down. 'The council ought to do something. He's throwing food into the road and the stupid birds are going after it.'

As she spoke, two buses screeched to a standstill, forming an instant traffic jam. A line of cars hooted and honked at the geese who stood their ground and honked back. The tramp sat back in quiet satisfaction and enjoyed the scene, munching on a bit of hand-rolled cigarette.

'I am Larkin Recruitment Consultants,' Ron yelped suddenly, getting through on his telephone call. 'I want Darling. Who are you?'

'Mr Darling's PA,' Sophia heard a voice squeak on the other end of the telephone line. 'Mr Darling is in a meeting.'

'Then I'll wait until he's back from his meeting or the lavatory or wherever he's gone. No, he can't call back.' He put his hand over the receiver. 'Personnel are always in meetings when money comes into it. Never want to have to go back to the boss and tell him if he wants the right man they're going to have to cough up more dough.'

He waited, fanning himself impatiently with an empty A4 file.

Larkin Recruitment Consultants' head office was a stifling, telephone-box sized room. At five foot ten, Ron's head scraped the ceiling. He had a fan going full blast, ruffling papers. Two desks pushed back to back, two grey typing chairs and a bank of metal filing cabinets filled the tiny space. Sunlight pouring in through the Veluxes heated the wooden floor, the air smelling of honeysuckle and traffic. Darling evidently came back.

'What do you think this is?' Ron bawled, reading spectacles perched on the end of his large nose, thumbing several sheets of neatly typed paper in disgust. 'A marriage bureau? I've got him interested and willing but he won't budge until he gets the right package. And this isn't it. Quit playing the reluctant virgin and come across with the goods.'

'Your turn to be rude back,' murmured Sophia to herself, putting paper into the photocopier. 'It's called negotiating.' She pressed a button and the photocopier began flashing and whirring.

'Of course he speaks French and German,' Ron snapped down the telephone. 'And in any case, everyone in Brussels speaks English. Romanian? Buy him a Linguaphone course and a Walkman. Fluent in three weeks. Failing that, buy an interpreter. Which you do anyway. What's the matter with you?'

'I read those ads too.' Darling sounded amused. 'The point is, not all contracts are negotiated in Brussels. Far from it. We could require Romanian, Hungarian and Serbo-Croat – not that anyone admits to speaking *that* any more – and Polish and Russian would be even better.' Darling always enjoyed winding Ron up. 'But we are exceptionally reasonable people here and a bit of German will do.'

'Course he has German,' Ron roared. 'He's a fucking *scientist*.'

'Scientific German can't ask the way to the *Bahnhof*.'

Darling tired of the game. The candidate was the best person for the job and they both knew it. Interpreters cost a fortune and went with the job. The rest of it was academic, but they would stab at each other until they drew blood over details; pay package, private health care, first-class travel, share options, the whole deal including Ron's profit.

Ron was bawling again. He never talked if he could bawl instead. Sophia sighed. With bills due next month, that he made a profit was the only thing that mattered.

Josephine had complained about the bawling. 'If Ron *must* telephone people in New York or wherever and shout his head off, could he try to remember there is a telephone cable *all the way* across the Atlantic, and they can hear him perfectly clearly? Try to get him to bear in mind that he makes phone calls, like Garcia does, at times when other people are trying to sleep. Would you *please* keep your windows shut.'

'Too hot,' said Sophia. 'Ron sweats.'

'I thought the whole *object* of that illegal conversion that we're all conniving at was that he wanted complete confidentiality when he's poaching people from their employers. He shouts so much, the whole neighbourhood can listen in.'

Sophia smiled sweetly.

'It is lucky that I like you because where your husband's concerned, sometimes I find myself contemplating homicide,' her next-door neighbour exclaimed, marched up her own front door steps and slammed her door.

Chapter Eight

The third house in the terrace had been converted, some years earlier, into flats, evident from the brass entryphone next to its scuffed black front door. A row of names was neatly printed next to the entryphone buttons – Howarth, Quinlan, Hassall-Hammond, then, at the bottom, for the ground-floor flat, scrawled in bold red capitals, BABE'NBARRY.

The whole façade was somewhat in need of maintenance and a coat of white paint.

'They're supposed to have a complete face-lift every seven years. It's in their lease,' Sophia complained to Josephine.

'Hark who's talking! In any case,' Josephine added, 'sooner or later someone will go busybodying around and list these buildings. Then we'll all have an obligation to keep them up.'

Sophia darted a glance at her. 'No doubt that was one reason you were in such a tearing hurry to get Emilia's extension on. Before they turned you into a historical monument so you couldn't put a carbuncle on your house and get away with it.'

The courtyard was a sociable place. People sat on the bench underneath Josephine's dining room window to have a cigarette, chat or, like Hosannah, just watch village life go by. Sophia and Josephine often bumped into one another and stopped to chat.

One Saturday afternoon in late June, Josephine, in bagged linen trousers, a mustard jacket, her hair scraped into a wide green Alice band, met Sophia coming home from Sainsbury's.

'New King's Road. Beaumont and Fletcher. What do you think?' She took a bundle of fabric swatches out of an enormous handbag and held them out for Sophia to inspect.

'For you?'

'For Samantha Gilmour. Ideas for bathroom curtains. She likes

Designers' Guild but that Georgian cottage of hers asks for something more traditional. We'll end up compromising.'

'And how many bathrooms has poor little Marie Antoinette got to cope with in her playhouse this time?' Sophia inquired sarcastically.

'Four,' Josephine admitted reluctantly.

'Oh *dear.*'

Josephine stuffed the swatches back in her bag to give Sophia time to stop sneering.

Samantha Gilmour had four bathrooms in her new place just down the road in the country. The Gilmours also had four bathrooms over the way, on the far side of the common. Josephine had counted three in the farmhouse in the South of France, had never visited the Caribbean pad. It was a pity Hosannah never visited the Gilmours; it would have put her notions about capitalist wealth in an undreamed of new perspective.

'There should be a law against it,' Sophia said jealously. 'Anyway, why are you running around the New King's Road for them?'

'Their country cottage is actually a big, rundown house which needs renovating. They asked me to do the interior design.'

'Well now.' Sophia's little pixie face looked calculating. 'Good for you. Garcia and Emmanuel Gilmour were at school together, weren't they?'

'I did not get the job because of Garcia,' Josephine said coldly. 'He had nothing to do with it. I submitted ideas and estimates. And they liked them.'

Sophia, in black leggings, black plimsolls and a huge yellow jumper, looked like a wasp and had a waspish expression. 'Your builders have wrecked our honeysuckle,' she changed the subject crossly.

'And the Gilmours' builders are busy wrecking their garden, too. Builders do. It'll grow back.'

But Sophia was still thinking about Emmanuel and Garcia. 'They caroused around playing hockey, didn't they?'

'They played a lot of sport. Yes.'

Sophia scented something in Josephine's voice, a vague sense of unease.

'They did a lot of things together. Got drunk. Got selected for the Olympics. Turned the Olympics down. Too busy making money.'

The real team sport in those days had been practical joking. *Terrible* jokes, ruthlessly planned and carried out; a few victims still hated Garcia. 'They deserved to get arrested any number of times,' Josephine went on. 'But the only time they did, they were racing stolen milk floats down Brighton seafront. Blind drunk at three in the morning. Garcia paid Emmanuel's fine because he was the one with money at the time.'

'Sporting brotherhood,' said Sophia, suddenly wistful.

'Sporting Mafia,' Josephine shot back. 'Don't start romanticising that gang, Sophia; they're worse than the Triads.'

By unspoken consent, they picked up their bags and went inside their respective houses.

When Josephine and Garcia were first married, they lived in a flat. Sprawling and roomy, it occupied the third floor of a five-storey block just across from one of the gents' lavatories in Hyde Park, not far from the Albert Hall.

Emmanuel found it for them, rang them up in Spain on their five-day honeymoon, told them to come back, quick, he'd found them a fantastic place to live, at a peppercorn rent. It was a fix such as wouldn't come twice.

Garcia spent all day telling the airline his mother was dying and he *had* to change his tickets. As they flew home, he said airily that he couldn't have afforded more than two days in Spain, and anyway, having somewhere near Emmanuel and all their friends that was amazingly cheap and convenient more than made up for a bit of lost honeymoon – he leaned over the uncomfortable aircraft seat and kissed her nose – didn't it?

They were all skint in those days, just down from Oxford, starting out, lawyers, doctors, dentists, teachers, bankers, businessmen, architects and accountants; they had all the professions between them. Emmanuel lived in a top-floor flat just round the corner from the snip he had found for Garcia. He let his rooms out, to pay the rent. An entire hockey team often dossed there, mostly men he had known at Oxford. If there wasn't room, they dossed next door, with Garcia. After the game, pissed as newts in the decaying prefab that smelled like a cross between a brewery and a French urinal that was their clubhouse, they stayed drunk from

Saturday afternoon to Sunday night, and behaved, Josephine said, when she lost her sense of humour, like the monkey house in the zoo. Garcia became a legend among cabin crews in several airlines for running on to mid-weekend flights straight from the finish, still in muddy strip, covered in bashes and bruises.

'Ridiculous,' Josephine muttered, left to hold the fort and clear up the havoc.

'Ah,' Garcia would say in later years, nostalgia in his eyes. 'But wasn't it bloody *brilliant*?'

When the clubhouse closed, they hurtled back for *Match of the Day*, a whistling, yelling convoy of mini mokes and smoking tyres down the Kensington Road, the Beatles belting out. Sundays, they played golf.

'Is there a pitch and putt in Hyde Park?' Josephine had asked innocently the first time Emmanuel got out the clubs.

'You want to play?'

Naive, puzzled, she took the club in her hand and flushed when they all howled with laughter.

They teed off from just inside the front door. The second hole was down the hall, round a tricky corner, to the lift. In the lift, out of the lift. Fourth hole needed careful judgement, through the front door and down the steps. Across into the gents' lavatory in the park, then it was uphill all the way back again. The gutters were the rough and the drain was the water, for which there were severe penalties because if the ball went in the drain, it was lost for good. The lavatory brush holder, wedged on its side, back in Emmanuel's bathroom, was the eighteenth hole.

Garcia once put the ball on to the camber of the Kensington Road where it balanced in a way that should have been impossible, right on the middle. He was out there on his hands and knees sizing up the next shot, with buses and traffic racing past, when Josephine, hearing shouting from the street, ran out to look. Emmanuel, waving a seven iron over by the gents' lavatory, was looking back, beside himself with laughter.

'Oh my God, he'll get killed,' she shrieked.

'Not him,' Emmanuel roared back, pointing with his iron.

A police car had parked at the side of the road. Garcia, vaguely aware that everything had stopped, looked up, annoyed at being distracted from an exceptionally difficult stroke.

'Tricky one, sir,' said one of the three policemen who had scrambled out of the patrol car. The other two set about holding up the traffic. When it was at a standstill, the three of them went down on their hands and knees and gave Garcia some serious advice. In the event, the ball flew sweetly straight into the lavatory.

The police clapped him on the back and climbed into their car, leaving the traffic to clear itself, which seemed to take for ever.

Then they'd loll about drinking beer and watching sport all evening on television, Josephine remembered, while she and a group of tolerant, misguided girlfriends who had not yet heard of feminism made vats of spaghetti bolognese and lugged gallons of cheap Chianti from the nearby off-licence. She had felt as if she was running an upmarket soup kitchen. Once word went out on the grapevine that Emmanuel and Garcia were keeping open house in Kensington, there was seldom a moment's peace.

After a while, there was a spate of weddings, then a spate of babies.

'What about us?' Garcia suggested, not wanting to be left out, and broody.

'The way we live and babies don't mix,' Josephine answered.

'We can make it.'

'*I* can make it, you mean. You won't change just because we've got a baby.'

They talked to and fro, to no avail, for months. Then her pills went missing.

After the row that followed, he was contrite. Garcia in a contrite mood was enticing, humble and at his most manipulative and dangerous. Josephine, seduced, absolutely against her better judgement, gave in.

To become a single mother.

Garcia, absent more than most divorced fathers, doted on Emma, spoiled her shamelessly.

'It's to stop himself feeling guilty,' Josephine cried to Emmanuel's wife, Matilda. 'The next minute it's "I've got to hop on a plane, and why won't you come with me?" You can't do that with a toddler.'

'Garcia's wonderful with her,' Matilda said easily.

'He winds her up, you mean,' Josephine snapped. 'It's easy to be

Mr Wonderfully Exciting when you don't know what a routine is, you're mostly twelve thousand miles away and never around long enough to clear up the mess. It takes me a week to settle Emma down when he goes away again.'

Matilda, pregnant with her first child, didn't have a clue, just smiled like a beautiful, sensual, lazy cat. Two years later, she and Emmanuel were the first of the gang to be divorced.

All Emmanuel's wives were blonde: Matilda strawberry, Vanessa ash, Samantha silver. They were all beautiful, and younger than he was. Emmanuel's ex-wives turned into his best friends.

'And they don't seem to *mind*,' Sophia sighed. 'Ron's ex-wives only speak to him when they have to. When it's something to do with children.'

'They don't mind at all. It was hysterical,' Josephine said, back in March, tanned, hair bleached, clear-eyed and radiantly healthy, with the year's best skiing story to tell, to Sophia's unspoken envy. She had gone round to borrow some milk for tea and to give Sophia a couple of bottles of duty free wine and a carton of cigarettes.

'Who wants tea?' Sophia said, taking the bottles and fetching a corkscrew.

They sat drinking their lunch, Ron shouting faintly in the distance, hidden away in his eyrie.

'Garcia said he'd meet me in the airport. He was late.' He always caught planes at the last minute and when she was with him it made her anxious. 'When I got to the check-in, it turned out the plane was delayed. Garcia was on the way from his office and nowhere around, so I went through to wait in the lounge.' Josephine poured them a second glass of wine.

'And I bumped into Vanessa. She had Susannah with her, and the two little boys, and a new baby. And the nanny. And it turned out they were waiting for the same plane as us. Then her husband came in and said the plane was more delayed than they thought so we had some more drinks, then there was a whole lot of commotion and Matilda came sweeping in in an absolute flood of people, the four kids, her mother, her mother's boyfriend, her current husband and his son.'

'And *his* first wife?'

'No,' said Josephine, puzzled. 'Just the nanny. Then Emmanuel came rushing through with Sammy in tow, tripped over one of his stepchildren and practically fell into Vanessa's lap.'

'How *embarrassing*.'

'Absolutely not. By the time Garcia turned up and our flight was called, we'd taken the lounge over and were having a party.'

'You must have had such a lovely time,' Sophia said sadly.

New husbands, new wives, former husbands, former wives, original children, new children, stepchildren, babies, nannies and God knows what. They drank Swissair's first-class lounge's champagne supply dry, went roaring off to the plane together and had a *brilliant* holiday.

Until they came back.

Garcia had come home, dumped his ski gear, showered, repacked, sworn at his faxes, kissed her and gone back to Heathrow to get on another plane.

Strangely restless, obscurely agitated, Josephine stood in her glorious kitchen, listened intently. The lunchtime wine she had drunk buzzed in her ears against the silence of the empty house. She drew a finger absently across a surface. Dust. When they went away Hosannah took every kind of liberty. Even Hosannah would have been welcome company. She went out, along the passage, upstairs and looked at her desk, piled with work, then walked around the big house, aimless. It closed round her like a giant shell, all sound of the world beyond receding. Maybe, she thought, this restlessness was how you felt in prison when they locked your door and sealed you off.

Josephine gone, Ron blessedly quiet, and all the PGs out, Sophia sat thinking about how it must be to live in that charmed circle, with men like Garcia and tall, clever, blindingly sophisticated Emmanuel who got on with all his wives, who seemed not to know what it was to be lonely and jealous.

She opened her eyes with a jerk as an unwelcome image blossomed on her eyelids: a Prince Charles *Doppelganger* at this moment roosted up in the attic above her head, like a big-eared, chain-smoking, whisky-swilling, depressed, Prozac-gobbling bat who had once seemed to her the most exciting man she'd ever met, until the gilt came off the gingerbread. While the charmed circle, in her imagination, flew around the world making millions, he was up there in the attic, morosely trying, like everyone else, and mostly failing, to earn a daily crust.

Chapter Nine

Barry, of the bright red BARRY'NBABE on the ground-floor button on the end house's entryphone, was one of Garcia's best freelance designers. When he rang the doorbell one mid-afternoon in early August, Josephine was absorbed in modifications to the electrical design for Samantha Gilmour's country kitchen.

'I brought some stuff across for Garcia,' he said, following her in. 'Not urgent. When he gets back.'

'Tea?'

What he really had come for was company. Barry was a gossip.

'Have you heard, Luvvie's walked out?'

Barry threw himself into a chair and watched Josephine put the kettle on. 'Well, not exactly walked. Melissa threw the poor little dear out on his ear.' He shuddered. 'They had the most *enormous* row.'

Melissa Howarth, the top button on the entryphone, was an actress the wrong side of fifty. Byron Terrace was her home when she wasn't up North with her hair in curlers, filming for *The Street*.

'What did they row about this time?'

Barry snickered. 'Melissa's face-lift.'

Josephine ran a finger along her jaw surreptitiously.

'I don't think so, dear. Not yet,' he said unsympathetically, catching the gesture. 'Anyway, Melissa has been consulting our good friend Andrew about rejuvenation.' Andrew Quinlan's name was next to the first-floor entryphone button, directly over BARRY'NBABE. A plastic surgeon, since his divorce he had lived alone, a sparsely furnished, impersonal bachelor existence. 'He sent her to see a friend of his who does chin and jowl jobs and she came back all excited about looking twenty again.'

Josephine's eyes widened. 'Must have been some sales pitch.'

'Quite. They really got fired up, I could hear Luvvie going "You can't afford it, you silly bitch." Melissa goes, "I can afford it if I stop affording you."' Barry parodied Luvvie's trained, beautiful, drawl: '"Don't talk as if I'm some kind of gigolo or toyboy."' Falsetto: '"Would poodle suit you better?" I think he smacked her face,' Barry burbled. 'If he's bruised her, it'll show up, won't it, on the telly?' He sat back, sipped his tea and beamed with malicious enjoyment. 'Only actors would do it. They had all their windows open and it was effing this and blinding that.' He began to laugh. 'She started chucking his clothes out. The courtyard was getting littered with boxer shorts. Gordon was playing his head off in the background, just like watching a film with a soundtrack. Ron came out and said it was arias from *Ada*. Remember Ada in *The Street*? She used to look a bit like Melissa's going to, if Andrew doesn't get in first.'

'*Aida*, I expect,' said Josephine.

'No. Ada. It was that actress that died – Vera . . .' His voice died away thoughtfully. 'Doesn't matter. Gordon had his loud pedal through the floor, banging away while they banged each other. It was a scream.'

'Hilarious. Comic opera,' Josephine said. 'Is Melissa all right?'

'I don't like opera,' Barry remarked comfortably. 'Give me Andrew Lloyd Webber. Luvvie came out eventually with his little suitcase and picked up all the boxer shorts and went away. Haven't seen Melissa since. Gordon must have hated it. If it got in the local paper that his next-door neighbours get into brawls, his parents would take their kids away.'

Gordon Hassall-Hammond was the last name by the entryphone, and taught piano on the second floor.

'Anyone who scared easily wouldn't go there in the first place,' Josephine retorted.

A kind and gentle man, Gordon Hassell-Hammond had the looks of a troll.

'Inbreeding,' Barry suggested, pouring the last of the tea. 'Poor old Gord. The original mouse that roars. What would you do if you were five feet five inches tall with feet as flat as a goose's, a pot belly, grey hair standing on end like Beethoven's, warts on your nose and could play the piano brilliantly but not *quite* brilliantly enough to be a concert pianist, and most people thought you weren't precisely quite all there in the head?'

'Top myself, probably,' said Josephine cheerfully. Irrationally, she lowered her voice. 'But we shouldn't talk about him like this. He'd be terribly hurt.'

She need not have worried. The Honourable Gordon Hassall-Hammond, eldest son of Lord and Lady Randolph Hassall-Hammond, wasn't paying attention to anything, even had they been anywhere within earshot. He was much too busy.

'Forty-five, short, fat, bald, lonely Lord with title and visiting rights to stately pile but no actual expectations (death duties and elder brother) descended directly from Charles the First via Uppingham, Royal College of Music and the dole office, now in steady work as private pianoforte teacher, accompanist and would-be composer with own flat South London, seeks similarly short person with kind heart, patience and passion for opera and classical music, to be his Lady.'

Gordon sat, a copy of *The Times* on his knees, chewing the end of a blunt pencil in an agony of indecision. All the males seeking commitment and long-term relationships in the 'Saturday Rendezvous' column described themselves as executive, home-owning, good income, happily divorced, youthful in outlook, own hair and teeth. To a man, they were tall, into candlelit dinners, theatre, long country walks and fun. And GSOH. He concluded it meant Good Salary, Own Home.

Funnily enough, he noted in surprise, they were all looking for the same person: a slim, sensuous, fun-loving, non-smoking dream woman of around thirty, who would enjoy everything they did and make their lives complete. And fun.

Gordon contemplated what, with desperate honesty, he had written in his crabbed, pernickety, forward-sloping hand, more used to writing crotchets and quavers than advertisements for a wife to ease his solitude, which he had once enjoyed. He wasn't divorced, had never been married; teaching and music had been his life. Of late, for no reason he could make out, that sense of self-sufficiency had soured and darkened to aching loneliness. He pencilled in 'GSOH'.

'Drivel.'

He tore it up and added the shreds of paper to the pile in the wastepaper basket by his grand piano.

'Honourable bachelor, young forty-five, seeks sensuous lady for making beautiful music . . .'

Garbage, bullshit and crap; *The Times* had columns of it. He scanned the paper again, wondered that they could print such rubbish. Garbage. Guiltily, he glanced round his chaotic sitting room, every surface cluttered with sheet music, books about music, bits of libretto scribbled on the backs of envelopes, full-length librettos and scores. The top of the piano was piled with dust, half-drunk mugs of tea, pens, pencils, several metronomes, all broken except one, crumpled fistfuls of receipts that should long since have been filed for his accounts, a silver-framed photograph of his parents standing outside the ugly, windswept, grey stone family seat on the Lincolnshire coast (he'd rather get the plague than go back and live in it), a silver-framed certificate from the Royal College of Music saying he had a Master's degree, more slews of music books, a pile of unopened bank statements and a tax return for the self-employed from the Inland Revenue that was months overdue.

The carpet was littered with newspaper, the fireplace, a glory of Victorian black-leaded iron and flowered tiles, had not been cleaned out since the last time it got cold enough for him to light a fire. There was a serious smell of cat.

Uneasily, Gordon tried to view it through a woman's eyes. Never mind fun in the firelight and candlelit dinners; what woman would want evenings here of any kind, where she would have to scrape ginger fur balls off the seat before she could sit down in a chair? He chewed the end of the pencil frantically and faced up to facts. Radical measures were needed, a clean sweep and a new start.

'I'll get a cleaning woman, put an ad in the post office. And *you* will get a visit from Andrew,' he growled at Tom and Jerry. 'He does neutering. Stop all that spraying. Stop the stink and caterwauling. Disgusting. Sophia Larkin tells me there's a new litter of orange kittens at the bottom of her garden.'

The threat hung in the air.

Two ginger toms sprawled on the sofa in nests of matted yellow hairs stirred uneasily, opened one eye each, pulled in their paws protectively, scratched briefly and urgently at biting fleas, flexed their claws and went back to sleep.

He got up, found a mug on the piano, and went into the kitchen to make tea. While he waited for the kettle to boil, it dawned upon him that truth wasn't a prerequisite in the rendezvous column. Inspired by this insight, he went back into the sitting room and wrote rapidly: 'Musical peer, forty-five, bachelor, medium build, own home South London, seeks kind, musical lady to share duets. Looks and age are not important but intelligent, warm, affectionate personality is.'

None of the other ads mentioned intelligence, he noticed, pleased, which helped his stand out a little more.

His modesty didn't entirely do Gordon justice. He was more than just a Grade One to Eight teacher, was heavily in demand wherever singers needed a pianist to accompany them, from Berlin to Birmingham, from Wigan to the Wigmore Hall.

The agent who handled his bookings kept urging him to go for better things. A shrivelled Scotsman no taller than Gordon, fine sandy hair arranged across his freckled head, he looked top heavy due to a high, bulbous forehead and an exaggerated, trimmed and waxed gingery handlebar moustache.

'Give up teaching so you're free to travel and I'll see you get enough work to make up the money,' Finbar Macbeth urged.

'You mean, if I make myself completely dependent on you, you can up your percentage,' Gordon growled.

'Me? Would I do that to someone I represent?' The handlebar moustache quivered with indignation.

'Naturally.'

'Ever *really* thought about trying the concert circuit?' Finbar suggested wistfully, as he always did. 'I could lay on some venues; suck it and see.'

'I'm not good enough for the venues that count,' Gordon answered bluntly, flexing long, strong, wiry fingers, surprising on small, rather feminine hands. 'Good enough at what I do, but I'll never turn into an Ashkenazy and make your fortune. Bad luck.'

The little Scot nodded glumly. Their exchanges were always the same, once a year over lunch in the Savoy, for which Finbar paid with a pained expression.

'Anyway,' Gordon shot as they parted, 'I *like* children.'

The children themselves generally had to be bribed the first few times, and shoehorned through his front door, on account of his abrupt manner and alarming looks. But they got along, he got results, they passed their grades and he always had a waiting list.

In Josephine's kitchen, Barry stood up to go, sat down again.

'Seen Babe lately?' he asked casually.

'I've seen the hair, if that's what you mean. Bit garish.'

Barry nodded glumly. 'He's got the wanders again. Dockers – anything hairy that drops its aitches, drinks beer and has tattoos all over it will do.'

There never seemed much to say about Barry's sexual tastes if you weren't gay, not into S&M. She was very afraid that one day Barry, out of perverse, blind love, was going to end up with AIDS.

'I have to earn my living,' she said, getting up to signal their gossip was over.

'You do not,' he said indignantly.

'Well, I want to,' she answered evenly.

'What does it feel like to be able to have anything you want?' Barry inquired nastily since she wouldn't help him over Babe.

'I wouldn't know,' she said mildly. 'But I do know that I'm nearly forty and tired of watching my life go past just waiting for Garcia to come home so that I can wait for him to go away again.'

Talking of S&M, here's Mr Vice himself.

Barry, letting himself back into his house, his key in the battered black door, nearly voiced the thought aloud, seeing Andrew Quinlan, the portly, pink and baby-faced plastic surgeon with plump, moist hands, short tubby legs and fat bottom coming through the courtyard gate.

Mr Quinlan, rosy, aftershaved, starched, pressed, pinstriped and urbane even off duty, normally had a chuckling, tormenting and perverse sense of humour which tortured his nurses and junior staff and gave him an immense amount of pleasure. That Saturday it had gone missing.

Barry flew indoors before the surgeon could cross the courtyard and say hello, then peeped out and watched him stamp up the front steps, porcine face black as thunder. Barry hastily dropped the lace curtain he was twitching. He didn't like Andrew Quinlan even when the man put himself out to be charming; the thought of him in a rage made goose bumps prickle up and down the fine fair hairs all over Barry's arms.

Andrew was in a vile temper. He had had a long and tiresome lunch in the Ritz, drank too much claret, then endured an hour in the foyer drinking tea and listening to piano music and Caroline outdo each other's droning.

The lunch had been meant to please and placate his ex-wife. Instead, it had given her an opportunity to abuse and threaten him until they parted on worse terms than ever.

They emerged from the Ritz, her not in the least placated, him in the blackest of moods, all trace of his usual provocative sense of humour – sick, Caroline called it – gone strictly to the birds.

'You think I'm making a fortune,' he said bitterly. 'I'm not. My friends all want nip and tuck for free or on the never-never, and I get tired, turning them down.'

'What friends?' Caroline demanded incredulously.

'One or two. Particularly the lovely Melissa who is so plainly terrified of ageing. Well, why not? Snip, snap, Melissa, my dear. I can see you nicely nipped and tucked where you least expect it.'

Caroline edged away. 'You are *horrible.*'

'I'm realistic.'

When he told them he was a plastic surgeon, women instantly assumed he did bee sting mouths, liposuction, tit, bum and nose jobs. He let them think what they liked. His speciality was more arcane altogether and the private work made a great deal of money. Caroline wanted a bigger share of it, had spent the whole wretched lunch threatening to go back to court to get it.

He slammed his front door, slammed an open window on the world outside, poured half a glass of whisky and threw himself into a chair.

'Damn you,' he observed, saluting her and swallowing most of it in one go.

He had been to see his solicitor.

'I won't pay my wife to live in luxury with her lover in my

ex-home in Surrey, driving my ex-BMW and disposing of my ex-daughter to an expensive boarding school. Bloody neglectful mother. Can't we argue she's unfit? Spike her guns so she'll come to an agreement?'

That argument had gone down like a lead balloon with the divorce judge. Annabel told the court officer she adored boarding school and wanted to live permanently with her mother and Rupert. She did want to visit her father – sometimes.

'That seems straightforward enough,' said the Registrar, endorsing previous decisions that Annabel was old enough to make the approaches herself. He refused to make Andrew an access or visitation order.

The malt burned in his throat. Caroline had the upper hand all down the line because she had his marital home, his car, Annabel and the photographs. Now she wanted the money she claimed he owed her; at the end of the day there was no damn choice.

He had tried to be pleasant, calm, not to aggravate the situation. He had faced her frankly across the table, the piano warbling, china tinkling, voices buzzing discreetly all around, his head aching.

'Are you absolutely determined to keep making the legal profession wealthier than it already is by hounding me?' he asked, exhausted by her stubbornness, her refusal to let go and give up. 'You can't win. Not in the end, you know.'

'I'm not hounding you. You owe me a lot of money. I keep writing to ask you what you're going to do about it and you have ignored me.'

'Taking me to court,' he said in disgust.

'Taking you to court was the nice way to do it,' she replied.

'Blackmail is illegal,' he answered, keeping his voice very low. 'I don't believe you understand. You could go to prison.'

She was thinner than when they had first separated, lines around her eyes, reddish hair cut very short, a sharpness, an edge to her that he didn't remember being there when they were together. He supposed he, and disappointment, had planted the bitterness in her.

'I can't *help* being what I am,' he went on with quiet intensity. 'I've fought it, and it doesn't work. I am genuinely sorry.'

She didn't seem to hear. 'I have had arrears awarded against you, and costs, and I intend to get them, Andrew. I'll ask for the money to be collected from your employers if I must.'

'If you hound me or interfere with my salary, I'll go and work abroad. I can work anywhere. Johns Hopkins, Cape Town, Casablanca. Especially Casablanca. A lot of transsexual surgery in Morocco. You try getting money out of there.'

'The photos,' she said.

'The photos,' he said calmly, 'will cut no ice in Casablanca. They'd turn them into postcards and sell them to the tourists.'

'You won't go and work in Casablanca. You couldn't stand the heat. Or the Arabs.'

She had found the photos on his fortieth birthday, looking in his desk for Sellotape to wrap his present with. It had been entirely his own, careless, fault.

'OK. How about Peter Tatchell? I'll be selective, send him just the ones with men. How would you like to be *outed,* Andrew?'

Well-known reconstructive surgeon, Fellow of the Royal College of Surgeons, counsellor to the psychosexually distressed and giver to several children's charities. Mr Tatchell would think Christmas had come halfway through the year.

'That won't destroy my career,' he said, laughing with fury.

'No? Everyone would start worrying about HIV. They wouldn't touch you.'

The pianist stopped to change his music and in the brief moment of quiet Andrew heard muted laughter from another table. He could hear the laughing and whispering and sniggering behind his back. Oh, they'd enjoy repaying some of his taunting jokes.

'Think of your reputation and the rooms in Harley Street. Poor Andrew, you wouldn't be able to afford any more fun and games and before you knew it you'd *have* to go to Casablanca.' She was smiling gently at him, but the smile didn't reach her eyes.

He reached into his breast pocket and drew out a cheque book. 'If you give me the photographs and the negatives.'

Caroline laughed. 'Don't make me do it. Truly, I deeply disapprove of what Peter Tatchell does.'

If they hadn't been in the Ritz he might have murdered her. Since they *were* in the Ritz, he gave in and wrote the cheque.

[illegible]

[illegible]

[illegible]

[illegible]

[illegible]

[illegible]

[illegible]

Chapter Ten

Business trips were like having babies, Garcia thought. According to women, every time you had one, you vowed never to have another. Then you did.

By the time flight BA 002 was halfway across the Atlantic on a Friday afternoon, bringing Garcia, accompanied by Millie, home to London after a month away, the Texan voice two rows behind was like a dental drill, going through his skull. It had gone on, a high, nasal, penetrating, migraine-inducing drove, for hours.

'. . . point five per cent of the first shipment. I heard Geoffrey ask Zack three times, do you know what you're agreeing to? And Zack says, sure I do. Point five of one per cent.' The fat Dallas businessman slapped a hand the size and texture of a wet salmon on a vast knee, a gesture of disgust. 'Now it's, OK, you guys, the deal's point three per cent. I heard him ask Zachary three times. Three times, he said, Zack, you just gave them point five per cent, do you know what you're agreeing to? And what are they offering? Point three per cent. Assholes.'

At the very front of the cabin, Garcia sighed and squinted over the back of his seat at the redneck bawling through his blunt nose at his secretary, trapped in the window seat, colourless and efficient. Long, thin, beaky-faced as a middle-aged stork in her good and sober suit, she had a greying pony tail, her only concession to colour a magenta chiffon scarf tied round her ruined neck.

Her employer had shouted dictation at her in the lounge at JFK, shouted instructions about the hotel where they were to stay as they sat on the Tarmac waiting for permission to go, shouted until they were halfway across the Atlantic about the board meeting they were coming to attend. His fat lips sprayed Stilton cheese, biscuit crumbs and vintage claret. Her soft, lined cheek almost brushed his jowls as she leaned towards him in the narrow aircraft seat, struggling to make out his words through the numbing roar of the engines, looking into his face and lipreading with the intensity of a lover. A stewardess bent across them to fill the secretary's glass with fizzy water. The Texan, like the engines, roared on.

'Fancy wasting food and wines as fine as these on people who invented McDonalds and root beer,' Garcia complained.

Millie, in the seat next to him, was absorbed in a plastic folder full of figures. She was on a slimming diet and interested in neither food nor xenophobia. Garcia pushed his own half-finished plate of food away. Across the narrow aisle, thin as a stick and huddled inside a cashmere trouser suit and dark glasses, Joan Collins pushed her own plate away, plugged her earphones in and ignored the efforts of the minder sitting beside her to entertain.

Gnawed by boredom and anxiety, Garcia tried to distract himself by staring fixedly at the two signs glowing on the bulkhead in front of him, watched their flight data changing.

Speedbird 002 was travelling at a little more than twice the speed of sound and at sixty thousand feet had drifted to the very top of its long parabola across the Atlantic. The fact that he was in Concorde no longer thrilled him as it used to.

He fingered his nose, eased his headache and wondered whether to ask the stewardess for aspirins. The thought of needing aspirins depressed him, made him feel old and tired and jaded. As did the implications of the frightening news he suspected was hidden in the figures lying in Millie's lap.

He had first flown in Concorde in 1980, a couple of years after it came into service.

'I flew supersonic,' he yelped, hurtling through the front door of the flat. He had whirled around the hall, punching the air. 'Better than sex.'

'You're hyper,' Josephine said shortly, as two-year-old Emma caught his overexcitement and burst into tears.

He followed Josephine into the kitchen and opened a bottle of wine. 'Here's to being home.' He waved his glass. Red wine painted a supersonic parabola across their kitchen wall.

'Hyper, manic, uncontrollable and impossible,' she added for good measure, snatching a dishcloth and lashing at the stain.

'Perhaps super sex on British Airways is why you haven't been home for several weeks.'

Garcia got the part of the message he wanted to hear, put Emma in her cot with a packet of chocolate biscuits and dragged Josephine into bed.

But that August he brought his mother over from Seville to look after Emma and took Josephine to New York on the Concorde, and gave her dinner at the Rainbow Room for her twenty-sixth birthday.

'What did you do?' he asked; he had been in meetings all day.

In those days, she had waist-length hair piled on top of her head, Elizabeth Taylor eyes, deep blue-grey, heavily lined with black.

'Shopping. Wandering. Soaking up the *pzazz*.'

'*Pzazz* in my bank account?'

Josephine shook her head and laughed. 'I was in a pharmacy near Grand Central buying shampoo. There was a bit of a commotion, and there was a skinny little . . . person . . . trying to buy Tylenol at the counter.'

The waiter filled their glasses.

'What's funny about that?'

'It was staggering up and down in its high heels and tight skirt, with its jaw wired up. It had obviously had an *awful* fight with a handbag.'

'Stay away from Grand Central,' Garcia said crossly. 'I've told you.'

'It was hissing through its teeth at the pharmacist, who was trying to call security, when it shoved its handbag on the counter and took out an iguana.' Josephine clenched her teeth and whispered, "Tylenol ain't fer me. Fer her. Got a headache." When I went out, it was touting the iguana around the make-up aisle saying gimme ten dollars and she's yours.' She spluttered with laughter.

'That's New York,' he said. 'It's good you enjoy it so much. It'll make it much easier.'

'Make what easier?'

He leaned towards her, took both her hands and beamed.

Josephine dragged her hands away. 'Why do I smell a rat?'

Garcia signalled the waiter, ordered a bottle of Krug with dessert.

'Millie's apartment block is very safe, and you can shop,' he said obscurely as the waiter went away. 'You'll be fine.'

'Why do I need to be fine?' Josephine asked. 'Why are we pleased Millie's apartment building is safe?'

'Because I'm looking for an apartment here for ourselves.' He ignored her sudden stillness, his black eyes glowing with enthusiasm. 'Can't invade Millie every time you want to come over and we can't have Emma in hotels. My staff will use it instead of hotels and the company will pay expenses. I've put some details of possibles for you to look at. Midtown, so I can walk to work.'

'Walk to work. And where are you going, that I am to spend the rest of my trip keeping myself occupied shopping and looking at real estate brochures?'

'San Francisco,' Garcia said airily. 'We leave at six. You needn't wake up.' He looked at her across the table and blew a kiss. From the other side of the room, the waiter watched and sighed. They made a beautiful couple. Could be right off the cover of *Hello!* 'Work, darling. The client is paying for the tickets.'

'I knew it was too good to be true,' his wife said and picked up her glass as if to toast herself. 'I have been reading Erica Jong and I realise I have a workaholic for a husband. But I don't think Isadora Wing had a two-year-old and her mother-in-law waiting at home. Happy birthday to me.'

Garcia stroked her knee under the table as if she was a touchy cat. 'I love you so much,' he murmured.

She removed his hand. 'You keep dreaming your little supersonic dreams, darling. Personally, reading Erica Jong, I think the time has come for a few zipless fucks.'

After that, San Francisco had been a welcome escape, and very good business. Garcia stared at the glowing panels in front of him again, to drive out the disagreeable memory of the rest of that long-ago birthday. Josephine had turned excessively moody and gone back to London early, claiming to be in a wholly irrational, subsonic depression.

He shifted uncomfortably in the narrow seat, eyed Millie uneasily. She was still reading.

He had always imagined that Concorde would fly in an eerie silence, that at supersonic speeds they would outfly the noise of their engines, flee like a shooting star, slide soundlessly round the curve of space before their own sonic boom.

It was not so. After three and a half hours in a long, narrow, floating grey tube with tiny windows, claustrophobia tight in his chest, the flights generally left him nerveless. Except for the first eight rows of seats, its vast engines drowned all conversation held at other than the top of one's voice. The further back, the worse the noise and the more jarring the landing. He still loved it.

'How do you stop a plane shaped like a dart?' he had asked the captain the first time he had pushed his way through the queue of fascinated men wanting to peer at the cramped and crowded flight deck. It smelled of male sweat and aftershave, four large men in a very small space, shirt sleeves rolled up in the heat. The nose and visor were up in supersonic flight, the visor with its small windows protecting the windshield from heat and wind. Banks of instruments glowed in the subdued light like some fantastic, electronic Milky Way.

'We *are* a dart,' the captain agreed, turning round in his seat to talk to his passengers, gawping over each other's shoulders. 'You are right. We would fly and fly and fly, so we have to stall and slam our back wheels hard into the ground. We stop pretty quickly.'

Garcia had lingered, asking questions, until the captain got rid of him by inviting him to sit in the jump seat for the landing.

Descending into Heathrow, body webbing straining round him as the plane fought its own forced landing, had been magic, sending him home high as a kite on adrenaline, to spray red wine on the kitchen wall.

Smacking around two hundred and forty thousand pounds into the Tarmac at about a hundred and seventy knots jolted the spines of those in the tail end.

Thinking of spines, his ached, Garcia realised, wishing he could get up and stretch his legs, ease the tension in his chest, get some air. There wasn't room. Stewardesses would start falling over him and there was a queue for the loo blocking the aisle. Those at the back by the lavatories probably had ignorant PAs, feeble travel agents or not enough clout with Special Services at Kennedy to get themselves better seats. To be right at the front it helped to be a king, queen, head of state, Joan Collins or Millie and Garcia. The big mouth with the secretary bird was well inside the coveted first eight rows, so he wasn't doing so badly. Garcia yawned and peered across Millie out of the small window. It would be uncomfortably hot were his face close enough to touch it. Travelling at a little over Mach 2, the outside of the aeroplane's skin would be hotter than boiling water. He could just see, if he half rose and craned his neck, the pronounced curve of the earth below, dark on dark, the sky deep navy blue, as they glided along on the very edge of space.

He had tried to describe what his company did and what Concorde was like to Sophia Larkin the day they moved into their house in Barnes and he had just met her for the first time.

Coming back from the Barnes Wine Shop with a celebratory bottle or two he had tripped over her sitting on the step out to the pavement, with her eyes shut, small hands folded in her lap, as if she was praying.

'You OK?'

She was a small woman with the narrow, compact build of a busty child. Her peroxided hair was tied back with a scarf and she was huddled in a brief, pillarbox-red PVC raincoat tightly belted round a tiny waist, her feet bound into silver platform sandals.

'Locked myself out. I've phoned for help from the call box. My husband says I'm daft as a brush.' She jerked a thumb behind her. 'Middle house. You've obviously just moved in. Nice to meet you.' She looked like a worried, disconsolate little pixie, the shiny red PVC slicked with drizzle that was turning to rain.

He rattled the carrier bag of wine in his hand. 'Come on in and meet my wife, and have a drink.'

'I shouldn't. I've got Uncle Harry.'

He waited in the drizzle.

'Uncle Harry's dying in my dining room,' she said apologetically. 'Cancer. He's too ill to answer the bell.'

Garcia raised the carrier. 'Poor Uncle Harry. All the more reason, I'd have thought, for a drink.'

By the time Ron cut short a meeting with a client and came home to let her in, she was helping her new neighbours unpack tea chests in the high, dingy front room, its floor a sea of crumpled newspaper and piled books. Emma was sprawled on her back asleep in a roomy travel cot in a corner, snuffling. Sophia didn't care much for small children. She made half-hearted remarks that failed to strike the right note of enthusiasm, then unpacked the whole of the *Encyclopaedia Britannica*, perched on the pile of books and ate a lot of crisps out of an orange plastic colander while Garcia talked and emptied their third bottle of Chablis into mugs. Josephine interrupted Garcia.

'What he's not telling you is that he spends half his life hanging around in airports or throwing up with jet lag and has insomnia. He has to take sleeping pills and sleep with the light on like a baby because he might not remember where he is and try to go to the loo in the night and fall down the stairs instead.'

Garcia took his opium pipe collection out of a case and spread them on the floor.

'Do you use those?' asked Sophia, impressed.

Josephine examined Sophia curiously. 'Not many people know what they're for.'

'Jo uses them when I get too much for her, don't you, darling?' Garcia grinned and opened another bottle of wine.

'There are times,' Josephine said, grimly.

Like the time Garcia called from Tokyo and woke her up. She had just given up her job in an architectural practice, had almost finished preparing the nursery, was enjoying a deep and exhausted sleep. By the time the preliminary endearments had rattled tinnily down the line, she was awake enough to be suspicious.

'There is a reason behind this enormously expensive telephone call, and I suspect it isn't homesickness or love.'

'It *is* homesickness. I love you and I miss you like crazy.'

'And?'

'Well, there *is* one other thing. We can manage a few extra people next week, sweetie, can't we?'

After a delay in which the cost of the call went through the roof, she said coldly, 'I'm having a baby sometime in the next two weeks. Why?'

'Because you are sexy and beautiful and clever and—'

'Don't bullshit. Why the people?'

'We have to bring them to London and the cash flow can't quite afford Claridges, which is what they expect.'

'What they'll expect is bedrooms,' she snapped. 'We only have four and one is turned into a nursery and has ducks all over its walls and ceiling.'

'They'll share,' he said blithely. 'Take the cot to bits, put the teddy somewhere else and take the mobiles down, just for a day or two. They can count ducks while they try and get over the time difference. It'll send them to sleep.'

She was speechless with offence.

'It's the biggest compliment you can pay a Nip,' Garcia wheedled. 'Invite him to your home. We've got big projects coming good that we've been nursing along for *years.* Staying with us will more than make up for not affording Claridges. If the deals go through we'll be able to afford to look at houses. You can go round the estate agents and draw up a list.'

The bribe.

'*Japanese,*' she said through her teeth.

'Friends,' he said indignantly.

He heard an ominous silence.

'They're not so bad. Don't worry about grub, we can feed them Chinese takeaways and plenty of whisky. Millie will translate. Next problem?'

'Millie will be here too?' In her mind's eye, she could see his martyred expression. Of course Millie would be here too. 'Whatever I say, they're coming, aren't they?'

''Fraid I already invited them, my darling. They were thrilled to *bits* and you're an absolute *gem.* Don't go and have the baby yet,' he said happily and rang off.

Later that day she waddled to the twin-bedded nursery, took down the exquisite, spinning mobiles she had spent hours making and took off the lovingly stitched covers from the little white cot. Yellow ducks marched across the walls, yellow curtains framed the window, butter-coloured carpet lay in the floor. The cot came from America, a gift from Millie. She and Garcia had shopped for it together and brought it home export wrapped in the hold of a plane.

'A doormat and someone with big boots have a lot in common,' she told herself furiously. 'Am I really going to give in to this?'

Finally she did what Garcia had asked and dismantled the cot.

'How *can* he?'

Emmanuel had come round to beg a bottle of brandy because it was Sunday and the off-licence was shut.

'GGIL must be short of cash,' he said, helping himself to an unopened bottle of Garcia's best cognac. 'Feed 'em plenty of Scotch and they'll be happy.' But he gave her a big hug before he went, stroked her hair, and told her it would be all right. 'I'm just over the way. Yell if you need me.' He pointed at her enormous belly. 'He won't miss it, you know. He'd fly home from the moon, for that.'

She suddenly felt herself close to tears. Later, getting ready for bed, she remembered his warm arms, the tender touch on her hair. Aching with loneliness, she looked at her huge belly in the mirror, and her mind wandered. If it weren't for that . . .

The four small men bowed incessantly.

'It's macho to booze,' Millie yawned as they chattered their way through a bottle of duty-free Glenfiddich the evening they arrived, dead on her feet from jet lag.

Josephine longed to fall, distended belly and all, into Garcia's arms. Garcia fell into the Glenfiddich instead. She left them to it and fell by herself into bed.

No time later, it seemed, she stood in her kitchen doorway rubbing her eyes, barefoot, terminally pregnant, tousled and pale from sleep. What had woken her was a powerful smell of frying bacon and the fact that the Kensington flat was lit up like the *Marie Celeste*.

'What do they think this is? A boarding school midnight feast?'

Four small, jet-lagged Japanese businessmen in kimono dressing gowns roosted round her kitchen table, munching bacon butties. Millie in grey socks and a Ralph Lauren robe was stabbing like a heron in a fishpond with a pair of tongs into a smoking grill full of sausages. As one, the Japanese rose and bowed like energetic baby chicks, beaming.

'What are you all eating?' she demanded stupidly.

The green digital clock on the oven said it was four o'clock in the morning. Even the traffic on the Kensington Road was still quiet. The Japanese stopped bowing and watched her expectantly.

'They're starving,' explained Millie, shovelling sausages on to a plate. 'It's lunchtime for their tummies and if they were in a hotel they'd call the night desk. As it is, we are offering twenty-four-hour room service. What they really want is sushi and green tea, but we could only find wieners in the freezer. I told them, eat up, you guys, this is a great English delicacy.' She licked grease off her fingers. 'I don't know that they believe a word of it but, being Japanese, they are abnormally good-mannered. We were doing our best to rise to the occasion without disturbing you.'

Millie slid the plate on to the table. There was a little flurry of laborious, garbled interpretation and the Japanese nodded solemnly.

'This isn't a hotel,' Josephine announced ominously.

Garcia instantly got up from his chair and came over, put his arm round her protectively so that he could turn her away and hiss in her ear.

'Making them welcome in our own home is—'

'The biggest honour we can give them,' she hissed back, tight-lipped. 'I know all that stuff. What it means is, our home is *cheap*.'

'*Not now*,' Garcia growled, making it look as though he was kissing her earlobe.

'They *love* ketchup,' Millie cried, planting herself opposite four pairs of uneasy Japanese eyes unused to embarrassing public displays of affection, smiling until she thought her face would crack. A lot of money was riding in this trip, and on the feelgood factor of the flattering invitation to stay in Garcia's home in Kensington instead of Claridges. Josephine couldn't be allowed to spoil it.

'Join us,' Millie invited.

'In a minute,' Garcia said brightly, grabbing his wife's arm. 'You need a robe, darling.

'Be nice,' he begged, in the bedroom. 'It's not their fault. They'd do as much for me, and think of the money.'

'I don't care about the money,' she said sullenly. 'I don't know which is worse, running a bed and breakfast for the two of you or Millie *in my kitchen* telling those wretched little men that burned chipolatas are traditional English cooking. She who eats out in Manhattan every night is suddenly a *cook*?' She dragged a dressing gown across her bump and glared, red-eyed at waking suddenly from a deeply weary sleep. The baby kicked in protest at being woken from its own sleep.

'Come here,' he said. 'I mind as much as you that I've come back after weeks without you and I'm stuck in there with them.'

'Are you going to be here for the birth of this baby?' she snuffled into his shoulder.

'Absolutely. Definitely.'

'*Promise.*'

'I promise I will be there.'

Like a small boy, he crossed his fingers behind her back. *If I can.*

Millie put two incinerated pork chipolatas into a bun, patted the back of a chair. 'Eat for two!'

Josephine felt Japanese eyes turn away from her dishevelled state and pregnant bump.

'I could get this down without throwing up on the spot, Millie,' she muttered, giving in, 'only if I have enough hot chilli chutney on it.'

'You need *three* of these?' demanded Garcia, bringing out jars of Mrs Gheeta's hot chilli pickle from a cupboard.

'Not all at once. One will do.'

He put it down and touched her bump lightly. 'Babies,' he said to his visitors. 'Cravings. Funny foods. Coal. Hot chilli pickle. Eats it by the jar. Haha. Yummy.' He made a gesture, showed them the jar and kissed his fingers in mock appreciation.

'Aaaah.' A collective smile beamed on Japanese faces, an eager, understanding nodding of heads.

'Garcia, I don't think . . .' Millie cried.

But the damage was done. A few moments later four of the most up-and-coming men in Japan's booming retail trade, the core of Garcia and Millie's growing network of business contacts, were chewing stoically at four thirty in the morning on burned hot dogs lathered with red-hot lime and chilli pickle, a look of frozen shock upon their faces.

'Do you realise what you and Millie have done?' demanded Garcia distractedly, noticing it was already getting light and seriously worried about severe loss of face in the event of an all too likely outbreak of serious diarrhoea.

'I didn't do it. You're the ones who can't sleep. Schedule junkies, both of you,' she yawned.

'I'm addicted to success,' he said, getting into bed. 'What's wrong with that?'

'To adrenaline and go, go, go,' she corrected, putting out the light. Grey dawn crept round the curtains. 'Always looking for the next fix,' she added drowsily. 'Bad as smack.'

'Smack?' he said, waking up in astonishment.

'Heroin,' she said sleepily. 'And you've got the worst deal. You and Millie have to buy Concorde tickets to get your high. Lot more expensive than smack.'

She was asleep.

Pregnant women have bizarre ideas, he thought, and went straight to sleep himself.

Ten days after the Japanese went home, Emma was born. Garcia made it to the hospital. The next day.

'I don't want a nanny,' Josephine said, pushing away the Norland brochure, once she started speaking to him again. She looked down at her sleeping baby. 'I couldn't leave her, not for five minutes.'

'You'll need a nanny when you come overseas with me.'

'No.' Josephine stroked her daughter's soft skin tenderly.

'You cannot bring an infant to places like Japan and Djakarta on a business trip.' Garcia sounded scandalised. 'Have some sense.'

She smiled serenely. 'Of course not.'

'I thought, once you'd given up work and got a good nanny, we could travel together!'

Josephine looked at him as though he was mad. It was a long time before he believed she really meant it. When Emma was two, Garcia was adamant that it would be the perfect compromise for Emilia to come to live with them.

'Now I've got *two* children,' Josephine sighed, knowing that where his mother, who had accepted with alacrity, was concerned, she didn't stand a chance.

Chapter Eleven

'You should have been an airline pilot, Daddy.' Ten-year-old Emma, so like her father, was doing arithmetic on a bit of paper. 'You must have spent about five years of your life in aeroplanes.'

Garcia stared at her. 'Have I?'

She showed him how she had worked it out.

'You just gave me an absolutely brilliant idea,' he said.

'He went careering headlong into a love affair with small planes,' Josephine told her friends gloomily. 'It was Emma's fault for putting the idea into his head.'

'We're going to Versailles for lunch,' he announced one Easter morning.

'Who is?' Emma was home from school and had promised Emilia she would take the dogs for a walk.

'You is.'

'But—'

'No buts. You and your mother are coming.'

'Oh, yes?' said Emma, looking round Biggin Hill Executive Terminal. 'On a Love Air Day Trip? Thanks, Dad.'

'I don't think,' Josephine began, but Garcia flung out an expansive hand and pulled them over to the window.

'Meet Robin,' he announced, in a tone that meant 'Meet the new love of my life.'

They stared.

'Oh dear,' Josephine muttered.

Garcia was almost hopping up and down, beside himself with enthusiasm and excitment. 'Cruises at one hundred and forty knots and can fly to Venice without refuelling,' he crooned. 'Brand new and as much wizardry under the bonnet as a seven four seven. What do you think?'

'What I think is that seven four sevens have four engines and feel safe. *You* may be going to Paris,' answered his wife, peering through the window at bushes bending in the wind as the little red and white French four-seater sat gleaming and spotless on the Tarmac beyond. 'I most definitely am not going anywhere in a gale in a winged Robin Reliant.'

'Roeban,' Garcia said furiously. 'Made in Dijon. Not *Robin* and no relation whatsoever to a Reliant. And the wind is fifteen knots. That's fine.'

A terrible premonition crossed Josephine's mind. 'Who drives that thing?'

'I do,' Garcia crowed with delight and hugged himself. 'With an instructor. I've been having lessons.'

'Marie Antoinette was ahead of 'er time,' burbled the coppery-haired little guide with a PhD in the French Revolution and prettily accented English, shepherding her flock of sightseers on a tour of the King and Queen's private apartments behind the *grands salons* in Versailles. 'Court life for such a woman was not easy. Being a modern mozzer and wife, she 'ad many ideas zat many psychologists today would agree wiz. She felt frustrated and stifled by court protocol.'

They trailed behind her into the next cramped, bare little room.

It's like a larder, Emma thought, trying to imagine it filled with frilled and flounced Marie Antoinette, feeling the guide's description of private life behind the scenes was a little unconvincing.

'She would come to zese private apartments to spend time wiz 'er family and try to find somesing of a normal life,' the young woman chirped on. 'It was 'ere zat sometimes ze King and Queen were able to to see each ozzer wizzout courtiers present.'

'I read somewhere she was a very frivolous lady,' said an American with a videocamera trained on his wife. 'Look this way, Nancy.'

''Istory 'as misrepresented 'er,' the woman gushed indignantly. 'She was a ver' intelligent, compassionate person.'

They swept through narrow passageways leading through the suite of small, empty, bleak rooms where, she explained, Louis XIV retreated when the servants and courtiers had gone, for snatched moments of a warm and normal marital and family life.

'They'd have got stuck in those dresses,' Emma muttered, touching the walls of the corridor, so narrow she could reach them with her elbows. 'They'd be like corks in a bottle. Or they went around in their smelly underclothes. I don't believe a word of what she's saying.'

'What about "Let them eat cake"?' asked Garcia casually, wandering off and looking out of a window. Down below, all the statues marching along Les Tuileries had their heads tied up in sacking as though waiting for Robespierre and some ghastly mass execution.

'Someone else said zat.'

Garcia raised a black eyebrow in direct contradiction. The coppery Frenchwoman lost her professional smile and became earnest. 'Marie Antoinette would *nevaire* 'ave said that. She was too *sympathique*. Eet was someone else.'

'Ah.' Garcia looked puzzled. 'Any idea who *did* make one of the most infamous remarks in history, then?'

The woman looked as haughty as only the French can. '*Non*.'

She swept them onwards as Garcia ruminated with black amusement on the possible connection between the rise of European neo-fascism and Marie Antoinette's right-wing rehabilitation.

Josephine trotted after them and felt that she and misunderstood Marie Antoinette, if the guide was to be believed, might have quite a lot in common. And steak tartare for lunch in a Versailles brasserie, from the way she was feeling, had not been such a good idea.

Halfway across the English Channel, Josephine looked down and groaned, white as a sheet. The instructor sitting beside Garcia touched his arm.

'Your wife is feeling ill,' they all heard over their headphones.

'*In a bag!*' Garcia shouted, craning round, taking in her ashen face, Roeban about to be unspeakably sullied. 'Blue bag. Down the back of my seat. Don't . . .'

Two minutes later, Emma grabbed a plastic sack and threw up in sympathy with her mother.

'*Next* time . . .' Garcia began heavily, his grey BMW accelerating left out of Biggin Hill just before darkness, the lights of Westerham winking in the valley below.

'I want to die,' Josephine moaned, sliding down in her seat. She felt her forehead, burning hot as bugs from steak tartare crowned with raw egg rampaged into full-scale food poisoning.

'There won't be a next time,' Emma snarled from the gloom in the back of the car. 'That was absolutely *gross*, Dad.'

They had blamed it all on him. Now, thinking about his little four-seater sitting neglected in its hangar in Biggin Hill as he sat next to Millie on the three and a half hour JFK to Heathrow flight, he made up his mind. The video he had chosen bored him, and he found it hard to work on planes. Millie was much better at that.

He pressed his bell. 'Ask Captain Donaldson if I can sit up front for landing.' He gave the stewardess his private pilot's card, as he had many dozens of times before.

Waiting for her to come and tell him if the captain agreed to have him on the flight deck, he thought back. Getting on for thirty years of travelling. It had started quite out of the blue.

He and Jo had not long been married. He was working as assistant to the chief executive of a large Knightsbridge department store, twenty-five years old, with responsibilities, burning with ambition and hungry for success.

He invariably worked late. Leaving one wet June evening, unseasonably cold, he was undoing the clasp on his umbrella before diving down the stairs and out into the rain when he saw a small, patient Japanese, sitting outside the managing director's office on a sofa, a cleaner Hoovering around him as though he was not there, humming under her breath. The Japanese gentleman drew in his feet and the hem of his long black raincoat and continued to stare past her at the managing director's door with ineffable patience. Garcia went out of the door to the stairs, started down, went back, hesitated.

'Can I help you?'

The Japanese gestured.

'I'm afraid he's already left for the night. Someone should have told you.'

They both gazed at a spot on the floor. The cleaner disappeared on a cloud of almond-flavoured airspray. The Japanese managed to look regretful about the managing director's absence without a trace of real expression in his face.

'You could come in and tell me what you wanted, and I'll see him in the morning. You speak English?'

The Japanese looked up through lidless eyes. 'I speak English and I have appointment.' He had terrible, black and crooked teeth, marring a surprisingly pleasant smile.

Garcia shrugged very slightly, spread his hands, put on his widest, most winning Spanish smile, his own teeth gleaming white and gold, bowed from the waist and peered through his brows. 'Look, I don't know what's gone wrong, and I apologise.' He spoke firmly. 'I know I'm third best and you didn't come to see me, but he's not here and I am. You have come a very long way and I don't want you to waste any more of your time.'

The Japanese studied the top of Garcia's respectfully lowered head for a while with thoughtful, bloodshot eyes, then got off the sofa and bowed. Garcia straightened, bowed back. The two of them, like pecking clockwork pigeons, bowing themselves dizzy and narrowly missing banging their heads, backed down the corridor to Garcia's small and cluttered office where they had a very long, immensely productive talk.

Six months later, a wintry wind swept the concourse at Victoria Station, plucked at the ankles of rush-hour crowds streaming home from work, froze Garcia's ears as he headed for the Tube. He whistled cheerfully between his teeth. A pretty Sussex potter with fresh schoolgirl cheeks and long hair in an Alice band, who wanted to sell in Knightsbridge, had wined and lunched him most deliciously over a display of exquisite, original, collectable, very sellable pots. Garcia, busily planning how he would promote them, hurried past a bench, snapped his head round, stopped, wheeled back.

'Good heavens,' he cried. 'Do you always come to England to sit on benches?'

Startled, the Japanese businessman studying departures in a long black overcoat and yellow scarf leaped up.

'Goddard San,' he cried happily, hand outstretched.

In the raw and miserable cold, beneath the clicking departures board, announcements ringing in their ears, the pecking clockwork pigeons went hard at it all over again.

'Get a *heap* of Chinese takeaway and half a dozen bottles of plonk,' Garcia gabbled, standing at the telephones, watching the Japanese watching him.

'I've made stew,' protested Josephine, newly married and enthusiastic cook of inedible meals.

'I'm bringing home a Nip who wants to buy shirts,' Garcia hissed urgently. 'A *lot* of shirts. I can get them for him. There's dough in this, Jo, and I need a long talk with him in private. He won't want stew. Chinky takeaway will do.'

While Josephine put her stew in the larder and trudged through spitting, freezing rain specked with snow to the off-licence for the best French wine she could afford, then on to the Hong Kong Parlour for chop suey and spring rolls, the two of them sat on the Tube and came to an agreement.

'You come to Japan, Goddard San?'

Garcia bowed. 'I will come to Japan.'

An invitation to Japan, alien, unknown as the moon, and in the early sixties, its *huge* potential market virtually closed to Europe, was staggering.

So was the cost of getting there, particularly for one with an overdraft, a new wife, a cheap flat, a tidal wave of friends to feed and water, and not much else except reckless courage and naked ambition. *Joie de vivre*. Plenty of that. Cherry blossom, geisha, golden temples, exquisite gardens. But it was the prospect of business that beckoned. Now. He fingered the near-to-the-limit credit card in his trouser pocket and thought fast.

But not quite fast enough.

'Bloody hell, Jo,' he shouted through chattering teeth, on the one telephone call he could afford to make home, five days later, beyond the reach of an angry flexible friend. 'I was so busy dreaming about Buddhas and blossom I never stopped to think; it's midwinter in Tokyo, too. I didn't bring an overcoat and there are holes in all my socks!'

He had started his own company shortly after that.

The stewardess came back, handed him his card and said Captain

Donaldson would be pleased to see him on the flight deck. Beside him, Millie was typing into a laptop, frowning, two exquisitely black-stockinged legs up on the seat rest in front of her. She wiggled her Gucci loafers, an elastic bandage round one slim ankle.

Millie Hennessy was accident prone. Prone to other things, too; to flashes of business insight that left him speechless with admiration, tantrums that left him speechless with rage. They frequently left each other speechless with rage. Garcia considered he had no choice, being half Spanish, born in March, volatile by temperament, explosive by nature. *All* Ariens were fiery. People who goaded them with inflammatory remarks were asking for trouble.

Solving problems was his and Millie's business – design problems, retail problems, supply and demand problems, sourcing problems. Now, problems were threatening to spiral out of control. 'Control' triggered a memory of Emma, last time he was home, beginning the long summer holidays, yelling furiously, looking just like his mother.

'You're *embarrassing*,' Emma had howled.

'You'll be home before midnight, or I dock your allowance and ground you for a week,' he roared, out of patience with an argument that had bickered on and on all through dinner. 'And if it's embarrassment you want, I'll come straight round to Susan's house and drag you out.'

'Control freak,' she shrieked, stormed out of the kitchen, stormed back to snatch the portable telephone off its hook by the door to the hall, stormed upstairs.

'Control freak?'

'You've done her a favour,' Josephine said. 'She didn't want to stay over at Susan's house in any case. Now she can lie on her bed and rack up your phone bill complaining, and do it all in comfort with a clear conscience. You walked straight into it.'

'Control freak?' he spluttered. 'I'm an amazingly tolerant, indulgent, loving father.'

'Over-indulgent. Too tolerant. She needs a firm hand.'

Garcia stared, nonplussed.

'It's only abuse,' she pointed out calmly. 'Parents are *desperately* uncool and teenagers *so* much more sophisticated than in our young days. If you were here more instead of cocooned on seven four sevens you'd understand your daughter better. *And* what I put up with all the time. The only person she doesn't do it to is Hosannah.'

'Hosannah would put her over her knee and spank her,' growled Garcia.

'Might do no harm.' Josephine smiled brightly and for a moment he had an obscure, fleeting, frightening feeling that maybe he didn't matter any more, but then it passed.

Millie glanced up from her laptop, caught him looking sideways lost in thought, pulled a face.

'Bad?' he mouthed.

'Worse,' Millie said.

'That's exactly what I thought.'

Now they had begun to look into them, it was increasingly clear that the figures had been a mess for several months, not merely bad but bewildering, unaccountable and disastrous. Millie pushed her hair back and he read fear in her face.

'We are haemorrhaging money,' she wailed. 'But I can't see where, or why.'

Garcia said very quietly and clearly, 'I know. We've got a black hole, Millie.'

His visit to the flight deck forgotten, he tried to sound cheerful over the howling engines as they sank into the long descent towards London. Always look on the bright side, he reflected grimly. From the picture they were building from Tom Morrissey's last days in their office, there was no bright side and a great deal worse to come.

The first signs that they had something more than an accounting problem, something truly bizarre, had come out of the blue, two weeks before, in Tokyo, where his office manager requested a private word.

'I have paid it myself,' the young Japanese said, holding out a bank statement. 'The rent. Now, you see, I am overdrawn and please, Goddard San, I need one million yen.'

Garcia looked at the statement. 'You should have had this from London.'

'No expenses paid for four weeks.'

'None?'

The young man shook his head.

A couple of days later, in New York, Millie's secretary took him aside.

'We are late with the rent,' she said in her nasal Brooklyn voice. 'We've had no money through from London.'

'You too?' said Garcia, astonished. 'What is going on?'

'Not a lot, if you mean money transfers,' she answered. 'And that was what I was going to ask *you*.'

He fingered his cheek, feeling the prickling dead weight of his own exhaustion.

In response to the non-arrival of money from London, they had called Tom Morrissey who was vague and unhelpful, apologetic but couldn't explain what had happened.

'He's about to leave,' Garcia pointed out. 'Probably lost the thread.'

But the more they looked into what was going on, the more they worried. For two days, they worked nonstop.

At seven that morning he raced red-eyed to meet Millie at the airport, sick from New York taxi driving, anxiety, too much good Australian Chardonnay and lousy American sandwiches as he had carried on working the previous evening. Sun had speckled the sidewalks at five in the morning as he showered and shaved. Sixteen floors below his bathroom window, Park Avenue roared and honked.

The air conditioning hummed, making his apartment into an ice box. Outside, the humidity climbed to give New Yorkers another day of damp and sweating hell.

Getting into the car that arrived promptly at seven, his chest tight as an asthmatic's with anxiety, he felt unable to get his breath. Halfway along the freeway his stomach contracted violently and threatened to erupt. Meeting the silent, swarthy Armenian driver's eyes in the mirror, Garcia gestured him to stop.

'Let me get out and vomit.'

The man stared back, eyes like onyx, a heartless guerrilla in green and brown camouflage fatigues, broken old loafers, a Kalashnikov no doubt tucked down his dashboard. No Good Samaritan. Being a New York taxi driver was a form of guerrilla warfare, Garcia thought, swallowing hard, hating the man's indifference.

'Bankruptcy,' he murmured, as the crisis passed and the sign to Kennedy appeared overhead.

The word tasted of death.

'What are we going to do?' Millie asked.

'Work,' Garcia said, as the seatbelt sign flashed on. 'Call the auditors and the lawyers in again, have them go through the accounts with a toothcomb. We go on digging. No panic.'

They had already started throwing money at it, but even large amounts of money didn't staunch the losses. They got worse. A business that had taken twenty-seven years to grow was dying, with terrible speed. The stewardess came up.

'Thank Captain Donaldson for me, please, but I changed my mind.'

He suddenly had no stomach for it. It would all go, the first-class tickets, Concorde, seventy staff, worldwide offices, his reputation, his good name – the lot.

He could imagine that, but what he couldn't begin to imagine was admitting he had let them down.

And having to tell Emma and Josephine.

As the wheels unfolded below him, Garcia Goddard shuddered.

Chapter Twelve

The August day was going to be a scorcher, which should be lovely, but something about it was very wrong. When he came home from a trip they *always* made love. But last night Garcia had acted distant and distracted, had come to bed after she was asleep, rushed off to the office with Millie at five o'clock that morning.

In fact, except for a brief, rather violent hug, he had barely taken any notice of anyone except Millie, and he'd been closeted in his study with *her* for half the night.

Garcia always had the same recipe for confronting life. Work.

Josephine stood in the garden of Samantha Gilmour's beautiful Georgian house in Surrey and tried to shrug off the lead weight of her depression.

'Someone catch that bloody owl *before* it drowns itself.'

Watched by his alarmed owner, Bugsy Malone's untidy, downy brown head swivelled ninety degrees as he tracked the movement of a dried fir cone across an expanse of York stone paving leading from the high brick wall bordering their garden to the Gilmours' swimming pool.

The fir cone, teased out by a light breeze from where it had lain beneath a bush since last winter, rolled gently to and fro on the warm flags, half rotted, weightless. It had all the little darting look of a small, dark, indecisive rodent.

Bugsy considered, his stare a laser beam of concentration, concluded it was a rodent, gathered himself, shook his fledgling feathers, hopped clumsily towards it and fell in an ungainly heap over his own feet, the size of dinner plates. Disentangling his talons, the five-week-old baby eagle owl floundered, tripped, collected himself with a great flurry of untidy fluff and set off again with determination, heading straight for the cone rolling towards the edge of the pool.

'Who fuckin' let Bugs out, then?' A head with a shock of ginger hair, albino with sawdust, stuck itself out of the open master bedroom window and shouted urgently, '*Oi!*'

No one answered.

Rafe the red-haired carpenter swore, shielded his eyes against the sun blazing down on the deserted garden and watched his pet bird lurch closer to the water.

'Suppose I've got to turn the machine off, come down and put Bugs in his box myself. *More* of the client's time wasted, what he is paying good money for,' he threatened, seeing the site foreman amble out of the garage that served as site office and stockroom, the kettle whistling behind him, the stub of a fag glued to the edge of his lip. The foreman grinned, then frowned, glanced down, shook his head urgently at Rafe.

Rafe glared down at his boss's arm-waving. Behind him, the radio spewed synthesised Kylie Minogue, turned up high above the noise of his saw, in defiance of main contractor rules banning noise nuisances from site.

'What?' he yelled. 'Can't hear you. Go and get that stupid friggin' bird and put it in my van.' The midday sun reddened the back of his freckled neck, cast his shadow, black and sharp, on to the glass roof immediately below.

Hidden beneath it, sheltered from the glare by the vine trained across it, two women were on their way through the garden from the back door to the front of the house. Samantha raised both hands to shield her vision, to squint against the brilliance at the pantomine. Josephine, amused by the foreman's trying to warn Rafe that they were there, that he should mind his language and for *God's* sake not make references to wasting the client's time and money, forgot her worry for a moment

As the owl lumbered towards its fir cone, she asked, 'Where are your parents at the moment?'

'Finland,' Samantha said. 'Since about three months ago. Daddy's last posting before he retires.'

'Grim, I should think.'

'Not at all, if you don't mind mixed saunas and flagellation. Friendly embassy, friendly international community, friendly Finns, my mother says.'

My mother says. Everything Samantha's mother said was said

from some great distance. Josephine wondered possessively how far Emmanuel was a substitute for a father who was permanently absent in the Diplomatic Service. Samantha had been twenty-four and working as a Norland nanny when her employer's mother asked her to make up the numbers at a dinner party.

'Divorced for the second time, he's on his own. He upsets my seating plan,' Lady Forbes Ffrench had clucked. 'Would you be a darling and fill in? You'll find him charming. He's in business – chief executive of this and that, and *filthy* rich even with all that alimony. We love him dearly and I really don't know why he can't seem to hang on to his wives.'

Two sharp eyes had surveyed Samantha, porcelain skin, soft, baby-blue eyes and long hair done up in a complicated plait. A sweet, innocent face. Lady Forbes Ffrench had seen her dealing with her daughter who could be *very* difficult and demanding when it came to the children, and was not deceived.

'He should be very easy,' she added thoughtfully. 'He's got two daughters your sort of age.'

Despite, or possibly because of, his having daughters the same sort of age as her, Samantha and Emmanuel Gilmour found each other so easy they were married in less than a year. Father substitute or no, it seemed to work.

'Do you think it can swim?' Samantha asked, looking at Bugsy. 'I hope so, because I'm not going near those beak and claws to rescue it.'

Josephine kept away from birds of any feather: they brought her out in hives. Bugsy no doubt crawled with fleas and was only one of a collection of owls the builders brought and kept in the garage every day.

'I should think it'd get waterlogged and sink like a stone,' she answered crossly. 'But it won't fall in; bird-brained it may be, but it isn't stupid. I don't know what they think they're doing, bringing birds here. This is supposed to be a building site, not a sanctuary. I just wish they'd get on with their *work*,' she shouted suddenly, meaning for Rafe to hear her, which he did not.

Above her head, the carpenter failed to read the warnings from below, panicked, swore loudly and banged the windowsill with a section of door jamb to attract Bugsy's attention. Samantha tilted her head back, unable to see him through the vine that canopied the underside of the glass roof thickly, its leaves thick with tightly bunched, bitter-green young grapes. Sawdust, cement and pink plaster fell like talcum powder, settling in a fine film all over the garden, making everyone sneeze.

'They call that owl-fancying berk the wood butcher. One can see why. What will you do with this lot when you move in?' Josephine asked, following her gaze. 'Make your own wine?'

Samantha shook her head. 'The gardener who worked for the old woman who died here hung up his wellies when we bought it. He's eighty-six. He happened to wander past – in every sense – the other day when we were here, and we dragged him in and gave him a cup of building site tea. He isn't senile; he tipped it in the cement mixer when he thought I wasn't looking. He said, they look wonderful at first, then it's downhill to mould and shrivel. All promise and no performance, he said, no follow-through, no matter how exquisitely he pruned them.'

All promise and no performance. Garcia hiding in his study with precious Millie, and Emma in a furious sulk because Josephine wouldn't let her spend the day getting in Sophia's way and had insisted on dragging her down to Surrey.

'Bring your swimming costume and use Samantha's pool,' Josephine had said through gritted teeth.

'Everyone *else* is on holiday,' Emma whined.

'I can't go off on holiday in the middle of a project. Anyway, you're going to Seville with your grandmother at the end of the month.'

'*You* wouldn't want to go swimming with all those men staring.'

Josephine didn't have an answer to that.

'I wish I hadn't got Emma sulking and behaving like an ass, refusing to get out of the car. I wish that someone would put that bird in its cage, and I wish it would rain,' Josephine burst out.

Samantha turned in surprise.

'The heat gets me down,' Josephine mumbled, embarrassed.

'Headache. A3's a nightmare. Looking at half a million traffic cones through a heat haze makes your eyes go funny.'

'It does.'

Cones weren't the only things on the road that made drivers' eyes go funny. Samantha, driving down the same road that morning for the site meeting in a shiny black open-top BMW, wearing a T-shirt knotted under her breasts, a baby-blue bandana round her silver-blonde head and Ray-Bans on the tip of her nose, had Pavarotti blaring from the stereo and drove much too fast. Male drivers came over funny and caused havoc on the road around her.

'You're too young to remember Jasper Carrott's cone sketch,' Josephine went on. 'He said there must be an EEC cone mountain that needed using up. Even the Russians wouldn't take them, so we had to store them on the roads, which accounts for all the roadworks.'

When Samantha looked as vague as that, Josephine knew it meant she didn't get the point.

'Butter and beef mountains. The EEC sold them to the Russians, who subsidised food, rather than reduce the price so we could afford them.'

Samantha watched Bugsy trying to untangle his own feet. 'I like Jasper Carrott. Do you think he invented the Cones Hotline? One day I'm going to ring that number to find out if it's real and who invented *narrow lanes*.'

'Some ass in a powder-blue Jag with a precious number plate passed me doing eighty, hooting and yacking into a mobile phone. He nearly took my rearview mirror off. I hope he got done.'

'I passed that pale blue Jag,' Samantha boasted. 'But I didn't see you.' After a pointed silence, she added, 'Well, all right, so he was speeding more than you and I was speeding more than him. You *are* in a bad mood. I told you not to bother working on a Saturday. Why don't you tell Emma to take a long hike home via the railway station if she's being hell. Or you can leave her here, with me. Go home without her, open a bottle of something iced and fizzy and get pissed by the pool. Get a tan. Have fun.'

'It's not, on my own.'

'Where's Garcia?' Samantha's pale blue, mermaid eyes were narrowed.

Josephine moved out of shadow into sunlight, started towards the wooden gate leading from the back garden to the front. 'Working, as far as I know, like me,' she said over her shoulder, 'since he isn't at home. He got up at four o'clock this morning and I could hear him shouting at Millie as they left. So here I am at work, and I think we could get down to it now, Samantha.'

'*I* think you should go home and look for your husband.'

It was easy to see Samantha had been married for hardly any time at all to a man who doted on her.

'What makes you think my husband wants to be found?' Josephine asked lightly. 'No. We are going to look at boards, and you are going to consider the fabrics and carpets I've brought, and with any luck you'll like what I've put together and we will make some choices.'

'Are you at least doing something nice next week?'

They walked briskly round to the front of the house where the front door stood wide open, the hall floor piled with boards and bags of swatches.

'Barbecue. The neighbours and you.'

Samantha was scandalised. 'But it's your *fortieth*.'

Josephine stook stock still in the middle of the path, casting a short, black shadow. 'You think I want to *celebrate*? I'm nearly forty and I wish I wasn't. My only child is growing up, and my husband is mostly never there. I am faced with the rest of my life, so what shall I do?'

Samantha put out her hand, then thought better of it.

'I'm going to make a go of my business, make myself independent.' And one minute humming along, like Pooh Bear, in a fairly relaxed kind of way. Then I feel something creeping up on me, which feels absolutely *bloody*.

'I'm prepared to work *extremely* hard,' Josephine said fiercely.

Emma marched in through a big wooden gate leading to where they had left their cars, a Mickey Mouse T-shirt dragged down to her knees, over a bikini. She picked her way barefoot across the brown, dried lawn and disappeared round the side of the house.

'Eventually, she shows some sense,' Josephine said.

Samantha waited until Emma was well out of earshot. 'Do you want to tell me about whatever it is?'

Josephine's deep grey eyes were shiny, as if with fever. 'Not really, but I'm going to anyway. Garcia's having an affair,' she blurted. 'So, *you* tell *me*, Pollyanna, dear: for a woman in that kind of situation, what else is there for her to do?'

Chapter Thirteen

Josephine stuck her head into her big American fridge and hoped her flush of remembered embarrassment would cool off. She had exposed herself and Garcia as stupidly as if she had thrown herself on the floor like a two-year-old in a tantrum.

To her surprise, spoiled, indulged Samantha, who had no reason in the world to worry about anything, had put her arm round her and led her away from the curious stares of three builders emerging from the house carrying planks.

A painter looked down from scaffolding above their heads, lethargically spreading white exterior paint over the walls, whistling between his teeth.

'Are you *sure*? *Garcia?* You always look like the perfect couple.'

Half the perfect couple would have let Samantha's husband make love to her that time long ago, more than half in love with him all those years ago. Even now . . . She wondered wistfully whether they would have drawn apart, whether he would have taken the cognac and gone, or stayed. But she'd been pregnant.

Josephine, panicky, had an eerie feeling that Samantha could hear what she was thinking, read the disloyal images inside her head. She drew away clumsily, shrugged off Samantha's arm.

Awkward, they walked round the hot and windless garden, deliberately talked of other things, how the renovation had been fraught with conditions. A pile of worm-eaten wood from one of the floors they had had to replace lay waiting to be taken away and treated, to be used on another building of the same age, replacing like with like.

'Emmanuel was about to tell the builders to burn it but they threw the book at him.' Samantha quoted the formal, pompous letter from English Heritage and giggled. '"You will retile with original tiles, rebuild walls with original bricks or a match from stock from similar buildings, you will send all infested wood for treatment and preservation to us, and you will destroy nothing until we have inspected it and given our consent."'

All for a weekend home, Josephine had thought, trying to shuck off the awkward moment, regain her ground by being critical. This house deserves better than that. It should be loved and lived in by people who know that they are no more than custodians, beads on the chain of time. A house like this owns its owners. If it were mine, I'd never be able to leave it.

Clients often owned houses she would have loved herself: an occupational hazard. Vital to remember it was *their* lives that would be lived in them, to their taste, not hers.

'Are you going to be OK?'

Josephine made herself smile, tried to minimise the damage. 'I'm seeing bogeymen. Coming up to forty and neurotic. Take no notice.'

Samantha went to speak, thought better of it.

'Part of the problem is,' Josephine hurried on, 'at home it's worse than here. Emilia's annexe and changing my study has turned us into a building site. Only we don't do site visits, we live there. It isn't fun.'

It was hell. London in the long heatwave was crowded with tourists. Sophia was full up, crammed to the rafters with foreigners who came and went at all hours and who were noisily inconsiderate. Home was crowded because Garcia had filled it with stroppy builders who had taken half the roof off. Emilia was stalking around her new premises, giving orders, irritating the builders, who themselves had what was once called bloody-minded temperament and was now known as 'attitude'. Emma, dying to go and lie on a beach ogling boys, like her friends, was ungracious about everyone and everything and had more 'attitude' than the rest put together. Now, Garcia and Millie were hand in glove and acting strangely.

'The bloody poodles are the last straw,' Josephine said, making a joke of it. 'Rambo and Barney Darling torment the builders. Man bites dog. It's mutual.'

The dogs made sure everyone knew they were put out. Yap, yap, yap. Everyone in the neighbourhood, who wasn't away on holiday, was in a state of indignant unrest.

Eventually they had gone through the boards and Samantha had chosen her bathroom furnishings. By the time they'd finished, Emma had had all the owls out of the garage and the builders, downing tools to a man, were busy showing her how to fly Bugsy's father from a leather gauntlet on her arm. She had had to be bullied to go home.

Josephine cooled down, decided to take Samantha's advice, open something cold and bubbly, and sit, despite the dereliction of her garden by the now nearly finished building work, beside her pool.

'Hi, Mrs Goddard.'

She looked round the fridge door at six foot three of clean-shaven, brown-eyed, cleft-chinned, crew-cut, all-American male, standing by the back door. John B Denver Jr, spending the summer in London, boarding with Sophia, was, like Millie, from Connecticut, son of a merchant banker. His tanned and wholesome face split in a blindingly white, charming, ingratiating grin.

'Hello, John,' Josephine said repressively. 'If you've come about builders or dogs, don't bother. Just go away.'

'I have orders to tell you that your property is a disgrace to the neighbourhood,' he drawled. He put on a Jeeves and Wooster accent crossed with an exaggerated imitation of Sophia's poshest voice. 'One *does* not expect rubbish, skips, *or* radios outside when all one wishes to do is enjoy one's patio in peace. Emilia's dogs barking all the time are *ab*solutely the last straw. I woke up this morning and thought, oh my *God*, the council have let the common to the Gypsies; it's those bloody Lib Dems.'

'Sophia Larkin is my best friend and neighbour, and a miserable coward,' Josephine snapped. 'She is extremely kind, and if I had an emotional emergency there is no one I could rely on more. But she is also a crashing snob and a pain in the neck,' she hurried on, before the thought 'I am having an emotional emergency' could catch up with her tongue and spill out all over the place so that neither of them would know what to do. 'If she wants to stir up trouble, she should come and do it herself, not send the foreign help. You may go back and tell her I said so. Good day.' She picked up a bottle of Garcia's Krug and began to close the fridge door.

'Mrs Goddard, Sophia is distressed because your builders whistle at her and pass personal remarks.'

Josephine tried to keep eye contact with him at the same time as keeping a straight face. 'Do they?'

'Yeah. She says she is mortified.' His composure cracked and he began to laugh, a young, deep, overloud American laugh, all trace of Jeeves and Wooster gone. 'She is persuaded you are lowering the price of property on the north side of Barnes Common. Mrs Goddard, I have to tell you that Sophia and Ron are very seriously upset.'

'Seriously upset, my foot. Tell her to shut her Veluxes, and tell Ron not to shout down the telephone because I hear every word he says and *I* might get seriously upset,' Josephine snapped.

He was grinning like an idiot.

'Oh, all right. I suppose you'd better come on in.'

She led the way to her study, a newly plastered rectangle at the back of the house on the first floor. It had bare, stripped floorboards and two new radiators smelling strongly of paint. A draughtsman's board stood alone in front of a big Victorian sash window and on a table an AppleMac was shrouded in a transparent plastic cover.

'Can you lend me a hand with this?'

A pile of packing cases, full of papers, were stacked in the middle of the room.

'I was going to sit by the pool with a drink and look over some drawings. They're in here somewhere. So are the marble samples. But the cases are too heavy for me to lift down.'

Obligingly, he did it for her.

Josephine chuckled. 'Can you imagine walking into this every time you get up in the morning? Imagine if you had a hangover.' She held the marble square up to the bright, unshaded light. Glistening turmeric-coloured veins ran through the cold, polished stone. 'I have a client who wants it in his bathroom, floor to ceiling, except for mirrors. We spent a whole afternoon in Marble City, picking it out. Kuwaiti. *Pied-à-terre* in Knightsbridge. Money no problem and he could have the earth.' She shook her head. 'But he'd rather go for that.'

'We fought in the Gulf for those guys,' John B Denver Jr remarked. He fingered the stone with distaste.

From beyond the open door a movement caught Josephine's eye. 'We're in here, Emma.'

Her daughter slunk round the edge of the door, a moulded, sinuous vision in black Lycra bicycling shorts, black Lycra cropped top and enormous snow-white trainers. Her long, thick, tabby hair was tied in a knot on top of her head. Reaching up deliberately to fix it, she showed off several inches of flat, brown midriff and a neat belly button.

'Good grief, you look like a panther in a snowdrift,' her mother said acidly. 'Sophia's sent John round to complain.'

'Hi,' Emma said casually. 'I flew an eagle owl today. It sat on my wrist and walked up and down my arm. It's got the most enormous talons.'

Oh, *Lord*, Josephine thought. I had no idea.

The moment was loaded, stretched and sagged interminably as John B. Denver gulped, desperately tried to remember his manners.

'With your mouth open like that, you look really stupid,' Emma remarked in a friendly, unbiased sort of way, coiling like a cobra round the edge of the door.

'*Emma*,' Josephine hissed. She busied herself with her drawings, hiding a smile. John B. Denver Jr *did* look stupid, holding that chunk of blindingly ornate marble, his jaw dropped like a dozing passenger on a train, about to dribble. He rallied.

'*You* look *great*,' he said enthusiastically. 'Owls?'

'Samantha's builders run an owl sanctuary.' Josephine leaned over and took the marble sample gently out of his hands.

Emma did a studied imitation of Helena Bonham Carter's most suggestive, wide-eyed, innocent look, examined her nails, leaned on the end of her mother's drawing board and gazed soulfully out of the window.

'Er . . .' John B. Denver croaked. Testosterone, explosive as an IRA bomb. 'Would you like . . .'

Emma hunched her shoulders, examined her thumbnail minutely, didn't turn.

'Don't mind me,' Jospehine said. 'I'll take these down and open that Krug.'

'I've painted my room black with an American flag,' Emma said, treacherously forgetting Paul Scheinfeld and his football photos.

Looking sideways at a pair of size fourteen feet in Reeboks on the end of a very tall pair of faded jeans, her eyes travelled up, past a crumpled black Elvis T-shirt, came to rest ingenuously on John B. Denver Jr's enchanted face. 'You can come and have a look, if you like.'

'You will *not*,' her mother said promptly.

They turned as one, two young faces, pitying.

They only had to go next door and Sophia wouldn't care what they did. Josephine, cowardly, took her papers and fled into her garden.

'John B. Denver the Second is American, doing the Grand Tour and staying with Sophia. He is over-sexed, over-indulged and over our garden wall,' Josephine wailed later to Garcia. 'I think any minute he's going to be over Emma. I don't know what to do.'

'I doubt there's much you can do. She's sixteen, and we won't be able to stop her.'

He was writing faxes at high speed on the kitchen table, not really taking notice, his felt-tip pen going *squeak, squeak, squeak*. Mouselike movements, mouselike noise, mousewheel life, spinning faster and faster, almost out of control.

'Don't you think there should be more to life than working and making money?' she said suddenly.

'You don't need to work,' Garcia answered automatically, then his pen froze. Oh, God, that probably wasn't true.

'That isn't what I meant.'

'What did you have in mind? About Emma?'

She studied his absorbed, exhausted face. They were all so alike. 'We are a terribly self-absorbed household,' she said quietly. 'Don't you think?'

'No.' The squeaking pen began again.

First love. Agonising bliss. The heaven and hell of hormones. Emma on the pill at sixteen – should they let it come to that? A fierce ache in her own heart, for Emma's innocence and her own lost youth. At a loss to explain exactly what she had in mind, except it was something to do with protecting all of them, she resorted to sarcasm, smiled sweetly.

'That's all right, darling, never mind. I'll leave you to get on. When I've worked it all out, I'll fax you and let you know.'

Chapter Fourteen

'Not tonight, Josephine. Nor last night, nor the night before. You should have faxed him,' the emperor added sternly. 'About tonight.'

She was sitting gazing at herself in Samantha's big square stone fishpond, could see the emperor's reflection in the water. He was looking over her shoulder, frowning.

The foreman came down to the fishpond and headed Bugsy off, shooed him back towards the orange marble house.

The emperor began to laugh and fish nibbled her toes. The garden was full of people, luminous in bright moonlight, floating clothes bleached by the stars.

'The army say, make him talk. He'll talk all right. To everyone.'

Josephine struggled awake to find Garcia not there. She looked at the clock. Two in the morning. She had been dreaming about her birthday party, a silent, dancing gathering on Samantha's lawn. Then the emperor had come and pointed out that Garcia wasn't there, and it was all her fault.

You should have faxed him.

Drifting back to sleep, she knew that Garcia *would* talk to eveyone, just as the army said. He'd orchestrate everything, the life and soul of the party.

He was flattering Emilia, winding Sophia and Ron up.

'We're extending the building work,' he shouted, grinning.

Ron and Sophia went scuttling for Prozac. Josephine watched them grow wings, golden wings, to carry them back to cloud nine. Cloud nine, on cue, drifted past, a woolly, sinking sort of cloud that one could sleep in for ever.

Sophia wouldn't fly, became pouting and seductive, came on to John Denver Jr, who came on to Emma.

'*No.*'

But her voice wouldn't work. Helpless, she saw Bee and Abigail smile complacently, covered in overalls and blisters. Bee looked into the fishpond, said she only swam in soda water because she had to get back and finish pulling down their house. Barry was watching Babe, got up to the nines in a frock, all sequins and blue eye shadow, even though I told them, she cried, finding her voice, it's only a barbecue.

'I saw him as I left this morning, bleach and foil in his hair. Blue *never* suits him, and he will wear it,' she told a dozen goldfish, lined up along a lily leaf, gasping in their warm and soupy pond, their pump quite broken, suffocating. Barney Darling went by, pumping along on a skateboard. *Wheeeeeee.*

Breathless with tension in the hot, airless night, Josephine woke again, half laughing, half terrified, and came properly out of the dream.

'Garcia?'

She went down in her thin nightdress to find light under his study door.

'Are you coming to bed? Ever?'

He had his head on his arms, as though asleep, but he had merely been thinking.

'What are you doing up?'

'Not a lot.'

He got up quickly, came to her, and very gently led her back to bed.

Chapter Fifteen

'Mum?'

'Yes.'

'Do you think tragedy is catching?'

Josephine, tired after the overheated, broken night, looked up from putting sheets in the washing machine. Builder's dirt got trodden everywhere.

'Whatever makes you ask that?'

'Melissa says her friend has said that if she comes to see Melissa in London, will Melissa please not introduce her to Sophia.'

Garcia's drawn face haunted her. She had tried to ask, lying in the luminous summer night, what was wrong, but he had sunk instantly into a short sleep. How could a perfect couple, who never had problems, know how to begin to solve them?

Hey, baby, life's for living.

What about living on the dark side? Josephine, teetering on the edge of some deep and unknown precipice, wondered uneasily, not for the first time, if Melissa's friend might not be right.

Sophia was aptly named; her life had all the makings of Greek tragedy.

Her parents' divorce and her father's marriage to a stepmother she didn't get on with, whose will was an atrocious act of unnecessary vengeance, had turned her and Ron's lives upside down. One minute, limitless overdraft facilities, living on the most solid of expectations, sell in a seller's market for a cool million, invest and they'd be laughing on the interest. Next minute taking in PGs and recycling out-of-work executives – these days cheek by jowl with the cold tank in their roof space, subtly harried by the unseen owner in Australia. Ron headhunted for his living, using his only talent. Being an Old Etonian, he enjoyed arrogant attitudes, the result of limited intelligence but limitless access to the Old Boy Club. To hear him talk, he was in a cross between the KGB, industrial espionage and running British industry – *frightfully* important and confidential. Hence the attic. Private. Secret, even. In any case, all the rooms below were full of paying guests.

After the will came Uncle Harry.

Then Crispin.

Then Theo.

Josephine knew Sophia lived in fear of where it was all going to end.

Eighteen stone of Uncle Harry had come for the weekend, called the doctor out the second evening, bent double with a massive stomach ache.

'Greed,' suggested Sophia tartly. 'A pig. Needs to go on a diet.'

'A bit late for diet. Inoperable cancer,' said the doctor two weeks and a lot of hospital tests later. 'We can't do much except keep him comfortable and, ah, we've had a long talk with him.' He avoided Sophia's eye. 'Seems he's determined to come home.'

She was appalled.

'Let him,' Ron ordered, whispering later, in private, '*He's loaded.*'

It would spring their trap.

Uncle Harry lay shrinking and complaining and dying and griping ungratefully in Sophia's dining room for four months while cancer galloped through him. Having no other room, they took the dining table out, put a hospital bed in and ate in the kitchen.

'You could send him to a hospice,' the doctor suggested towards the end, 'if this is getting too much for you to cope with.'

Uncle Harry glared with morphine-crazed, shrunken eyes. 'You send me away to die, I'll come back and haunt you, so help me God,' he threatened, staring at Sophia.

'He wants to die at home. He has a right,' she said helplessly.

Noting the way her hands trembled, the GP shook his head, said would she like some Valium?

Uncle Harry resented being sick, resented dying, hated being nursed, hated Sophia for doing it, blamed her for his whole indignity.

After he left, a third of his former self, for the crematorium, she couldn't bring herself to eat in the dining room or hold a party.

'Bloody wills again,' she shrieked on hearing that Uncle Harry had left most of his money to his professional association. 'As if those bloody accountants haven't got enough already.'

She *knew* he knew how much, secretly, they'd counted on it. To want to profit from another person's death is a terrible, shameful thing. Out of sheer spite he'd be back to spook her and it would serve her right.

'She thinks the room is haunted and that he's waiting for her to throw a bash and defile his memory. She used to give some of the best dinner parties in SW13,' Josephine told Emma sadly, closing the washing machine. 'The irony is, we were all very sorry for poor Uncle Harry.'

Not all that long after Uncle Harry died, Crispin fell down in the gutter one day and didn't get up.

Massive stroke.

'He was blind drunk at the time,' Sophia cried, crying. 'How *could* he die in the gutter?'

'Your ex-husband was blind drunk the whole of his life,' Ron pointed out.

She wept. And wept. Couldn't seem to stop the tidal wave of her distress.

'You're married to me now,' Ron yelled, baffled, unable to comfort her.

The obituary took up half a page in *The Times* and the funeral was a big affair because Crispin had been quite famous. Some while later, the Royal Academy put on a small exhibition of Crispin's paintings and Ron could only just be persuaded to let her go.

Little Theo Larkin, Ron's younger son by his first wife, was, as Ron liked to put it jokily, two sandwiches short of a picnic. At his special school in Devon, out for a Sunday afternoon walk, he wandered down the gently sloping cliffs, bent to pick the pretty flowers. Straight over on to the rocks below. The offshore rescue boat found his little broken body on the rocks when the tide next came in.

After public outcry, there was a full investigation and the headmaster resigned his post. The uproar subsided into quiet, steady condemnation of the Larkins for sending Theo to an institution.

'It's the wills,' Sophia screamed. 'Everyone was going to leave everything to us, only they haven't. Don't they understand? Theo's mother is a sick woman, And me? I have to work.'

'Sophia is warm and sweet and kind,' Josephine said as the washing started going round and round. 'There's no one I'd rather have in a crisis. She understands them.'

'Sophia keeps waiting for a crisis.'

The remark jolted Josephine severely. 'And what else do you see in our dysfunctional daily lives?' she snapped, unnerved.

'Don't get stressed out, Mum.'

'I am not *stressed out*, Emma.'

Emma, not deceived by her mother's shrillness, put on her best American accent. 'John says they're kind of OK, but . . . he says, really, Ron's a dork. But he thinks Soph's cool.'

'Oh, really?' Josephine's mouth began to quiver with reaction. Sophia's American toyboy. The quiver became a snigger, then a huge, hysterical laugh. With Ron working at home, nearly always there, and the place crawling with visitors, it'd cramp their style. She couldn't seem to stop laughing.

'*Mum*,' Emma protested.

It would be a choice of on the attic photocopier or up against the cold tank and the roof struts, splinters in their bottoms.

'I just hope she shuts the damn Veluxes,' she gasped.

'You are *horrible*,' Emma observed coldly.

She was. Josephine struggled to sober up. In any case, Sophia, for reasons known only to herself, doted on Ron.

'You're right,' Josephine said, contrite. 'Sophia would never take a lover.

Theo's death, the greatest tragedy of all, ended with Sophia falling in love.

It was much worse than Uncle Harry. His dying in her dining room, plagued by cancer of the bowel and shrunken gums that wouldn't hold his false teeth was horrible but natural, as had been his lifelong, grouchy, grumbling, griping, spitting, dribbling bad temper.

In the funeral parlour Sophia steeled herself to behave correctly, peered reluctantly into his coffin to say goodbye and found to her relief that as a corpse he was not much changed after all. He merely looked a great deal healthier than usual, positively rubicund with make-up, nicely dressed in a jacket and tie, blessedly quiet. In death, Uncle Harry did one good thing. At long last he shut up.

Her stepmother, on the other hand, in the soberly carpeted Chapel of Rest, had had herself screwed down at once, having pre-arranged her economy-class funeral in detail down to the last tip for the hearse driver, leaving orders that she did not wish to be treated as a spectacle.

'More likely,' Sophia told the smoothly good-looking young undertaker, whose cold smile reminded her of pictures of Brad Pitt in the early stages of making *Interview With the Vampire*, 'she didn't want Dracula looking in.'

His smile chilled to freezing, straight out of a cold storage drawer, like most of his clients.

'Sorry. Joke. She'd be too vain to lie in state, anyway,' she whispered hastily, to placate him. 'She probably just worried that you'd forget to do her hair and not put her dentures back in.'

Theo's dying was worse than unnatural, it was *careless*.

His coffin was closed when they made their final respects. Sophia fingered the brass bolts.

'I wish . . .' she whispered.

Ron, who had identified the body, shook his head. 'You wouldn't want to look, believe me.' He retreated into a long, impenetrable and stony silence.

On the drive home she sat, her arms folded, all jammed up and unable to shed a single tear, as if blocked up tight with hay fever, or a tap with a perished washer, about to dribble.

Days went by and neither of them could sleep.

'No, Mr Larkin. Mrs Larkin. You'll simply get habituated.'

The young GP, the only one in the practice with an appointment free in less than a week, was fresh out of medical school and in his first, trainee, job. He had insightful, up-to-the-minute annoyingly know-all ideas about bereavement.

'You're twisting our arms,' Ron accused, refused any more prescriptions for sleeping pills unless accompanied by counselling.

The young man smiled, a fresh, natural, charmingly confident smile. 'There's CRUSE,' he said, looking up a telephone number in a directory of local services. 'It's run by people who have been bereaved themselves and have some experience of counselling.

They could help you talk things through. Better than relying on pills.'

'Send who you like,' Ron growled, holding out a hand for the prescription. 'We can always go private.'

This was not how patients were supposed to respond. The young GP pressed the key on his computer that printed out the medication.

'Call me Cindy,' the woman from CRUSE invited. 'Cindy Crawford.'

'How's Richard Gere?' Sophia asked, before she could stop herself. She heard her own voice go on flippantly, 'Are you still together, or are the rumours true?'

Mrs Crawford smiled, accepted a cup of tea without milk or sugar and refused biscuits. 'Unlike the other Cindy, I have to diet,' she explained. 'When I lost my own son, first I couldn't eat at all, then when I started comfort eating I found I couldn't stop.'

Mrs Crawford filled Ron's favourite armchair to overflowing with sixteen stone or more of firm, pink flesh covered with downy skin, like a great, fat, ripe peach. Ron coughed, put his cup and saucer down and swung himself round to stare out of the window, wooden-faced.

'You lost your son too?'

'We've lost four altogether,' said Ron from where he had his back turned to them. 'People, that is. Not sons.'

'When a child dies, it is desperate,' Mrs Crawford said gently.

Ron counted the PG's knickers on Sophia's rotary dryer as it whirled faster and faster in a gathering wind.

'Ours was an adolescent cot death,' Cindy Crawford went on. 'I went to wake him up for school, and there he was, stone cold dead. No one knows why.'

'I thought only babies had cot deaths.' Ron twisted round and looked at her hard.

'I used to think so too.'

Ron counted fifteen bras, started on the tights and cleared his throat in a way that Sophia knew meant he was about to leave the room, climb the ladder to the attic, fish the whisky bottle from behind the water tank and get drunk.

'We take it out on each other,' Sophia exclaimed, all in a rush. 'It's Ron's son who died. All I seem able to do is feel angry. It shouldn't have happened.'

'I felt furious with Nicky. I thought, you little swine, you've gone and left us deliberately.'

Over the back of his chair, she saw smoke rise as Ron lit a cigarette and went deliberately cross-eyed, watching smoke pour out of his nose.

'You think,' Cindy said, 'I shouldn't be angry. This person I loved just *died* and I should be sad and sorry. But when Nicky died, was I ever angry he'd let it happen to *him*. First I was shocked. Numb. When that wore off, I got so angry. I used to go in his room and yell my head off at him. You dumb, lazy *git*, I'd shout, couldn't you even be bothered to *breathe*? He'd never get up in the morning. You know? Teenagers can't get off the horizontal.'

The wind blew harder as the sun moved below the top of the window and glistened on the peachy down on her upper lip, glowed on her soft, fine hair.

'Grief can turn you crazy,' she finished.

'I'm cross with Theo for walking off a cliff, and I'm even angrier that those teachers let him. But I'm crossest of all with those other two wretches,' Sophia corrected her. 'By and large, I was so fed up by the time the others died, especially Uncle Harry, that I was really rather glad. Their going should have prepared us for what *this* would feel like, and it didn't because it isn't the same, at all. What was the point of all that dying,' she shouted suddenly, 'if it doesn't help when it matters? Why couldn't those wretches get *anything* right?'

Ron stubbed his cigarette out ferociously in a pool of tea in his saucer.

'You know so much more than most people about death,' Mrs Crawford suggested. 'In years to come, you might consider coming and working with us. The work does help give suffering meaning.'

The tide had come in and reverently laid ten-year-old Theo, with his mental age of six, on top of a flat black spur of rock, his shorts torn off, his sodden blue T-shirt emblazoned with bright, white letters. 'Carry Me Gently, I'm A Superstar'.

'If it's meaning she's after, then she'd better fucking apply,' said Ron in a strangled voice as he got up and stamped out of the room.

Later, he made a wholly unexpected and uncharacteristic apology. 'Sorry I shouted at that damn woman.'

'I think,' Sophia said cautiously, 'talking to her would help me quite a lot.'

'Fuck her and her counselling.' Ron sounded ragged. 'Since I haven't got to pay any more of Theo's school fees, we're going to have a holiday.'

The young travel agent explained the deal.

To call the kind of holidays they enjoyed 'package deals' made them sound cheap, Sophia thought indignantly, perched on a stool in Thomas Cook, trying to read the Miami brochure he was thumbing upside down. As though they took trips to Costa del Disco, their hotel a building site and beaches strewn with lager louts, empty bottles, used condoms and last night's vomit.

'Sounds like a dipso's wet dream,' Ron muttered.

'Everything, and I mean *everything* included. You can drink the bar dry. You want caviar and ice-cold champagne, or a bowl of Häagen-Dazs at three in the morning, you got it,' he cried eagerly, like the Burger King advertisement on the telly.

He turned the brochure towards them. 'Right on the beach, pool and spa. Massage, facials,' he said to Sophia. 'All that kind of stuff. Good food. Views. Every room has a balcony. Kind of place that attracts discriminating people.'

'You've been there,' Ron said sarcastically.

'Not as such,' the youth admitted guilessly. 'But the photographs are lovely. Someone who used to work here went there last year. Said it was brilliant.'

'And pricey.'

'It's all-in.'

'Who nursed Uncle Harry?' Sophia hissed.

'You.'

'Then I get to choose.' She pushed the booklet towards the young travel agent. 'We'd love to go.'

'Ought to ban children from aircraft,' Ron muttered.

The flight was long. A small child in the row opposite woke after the first couple of hours, amused itself by wailing, thrashing fretfully in its mother's arms. Sophia's head ached.

When food came round, Ron drank too many small bottles of red wine from the trolley and fell asleep with his mouth open, crammed uncomfortably sideways into the narrow seat. He woke, red-eyed and irritable, a crick in his neck and a bit hungover, and sat looking hangdog until eventually they landed. Sophia limped, her feet swollen like puddings, uncaring. Beyond the airport waited beaches with shady umbrellas, recliners, bar service and rolling breakers, warm, clear, transparent as pale blue stained glass.

'Champagne, pink gin, a martini full of ice or rum punch,' Ron muttered, following the signs to baggage collection. 'The question is, what to start with. I think rum punch.'

'Lazy days, romantic nights,' sighed the brochures.

'You start on rum punches and we won't be having romantic anything at all,' Sophia muttered to herself.

In the glossy photographs, couples gazed into each other's eyes, sipped cocktails at sunset, surrounded by flowers and attentive waiters, on the hotel terrace. Sophia sighed, hobbled as fast as she could, joined Ron at the line for immigration control. They had been slow getting off and were almost the last in the queue.

The immigration officer was small and neat and black. She stamped Sophia's passport, held Ron's in small, aggressively manicured hands, nails red and curved like a bird of prey's, tapped her computer like a woodpecker with the tip of a talon and inspected the screen for what seemed an unnecessarily long time.

'Is this your passport?' she demanded, swivelling to face him.

'Well, yes,' Ron answered. 'Of course it is.'

'Mr Ronald Larkin?'

'Yes.'

'Follow the line.'

He looked behind him. The last few tourists glared. He was holding them up. He looked back. 'Excuse me?'

'I can call security,' snarled the small woman, 'and have you escorted, *or* you can follow the line.'

'I think she means that one,' Sophia said, pointing to the yellow line painted on the floor behind them. It led across the immigration hall and disappeared into the distance.

'Why?'

The black immigration officer's expression was impassive. 'Follow . . .'

'The line. They have guns around here. I think you'd better do what she says,' Sophia whispered nervously.

Ron backed away, turned into the airport concourse and walked slowly, shoulders hunched, down the yellow line.

'What shall *I* do?' Sophia shrilled.

Several yards away, he turned and gave an exaggerated shrug. 'I'm busy right now, following a line, in case I get shot. Go to the hotel and if I ever get out of here, I'll join you.'

The remainder of the queue jostled forwards, Sophia moved aside and watched him walk away.

People sat or lay on benches. The grey room smelled of sweat and bad coffee from the battered drinks machine. Next to the machine, a middle-aged man in a crumpled grey suit sat by himself.

'Welcome to pound,' he said in a friendly Yorkshire accent.

'Pound?'

'Aliens and undesirables,' the Yorkshireman said chirpily. 'We wait in here while t' buggers fix to throw us out.'

'Why would they want to fix to throw us out?' Half a dozen bored and alienated faces ignored him. 'Why are they throwing you out, then?'

'Her indoors, at the desk. She says, why are you coming to Miami? I said, to get away from the wife who wants my brass. I was made redundant a month ago and I'm damned if she's getting half my miserable little bit of severance money. She wanted divorce in the first place.'

Ron sat down beside him.

'I thought she'd appreciate a bit of a joke, but she says, have I got a return ticket? Well.' He got up, tried to put some money in the drinks machine. 'Only takes foreign. No, I said. So then she spelled it out to me. Thought I was coming here illegally to try and work. On visa waiver. Whoops.'

'It is a State Department requirement that immigration officers have no sense of humour,' Ron said.

'Why are they throwing you out? Drugs?'

'Do I look like a drug smuggler?'

'What do drug smugglers look like?'

The other occupants of the pound looked discouraged, tired, fed up, bored, nervous and criminal. Ron had read that first-class travellers, middle-aged housewives or accountancy students were the kind that made good smugglers – less likely to get stopped by customs; perfectly ordinary, unnoticeable, like him. This lot looked as though they'd have condoms of cocaine in their stomachs. Hippies, addicts, Mafiosi. Except for the Yorkshireman who was probably smuggling worse than any of them.

Did the Prozac, Immodium, Hedex and Sophia's HRT pills in his case count as drugs?

Ron contemplated the intimate horrors of being body-searched and broke out into a sweat of terror.

'Mr Larking?'

'Lark*in*.'

A Sumo wrestler of a woman appeared in the doorway, as vast and solidly fleshed as the woman on the immigration desk had been birdlike and wiry, dark blue uniform jacket strained across her shoulders. Her hands had delicate pink palms and blood-red nails. Ron, appalled, imagined them feeling for packages in his most tender parts, and shuddered.

'Wake up and come with me.'

Her office was shabby, claustrophobic, the air conditioning turned up to freezing. She planted huge buttocks on a shiny metal chair behind a dark grey steel desk. Ron dabbed at his forehead and neck, sweating despite the cold.

'Mr Ronald Larkin. Have you been to the United States of America before?' Out of the enormous body, the voice was girlish, high-pitched and rather whispery. Marlon Brando. *The Godfather*.

Ron's mind promptly scrambled and went blank. 'No.'

She stared down her flat, wide nose at him, his passport open beneath the computer screen in front of her.

'I mean, yes. I have.'

'When?'

He tried to remember the year.

'A long time ago. If you look in my passport, the date will be on the entry stamp.'

'You ever been to Canada, Mr Larkin?'

'No.'

'You sure about that?'

'I don't think,' he said cautiously, 'that it's the kind of thing you forget.'

'You just forgot you'd been to the United States. Maybe you're just forgetting you've been to Canada.'

Ron rolled his handkerchief into a ball and tried to wipe his hands.

'I don't think so.'

'This your first visit to Miami?'

This was surer ground. 'Definitely. I'm absolutely certain of that.'

'Why have you come here?'

Ron relaxed. 'For a holiday. My son died recently and the doctor thought it would be good—'

'When did you last visit America?'

'It's just gone right out of my mind. If you look in my passport, the stamp will tell you.'

'There is no American immigration stamp in your passport, Mr Larkin.'

He thought irrationally, with a sense of grievance, someone must have moved it. He stared at the little red book lying between her enormous hands. He laughed with relief. 'I renewed it. I had one of the proper passports, the blue ones, which went out of date. The stamp was in the old one.'

'Why can't you tell me when you last came to America?'

'It was way back in the sixties,' he snapped, losing patience. 'I've forgotten the date.'

'There is no Canadian immigration stamp in your passport. When did you last go to Canada?'

'I have *never* been to Canada.'

She went away. Twenty minutes by the clock above her desk.

'What do you do for a living, Mr Larkin?'

He stared, controlled a suicidal urge to get up and run. They'd shoot him. *She'd* shoot him. *Brit gunned down in Miami shootout*.

'Headhunting,' he said tonelessly. 'I find suitable people for executive jobs.'

'Do you drive a truck?'

An eerie disbelief gripped him. Did driving Garcia Goddard's Range Rover, to take a load of PGs to a firework display the previous Fifth of November, count as driving a truck?

'Do you mean,' he asked cautiously, 'have I *ever* driven a truck?'

She sniffed and poked one finger languidly up her nose. 'What I am asking, *Mister* Larkin, is are you a trucker? Do you drive a truck? Period.'

He stood up. 'Look. Don't,' he yelped, 'reach for your gun. I'm not doing a runner. Look at me.'

'I'm lookin'.'

'I am five feet nine inches tall. I am stout and shortsighted and middle-aged. I have very clean hands and nails.' He held them out, implored her to inspect them. 'When did these hands last change a gasket? And you might not realise, being American, but I speak educated, public school English.'

She took her finger out of her nose. 'We're talkin' Canadians. Foreign.'

'Look.' He grabbed his jacket from the back of the chair, found his driving licence in his wallet and threw in front of her. 'My driving licence allows me to drive motor cars and bicycles, not heavy goods vehicles and trucks. Do I *look* and *sound* as though I drive lorries for a living?'

The black eyes stared up at him, then down at the passport on her desk. 'You got here a British passport, name of Ronald Larkin. A Canadian truck driver of that name just stabbed his wife to death. Last seen by his neighbour, drivin' off in his truck with his girlfriend.'

More death.

One flew over the cuckoo's nest. Miami airport. Perhaps this is how people finally go mad.

'I can't have killed my wife if she just went through your immigration control, can I?'

'The lady you are travelling with is not *necessarily* your wife.'

Extradition to Canada for homicide stared him in the face.

'You are not the Ronald Larkin we are looking for. You may go.'

No apology. No 'It's our mistake.' No 'Sorry to have confused you and scared the hell out of you.'

Before the monster behind the desk could change her mind, he grabbed his jacket, took a fix on the yellow line leading back to the immigration hall, and fled.

Chapter Sixteen

The All Seasons Hotel was three-quarters of an hour's drive from the airport, through late-afternoon traffic. The taxi driver's red neck was covered with stubbly grey hair. He drew into a gilded, panoplied, carpeted entrance framed by two vast stone sphinxes. Ron sat looking at the bristly neck, waiting for change from his fare. The driver appeared absorbed in something just beyond his windscreen until it dawned upon Ron what he had to do to get his change.

'Take three dollars.'

Silently, the driver peeled three dollar notes from the bundle in his fist, got out, lifted Ron's luggage out of the trunk and stood between it, its owner and the porter.

'Extortion,' Ron muttered, parting with another two bucks. A dollar a case.

The porter, behind his back, thumbed the palm of his right hand gently, and smiled.

The pyramid, faced with white stone and glass, was surrounded by palms, a glittering marble landslide of sea-facing balconies softened by a profusion of plants. Its gardens ended in a strip of sand laid out neatly with rows and rows of pale blue, cushioned loungers beneath white canvas shades.

The loungers were mostly empty, their sunfried occupants gone to their rooms. Cocktail hour approached, and the hotel guests showered and changed into après-beach. In the bar, overstuffed armchairs and sofas were filling up, a piano played softly, enervating as white noise, glasses chinked and clinked.

Sophia, still in smudged make-up and travelling clothes, was draped over a bar stool, a bottle of Californian Chardonnay, and two attentive fellow guests.

'I have called the airport,' she was saying distractedly as Ron walked in. 'No one would tell me anything.'

Suddenly she shrieked. 'What the *hell's* been going on?'

'I spent a couple of hours in the pound as an undesirable alien wanted for murder and I urgently need a drink.'

'My husband,' Sophia said, in a tone of wonder.

'Benjie and Sandra were saying I should . . . what do you mean, *murder*? You haven't killed someone, Ron?'

Ron caught the barman's eye.

'We were saying . . . what *were* we saying?'

'That if he didn't turn up soon we should try the embassy.'

Ron glared at the speaker and ordered a triple Scotch on ice.

'What were you doing?'

Oh, the bliss of the first gulp. 'It would take too long to tell,' he said, observing that Sophia's friend was a City type. Ron pigeon-holed him at a glance. All the usual signs were there: ruddy complexion that had nothing to do with fresh air, more with a fondness for wine, thinning, carefully cut hair, eyes that calculated life in percentages, pounds and pence. In an open-necked Ralph Lauren polo shirt, beige slacks and handmade shoes, sitting on a bar stool at the far side of Sophia, he was a big man, towered over all of them.

'Benjie McLaren,' said Sophia. 'And Sandra.'

Sandra smelled of Elizabeth Taylor perfume. She had dark, very shiny hair and the unnatural youth of the surgically lifted, gold-rimmed spectacles, gold sandals, gold buttons on a very short, very expensive emerald dress.

Sophia's new friends, Ron realised, ordering another Scotch and feeling better, were serious money. Benjie, when he spoke, had an educated, accentless, pleasant voice.

'We've been looking after your wife. She's been very worried. We were going to give you another half an hour then go to the police.'

'I was with the police,' Ron said dourly. 'Airport SS. To intervene with the authorities would have been about as useful as reasoning with the Gestapo. They are all mad.'

Sandra patted Sophia's arm reassuringly. 'He's here. Now we can all get on with our holiday.'

'I can see he's here,' Sophia said mournfully, looking into the bottom of her glass, finding it empty.

'Thanks,' Ron muttered.

'Benjie's a stockbroker,' Sophia said suddenly.

'I'm in the undertaking and embalming business myself,' Ron answered as the barman slid a third Scotch in front of him and asked him his room number.

Sophia's gave a small, anguished cry.

'Not really. Though the rate at which we've been using their services, I damn well should be.'

Benjie registered something that Ron, in his dementia, failed to notice. Sophia, hugging an empty wine glass to her breast like a shield against the world and about to fall, like a dazed parrot, off her perch, was a complete nervous wreck.

Josephine had a card when they had been away a week: 'We've met nice people – do everything together. Ron apparently dead ringer for a Canadian murderer and nearly got himself deported!!! Without Sandra and Benjie, don't know what I'd have done. Ron didn't take to them at first, now inseparable. Much more cheerful. Weather fabulous. Hotel same. Love, S.'

They played golf together, lay by the pool together, met in the bar each night, had dinner together and stayed up until two in the morning, drinking together.

'There were an awful lot of kids running around kicking up sand today,' Sandra complained at the beginning of their second week.

They agreed they should get away from the hotel, spend the day somewhere else, together.

'For peace and quiet, where's the best beach?'

The amber-skinned, perfectly groomed girl in reception smiled a big, warm, American smile.

'You're full of American families. Got no control over the kids.'

'A lot of Americans come here for their vacations.' She sounded pleased. 'There are no children on your floor, Mr Larkin.'

Sophia arrived and smiled sweetly at the girl. 'He doesn't mean it.'

Ron, aching over Theo, did mean it. Children *hurt*.

Sophia was wearing dark green linen shorts, her hair tucked underneath a wide-brimmed straw hat tied with a Jaeger scarf decorated with green and gold anchors. He could just see her upper lip, raised and pointed like a picture bracket, painted a neat ruby red.

'If you mean you wanna go topless or take all your clothes off,' the girl went on helpfully, 'topless is OK. We're not a naturist beach.'

'I wouldn't mind a naturist beach,' Sophia said boldly.

'You got a hire car?'

Benjie and Sandra had a hire car.

'Then I can tell you somewhere nice to go,' she offered, and bent under the desk to get out a map.

'You won't find me burning my private parts,' Ron growled and threatened to stay behind.

After a lot of buffooning and eyeing each other with covert interest, they agreed to give it a try. Just for the hell of it.

'*Oh*,' Sophia gasped as she peered over the cliff edge at the oyster-coloured sand and turquoise sea below. Immediately beneath her, sunbathers, some naked, lay in scattered groups. A two-minute walk to either side of where the path went down, the long sweep of the beach was empty. Recoiling, she went to lean on a tree beside their parked car, pale in the shade underneath her sunburned, reddened cheeks.

'Something wrong?' asked Benjie.

The others carried towels and a picnic basket prepared by the hotel down a sandy track through palm trees to the beach. He picked up an insulated wine box, put it down again.

'Sophia, you're literally shaking.'

Dim little Theo, born with a screw loose, fell to his death because no one was looking out for him.

'I'm fine. Just not very keen on heights.' She moved out of the shade of the tree into the harsh light.

'It's the business of the little boy, isn't it?'

Her eyes filled with tears and she didn't pull away when he drew her close. After a while, hand in hand, they walked together down the track, beneath palms and pines, the sand carpeted with miniature pine cones and dry needles.

'Better?'

'Yes.'

At the bottom, seeing Ron and Sandra five hundred yards away, laying out towels, planting big umbrellas in the sand, they parted.

They swam, sunbathed, read paperback novels, drank white wine and mineral water spritzers from the coolbox, swam some more, lay spreadeagled beneath the cliffs, red and slippery with oil, in the shade underneath the umbrellas.

Sandra had full, melon-like breasts. The triangle of pubic hair was the same glossy colour as her hair.

'Dyed,' Ron whispered in Sophia's ear, refusing to take his own shorts off.

Benjie had a long, heavy penis that flopped around, quite unlike Ron's. Sophia glanced, looked away, embarrassed. Not by his penis but by the fact that, on a naturist beach, it was almost impossible not to stare. She looked at them all, lying in a row, reading, three white bottoms and one pair of worn swimming shorts, and giggled. The sight was so silly, it cheered her up. They drank more wine, swam, the seawater a clear, delicate aquamarine, voluptuous against their overheated skin. A waterfall cascaded down the cliff as one of two large white houses visible from where they lay emptied some water storage tanks on to the sands below. Sophia rubbed half a tube of suntan cream into her body and gazed at the white mansion, all its windows shuttered. The small figure of a man came and went at the edge of the cliff, supervising the waterfall.

'I bet that's someone's country cottage,' Benjie said, smearing suntan oil on his own shoulders. 'Would be nice to be able to afford one of them, wouldn't it?'

Sophia got up and wandered down to the water's edge, scuffing her feet in the hot sand, looked back.

Ron lay on his back snoring quietly, his paperback open face down, plastered by suntan oil to his chest. Sandra lay on her side, facing away from the sea, sleepily absorbed in Danielle Steele. She turned a page. Benjie got to his feet lazily.

Naked, they waded side by side into the sea, swam out beyond the glassy shallows towards deeper water, glittering and darting with tiny, jewel-like fish, floated on their backs, eyes closed against the glare of the sun.

'Fuck,' Benjie said softly, opening his eyes and squinting at the sea around him. 'Look at that.'

Transparent, hardly bigger than guppies, glittering like spray drifting over the water's surface, fish leaped and turned, one gigantic shoal. They leapt and turned and weaved, a million swimming as one.

'You're crying.'

'Salt in my eyes.' Blinded by beauty and the glare of sun on sea, Sophia clutched at him, pushed against him by the gentle swell. The rest seemed as natural as breathing.

'Wanted to do this all week. I won't let you drown. No one can see. Come.'

As fish darted, leaped and played all around them, that was exactly what they did.

He pushed her away afterwards, to float on her back. She imagined, against the glare of her eyelids, the viscous little cloud of semen dribbling out of her. Millions of little Benjies, many millions more than the great cloud of fish. The thought was awesome.

Ron, superheated, woke, picked the paperback off his chest, stumbled to his feet and headed towards them.

Sophia turned to swim. As Ron plunged into the water, Benjie kissed her gently and swam away.

Chapter Seventeen

'It's for you,' Josephine said early in the morning, handing Garcia the telephone in the kitchen.

It was the young Japanese trainee with the smooth, flat face who had been writing faxes while Tom Morrissey sat, several months earlier, planning a whole new financial future for himself. He had come into the office very early to catch Tokyo on the telephone.

Garcia's face froze as he listened. 'I'll call you back,' he said abruptly and went into his study. 'We've had a fire.'

Millie, in a tracksuit, her hair tied back, was talking on his business line.

'*Millie.*'

She held up her hand.

'We've had a fire in the office,' Garcia shouted. 'We're lucky the whole building didn't burn down. A cleaner saw smoke coming from under Tom Morrissey's door and by the time they'd dialled nine nine nine and the firemen had broken the door down to get in, it was full of smoke and half his files were on fire.'

Tight-voiced, Millie told whoever she was talking to that she'd call back, and put the receiver down.

'When?'

'Last night.'

'How?'

'The firemen say a cigarette. In Tom's wastepaper basket.'

'Tom doesn't smoke.'

'Andy does.'

Millie rubbed her brow and tried to think whether Tom Morrissey's number two, a young accountant, was stupid enough to leave a burning cigarette in a bin behind locked doors. GGIL was a no-smoking office. No one smoked inside it. Ever. It was part of their insurance.

'Could it have been a cleaner?'

'The door was locked,' Garcia reminded her. 'Whoever it was must have left it smouldering in there when they went home.'

'How much damage?'

'A lot of his files are burned or partly burned. The accounts department computers are smoke-damaged beyond repair.'

That meant that their accounts records, all downloaded into the system at the end of each working day, were gone beyond recall.

'OK. We have back-up disks off site.'

He hesitated.

'We *have* got back-up disks off site?'

'Disappeared.' Garcia seemed to have difficulty speaking.

Millie froze. '*How*, disappeared?'

'I don't know. I only thought to check the other day. It's the first thing I should have checked when we realised things were wrong. I asked Tom Morrissey and he didn't know where they'd gone. He said he'd replace them.'

Her voice was flat. 'You mean we have no records?'

'No.'

'We should call the police.'

'The police came with the fire officers and didn't find anything particularly suspicious.' In a sense, who had damaged and stolen their computer records was immaterial. The storage space off site, where back-up disks should be, was empty, their records gone. Without records, they could never trace the causes of the chaos. They would be for ever left with nothing but suspicion.

'It has to be deliberate. We've been deliberately swindled.'

'Well, now, aren't you smart, figuring that out all by yourself?'

'I—'

'It's *you*. *I'm* over there, and *you're* over here,' Millie spat. '*You're* supposed to be running our head office. If you're dumb enough to give other people your money to look after and *invite* them to swindle you, if you're too dumb to be even averagely and normally suspicious, and too damn dumb to run an office, why should I pay?' Her voice rose. 'We've put a million of our own money into the company in the last three weeks, and it still isn't enough.'

Aghast, he watched deep rage, deep despair, running across her face.

'Asshole,' she added miserably.

She was starting to blame him. For the first time since they had found the black hole in their accounts, he realised the depth of fear and mutual acrimony that inevitably lay ahead. The greatest damage might not be to their bank accounts. As partners, they could be breaking up.

In the former convent garden below the Morrisseys' flat, the trees sang with birds in joyous early morning chorus, then for several moments they lost the battle with the noise from the engines of a 747 descending towards Heathrow, the morning sun catching the red and grey British Airways tail.

Janey Morrissey lay on her back in bed holding a watch in front of her face in the curtained gloom. She held her breath, let it out slowly and decided her contractions were coming roughly every fifteen to twenty minutes. She put the watch down as the next jumbo roared over.

She supposed she should do something, get up, wake Tom, pack her case, call the hospital. Instead, she watched the day brighten and waited for the next pain, curiously detached, passively winding and unwinding the watchstrap loosely in her fingers.

Directly above, tired passengers looking out of their windows for their first views of London could see matchbox streets crawling with the start of rush-hour traffic, windows and mirrors winking in the sun. As the seatbelt sign flashed on for landing, a fat blackbird sitting on the 'For Sale' board outside the house opened its beak and burst into hoarse and raucous song. 'Sold' in large red letters, 'Subject to contract' in very small black letters, had been nailed across it the previous day.

Tom was still fast asleep. Janey nudged him until he groaned.

'Still drunk? And I'm in labour. Brilliant.'

He still didn't stir.

A dog-eared manila folder lay on the table in their attic living room, a reminder of the previous evening's discussion. Stained with red wine, the table was strewn with pages of A4 covered in estate agents details.

'Got to have a Plan B,' Tom had explained, sorting busily through them the previous evening. He sounded brisk and organised, pleased with himself. 'Now we've sold this place, we are *buyers*.'

He looked intently into her face. 'Buyers are gold dust in today's housing market, Janey.' He pushed some of the sheets towards her. 'What do you think?'

They were small, two and three-bedroom houses, but in an expensive, bijou area not very far from where the Goddards lived.

'I think that now we've made an offer for that hovel in Chiswick and had it accepted, we shouldn't chop and change. Anyhow, we can't afford to live in Hammersmith or Barnes. What's the matter with you?' she asked irritably, rubbing her enormous belly. 'You're the one who is supposed to be so clever about money. Why don't you stop dreaming and throw that lot away?'

Because we have more money than you know, and I don't want to live in a hovel in Chiswick when I could live somewhere decent. With ghastly clarity, Tom had begun to understand how bank robbers must feel, all that money stashed away and no chance to spend it, living in fear of the raised eyebrow, the puzzled look. The question that must be avoided at all costs: how can Morrissey afford that?

He kept looking ahead, seeing a cul-de-sac he hadn't, in his desperation and relief when Garcia Goddard had given him his cheque book, been able to foretell. The end of the cul-de-sac was shrouded in darkness, impenetrable. In his dreams he faced it, heart pounding, terrified of his own guilt.

Recently, he could only get to sleep after several glasses of wine. He went on stubbornly sorting and resorting, doing arithmetic about fixed rate mortgages on the back of the folder and drinking wine. Long after she was asleep he had come to bed quite, quite drunk.

She put the wine glasses in the sink, filled the kettle, opened the blinds and pulled out the photograph of the two and a half bedroomed red brick Edwardian cottage they were buying. It stood at the end of a row of what had once been artisans' cottages, two storeys and a coal cellar, in the maze of streets off the Gunnersbury end of Chiswick High Road. The photograph had been carefully taken from the side of the house, masking its rundown condition. Repossessed by the bank who had lent the previous owners their mortgage, it had stood empty for over two years, its windows boarded against vandals, its long, narrow garden a neglected patch of grass, overgrown and full of weeds.

'It's a mess,' Janey had said when they first saw it. 'It's awful and I'm not interested and I'm not going in.'

'But we can afford it, with enough left over to do it up.' Tom put the key in the door. 'It could be very pretty.'

'Forget it,' she insisted, pulling Francesca away.

The downstairs, its windows letting in no light, was dark, smelled of vermin and damp.

'I'm depressed,' Janey said. 'I want Francesca out of here.'

'The bank know this house is depressing,' said Tom, determindly looking into each of the rooms. 'That's why they will sell it cheap. Doesn't matter so long as it's got potential.'

Upstairs, one bedroom was strewn with rubbish.

'A tramp's got in.' Tom kicked the newspaper and cider cans to one side, poked walls and window frames, opened cupboards littered with mouse droppings. He said, seeing her glum expression 'Use your imagination.'

'I am,' Janey snapped. 'I am imagining some filthy old man using the floor as a lavatory and what the vermin will sound like scrabbling under the floorboards.'

He stormed into the next room, kicked a dent in the damp plaster, swore and stormed back again.

'Sorry,' she said, keeping Francesca away from the mess.

'A bedroom each for the kids. A garden. Quiet road with only residents' traffic. No voodoo, no neighbours glaring at you every time you poke your nose outside the door.' He became plaintive. 'I've given up everything to get you what you said you wanted.'

She looked at him, puzzled. 'What have you given up?'

'We'll get a survey,' Tom said loudly, suddenly forceful. 'It's blighted, but only by recession. We'll make it very nice.'

'What with, Tom? We're already borrowing from Daddy. And what do you mean, you've given up everything to get me what I want? This isn't what I want.'

He had turned on her with such desperation, she hadn't said another word.

She tried now to visualise the look that had crossed his face as she stood waiting for the kettle to boil. Cold, bleak anger behind his hornrimmed glasses. Worse. Despair, a person she didn't know.

The estate agent's photograph crumpled in her fist as she leaned on the table, abruptly convulsed with another pain.

It's not going to be our house-buying chain that breaks, it's going to be my waters, she thought as the contraction passed and she heard Francesca wake, start talking and burbling to herself in her cot.

She dumped Francesca on their bed.

'You have to stay home and look after your daughter.'

The bright morning sun stabbed his eyes as he woke with a blinding headache. He slid straight back underneath the pillow.

'Go 'way. Hangover.'

'You can't have a hangover. I think I'm in labour. I have to go into the hospital.'

Tom went motionless under his pillow. 'You're a month early.'

Francesca climbed on top of him and began to ride piggyback, bouncing up and down.

'Dadeeee . . .'

'*Don't*,' he howled.

'Get *up*,' Janey hissed.

'Get *off*. I'm a broken reed,' he yelped, emerging from the pillow to drag Francesca off. 'I feel like death. Why are you a month early? Your mother was coming to look after Francesca.'

'I haven't done it deliberately. How,' she said patiently, 'would I know why this baby is coming early?'

'Don't try and lean on this reed until you've taken her away,' he said, pushing at Francesca. 'If you'd give me coffee and aspirin while I get dressed, I'll drive you.'

She got out of the car at the entrance to Queen Charlotte's Hospital.

'I'll go and park round the back,' Tom said. 'Will you be all right for a moment?'

'Go home. Give Francesca breakfast. I'll call you when I know what's happening.'

They argued briefly. Tom pulled away into Goldhawk Road as she turned into the empty outpatients department and went looking for a nurse. A cleaner was putting coins into the coffee machine in the corridor where she waited for her antenatal appointments, an electric floor polisher abandoned among stacks of plastic chairs.

Janey came up behind her and put her hand over the coin slot.

'Before you do that, would you please go and get someone quickly, before I have my baby all over your nice clean floor?'

A small, skinny black midwife in a blue dress and white polythene bib helped her undress and climb on to the couch where she examined her with thin, hard, pink-palmed hands.

'How many weeks?'

'Eight months.'

'Good,' beamed the midwife as if she had just won a prize.

A clock tick tock, tick tocked over the door.

'The doctor is coming,' the midwife said, patting her hand.

The pains came thick and fast.

Tick tock, tick tock. It seemed an age.

'How long do they think you'll be in here?' Tom asked a couple of hours later. 'Sit *still*, Francesca.'

Bored, Francesca clutched her mother's hospital counterpane and abseiled off her bed.

'I don't know. This is supposed to stop the contractions.'

They had put a drip in her hand and the rest of her in a white paper nightgown printed with pink daisies, open down the back and tied with tapes, like an undertaker's shroud. Her long dark hair was tied back with a piece of bandage.

'I look just about ready for embalming, don't I?'

'Hello,' exclaimed the occupant of the next bed, her curtains drawn, enthroned on a bedpan. 'Where did you come from?'

Francesca pointed obligingly.

'*Come out of there,*' Tom hissed from the other side of the pink curtain.

The very pregnant woman balanced herself on the bedpan, pulled up her sheet and looked anxious.

'Go and find your mummy,' she ordered.

'I can't stay home all day,' Tom said. 'Your mother is coming over at lunchtime.'

'Can't you take even one day off,' she said, 'to look after your child in an emergency?'

He reached out an arm round the edge of the curtain and yanked Francesca out.

'Lousy timing. This was not the moment for me to have a head like a piledriver and for you to start have contractions.'

Francesca ambled off to collect sweets from bored women sitting in other beds, came back with bulging cheeks.

'I *would* look after her,' he defended himself. 'Only, this afternoon I've got a second interview with another company and they seem very keen.'

She stared.

'I wasn't going to say anything until it was definite but I have to go for this interview because it's my best chance so far.'

'What are you talking about? What about GGIL?'

He studied the floor.

'For the past five months, I've been looking for another job.'

As Tom sat in Queen Charlotte's at half past nine in the morning and explained to his wife that, if he got it, his new job would bring a better salary that would go some way to affording renovations on the cottage, Garcia was opening his private mail: 'I'm sorry to have to notify you that two cheques, payable to your builders, have been returned. They have asked me to clarify the situation with you.'

Garcia called Richard Adams. 'What do they mean, *bounced*?' he demanded, incredulous. 'I never had a cheque bounce in my life.'

Richard spoke briefly, embarrassed.

'Have you asked Tom Morrissey?' Garcia snapped. 'He signs the cheques.'

'I don't think chasing your financial director is for me to do. But someone better had. I just explained to you, the builders appear to have been paid up to early last month, then everything seems to have stopped. And that last cheque bounced. By the time they catch up with their paperwork, I'm worried you could be seriously in arrears.'

'Have you talked to my wife about this?' Garcia asked abruptly.

'No.' Richard sounded surprised.

Garcia seemed to pull himself together. 'I'll look into it.'

'Tom isn't in today,' Emily told him when he summoned Tom Morrissey. 'He called in early to say he might be out of the office for a few days. His wife's gone into labour and they're in the hospital. Shall I tell him you'll call him at home this evening?'

Perhaps Janey's troublesome pregnancy was behind Tom's apparent failure to stay on top of his job, his negligence and his unprofessional behaviour. Garcia knew they would probably never get the truth, never pin the fire, the theft, their catastrophic losses on anyone, although it was certainly Morrissey. They would never have the money to pursue him in court. Garcia hated him with alarming intensity, would make him work out his notice to the last second, rub his nose in his mess like a dog.

'No. Have the florist send some flowers.'

He reached for the telephone to call Vivian. On Monday, unless a miracle happened, Vivian would stop being their financial adviser and become their receiver.

Very last thing, before he went home at ten o'clock that night, he called Emmanuel, his oldest friend and legal adviser.

'We are about to become insolvent.' Garcia's voice was dry. 'Vivian advises that we are unlikely to be able legally to continue trading beyond Monday. Millie has been screaming Chapter Eleven all day, and if we were an American company this couldn't happen. I have had to tell her over and over, we are solvent or bankrupt in Britian, and nothing in between. I don't know whether she actually hears me at the moment.' Vaguely, over his own, Garcia heard Samantha's voice.

'Samantha sends love,' Emmanuel said briefly, and waited.

'Vivian is ready. We need to meet with you.'

'Tomorrow is OK.' Emmanuel, thinking fast, scribbled notes on the pad Samantha kept by the phone. 'Fun birthday present for Jo.'

'*Shit*,' Garcia squawked.

'You'll have to tell her now,' Emmanuel said neutrally.

'This week, I have personally lost, er, let's see . . . about one point nine million. One point nine million. Happy fortieth, darling. We're paupers.'

'You are *not* paupers,' Emmanuel said sharply. 'Winding up your main company isn't pleasant, but you can't put it to Josephine like that.' Garcia *would* exaggerate. 'Look at it as cutting an albatross from your neck,' Emmanuel went on with deliberate cheerfulness. 'Without GGIL you're free to concentrate on doing what you've been saying you want to do, moving into consultancy, without that incubus in Islington devouring the profits the consultancy makes. This is what you could have done in a controlled way yourself if you could have brought yourself to let your baby go. When you're through with all this, you may decide Tom Morrissey has done you a favour, knocking it on the head.'

'It bears my name,' Garcia muttered. 'Has done for twenty-seven years. I'm ruined.'

'As your legal adviser, I tell you I do not agree.'

'The Japanese won't deal with a bankrupt.'

Emmanuel laughed aloud.

'The Japanese are so devious themselves they understand deviousness better than most. You'll have to play the game, go and explain you had a financial director who rotted the company from inside. They've had their own scandals recently, along those lines. They're aware these things happen.'

'A sorry tour, while they all sneer and enjoy my loss of face. Thanks. My secretary will call yours tomorrow.'

Emmanuel was about to snap back, jolt him out of self-pity, when he heard the telephone gently put down.

Chapter Eighteen

'Bastard.' The telephone in Andrew Quinlan's flat rang and rang. 'I *know* he's there. Casablanca, my eye.'

Caroline Quinlan left the door of the telephone box on the other side of the common to slam shut behind her when he didn't answer. Fired with all the determination of a woman who has not slept well for weeks for thinking about a hand-to-mouth future and resolved to get a lump payment in alimony as security against an absconding husband, she came storming into the courtyard through the wrought-iron gates just as one of Gordon's pupils, a pile of music tucked under his arm, was coming out.

'Seen that rat?' she demanded, waving a fist at the closed curtains of his flat.

Startled, he ducked to undo his bicycle from the railings, nervously dropped his music. The weird woman, in very posh trousers and a clingy top in bright orange, stood over him, looking so angry, her eyes sparked in a face nearly as brilliantly coloured as her blouse.

'I just had my piano lesson,' he stammered.

'No. You wouldn't. More nocturnal, rats. Sorry. Didn't mean to make you drop your stuff.' She backed away, flew up the steps and jabbed the intercom. No answer. 'Hey.'

His bike halfway through the gate, he froze.

'Which is your music teacher?'

'Mr Hassall-Hammond.'

She pushed a button.

'Yes?' came Gordon's voice.

'Hello, Mr Hassall-Hammond. I've come to inquire about music lessons for my son,' she said breathlessly.

The buzzer buzzed. She pushed the door and disappeared inside.

* * *

'Oh, *fuck*.'

Kneeling at the letterbox she could see straight down the small lobby, through the wide open door into his fusty, sparsely furnished sitting room, dim with the curtains closed. He lay on the floor, his feet out of sight, arms thrown to each side as if he had suffered some horizontal crucifixion.

'*Andrew*.'

She fumbled in her bag, dropped it in her panic, sorted a key from a purse, was shaking so much she could scarcely get it into the lock.

As she jerked the large plastic bag from his head, Andrew gulped, groaned, twitched, his eyes fluttering deep in their sockets.

'Don't you *dare* suffocate yourself, you stupid, copycatting bastard,' she yelled, heaving him over on his side and delivering a great thump to the side of his head. 'Wake *up*, damn you.'

He opened one eye a fraction, found shag pile carpet up his nostrils, his lacy bra ruined, twisted and torn under his armpit, the broken capsule of amyl nitrate grazing sharply into his cheek. His favourite scarlet suspenders had tangled when she rolled him over, were pinching painfully into his arse. Fuddled, drained by the satisfying violence of his climax and lack of oxygen, he lay naked and doggo and tried to roll with the blows as his ex-wife pounded and yelled abuse.

Above, in the top-floor flat, in a lull in the Hoovering, Melissa cocked one ear, looked puzzled.

'Can you hear anything odd?'

The cleaner, one of Mrs Bee's new recruits, ignored her.

'I said, CAN YOU HEAR ANYTHING? Are you deaf?' Melissa demanded, mouthing the words and miming elaborately, pointing to her ears and shaking her head.

'You don't have to take the mickey,' the cleaner whined reproachfully. 'They said they can't do nothing for me. I'm hard of hearing. Bells in the ears. It's tinnitus and they can't do nothing for it.' She sprayed Mr Sheen around Melissa's flounced and ribboned bedroom.

'You do that like Saddam Hussein conducting biological warfare,' Melissa remarked, dodging and coughing. 'Quick burst of anthrax, two of botulinus, let it mingle, and we're away.'

The cleaner, oblivious, began polishing the front of the fitted wardrobes with a pair of Luvvie's worn-out pants. They were bright red, Christmas trees and holly all over them, a stocking present from a couple of years ago, worn threadbare.

They had given each other silly presents in those days, had eaten themselves into a torpor, watched the Queen's Speech, finished half a bottle of port and spent the rest of Christmas Day monkeying around in bed. Melissa frowned, distracted from the disturbing sounds she had caught from downstairs; the sight of the pants was painful.

'You know, I miss Luvvie,' she said crossly, coughing with smoker's bronchitis and a second liberal lungful of Mr Sheen. 'Why did the silly fart have to take it all so seriously?'

'I did not,' said the cleaner indignantly.

'I said, I MISS LUVVIE AND WHY DID THE OLD FART HAVE TO TAKE THINGS SO SERIOUSLY?'

Her own bawled words brought blood to her cheeks and in her dressing-table mirror she saw her face redden with distress. It reflected, without make-up or clever lighting, an ageing character actress who, like the common barmaid she played, was dangerously close to becoming raddled, lonely and tired, and was losing a dignified fight to hang on to the very last of what had never been glamorous looks. Striking, yes. Good for the camera, photogenic, yes. But no oil painting.

Despite vanity and too many other faults to mention, including being absolutely impossible, she missed Luvvie. Without him, she had nothing more immediate to look forward to than Josephine's birthday barbecue on Saturday and learning a heap of repetitive lines spoken by a blowsy middle-aged tart.

The cleaner had downed tools and was taking off her rubber gloves, on the verge of a walk-out.

'I DIDN'T SAY YOU FARTED,' Melissa yelled in her biggest stage voice.

Two floors below, through his open window, her voice overrode a Bach étude and Gordon looked up, startled.

'Oh, didn't you, then?' the woman said, mollified. 'No need to shout.'

Melissa, dodging the aerosol aimed in her direction, fled to the kitchen, snatched a bottle of vermouth from the drinks cupboard and took the glass to the window. There she studied Sophia, mysteriously examining her front door closely with a hammer in her hand.

Luvvie would be sitting on a hard chair in a circle of hard chairs in that dreary warehouse behind the town hall in Hackney, doing a read-through. If she called, he'd make a big fuss about being interrupted, would secretly be glad of the break.

Depressed, she refilled her glass and reflected that her own week's break was almost over, she'd done nothing with it except have a row with Luvvie. She had to go back to rehearsals herself in two days' time.

'Now,' she admitted to a wasp that flew in and circled the neck of the vermouth bottle, 'is the time to kiss and make up. If only I weren't so bloody proud.'

The wasp crawled inside the neck, fell into the vermouth and thrashed violently around.

The cleaner planted Mr Sheen on the draining board. 'See you Wednesday.'

Melissa nodded, watching the wasp drown. I can drown myself in vermouth, like you, or swallow my pride and be the first to ring . . .

'Am I cooked?' Babe demanded, thrusting his head down. Barry, in old corduroys and a Marks and Spencer sport shirt, looked up from his drawing board, his back to the light streaming in through big French windows. At thirty-five he was already balding and had two deep frown lines above a long, splayed nose. He put down his pencil and contemplated the fairy dancing about their big basement living area, silvered head floating and glinting, tattoos writhing on a narrow, muscular back, tight buttocks convulsing in Calvin Klein snow-white knitted pants. His heart squeezed, moved by such beauty.

He merely said, 'It'll probably all fall out.'

Babe pouted a full, narrow mouth and wiggled his hips suggestively.

'Not now. Not with your head in Bacofoil and stinking of chemicals. Why don't you go and ask Sophia for an expert opinion?' Barry said patiently, picking up his pencil and getting back to work. 'And before you go, put some trousers on.'

* * *

Down in the courtyard, something glittery moved and caught Melissa's eye. She watched as Babe, dressed in jeans and what looked like several boxes of silver foil, emerged from his basement and spoke to Sophia who was preoccupied with measuring her front door.

'D'you want me to have a look?' Melissa called down as Sophia batted him away like a fly.

Babe craned his head back and squinted.

Melissa foresaw company, a good gossip and a sympathetic audience about what to do with Luvvie. Babe was a social worker, but she didn't hold it against him. He might even be useful. There was another bottle of vermouth in the cupboard, plenty of ice and some of Luvvie's beer still in the fridge.

'Come up here. Bring your shampoo and tongs and whatever and I'll do it for you. I'll let you in.'

The buzzer went. Babe darted into the basement, re-emerged, pranced up the steps with his arms full of cosmetics, beaming.

In the just-habitable annexe, Rambo and Barney Darling prowled restlessly, uneasy in new surroundings, inclined to escape, race round the corner and get under Hosannah's feet in familiar territory in front of the Aga.

'*Sit,*' Emilia told them sharply.

She sat herself in her upright chair by the freshly painted window, listening to traffic with a sense of grievance. Her old rooms had been at the back of the house, away from the noise. Until the dogs disturbed her, she had been absorbed in a letter, penned in a very un-English hand.

She read it, folded it, unfolded it, and read it again.

She said testily to the dogs, 'I don't know . . .'

In the fridge one of the bottles she helped herself to regularly, out of Josephine's fridge, was still half full. She filled a glass and went back to her seat.

'A widower. Like me. What do you think he wants?'

Barney Darling yapped hopefully and flopped, disappointed, his nose on his paws.

'What would you know about it?' she said, nostalgically speaking her mother tongue, the educated Spanish of the letter. 'We were *very* good friends.'

They had been friends as children, sweethearts as teenagers, briefly lovers as adults, then life took them in other directions and they both became other people's spouses. They stayed, through Christmas cards, birth announcments, now all too often deaths, in touch.

Now, he wrote, he was all alone in the shady, shuttered house on its hillside, overlooking Seville. Cancer, he wrote. She is dead one year now, and I write, at last, to tell you. It is lonely at our age, is it not, my beloved old friend?

Beloved.

Transfixed, trying to guess at the word's intent, Emilia unconsciously sat up straighter, patted her smooth white hair into place, took a mouthful of her favourite ice-cold Australian wine and silently toasted her dogs.

Babe inspected himself in Melissa's bathroom mirror and looked gratified.

'This'll make him sorry he turned me down,' he said, preening this way and that, viewing himself from all angles with a hand mirror.

'Who turned you down?'

'Barry.'

'What for?'

Babe looked cold and mean and ran his hand down the zip of his jeans.

Melissa chuckled. 'You are *such* a slag, darling. One day you'll try that nice man's patience one time too many and get yourself thrown out.'

Takes one to know one, Babe retorted silently.

They went back into the kitchen and Melissa picked up her hairbrush. 'White with a hint of yellow in daylight. Fashionable on people's walls a few years back and looks quite good on you,' she said, examining a strand of his hair. She sculpted the bleached mane into place with wet-look gel, stood back and admired her work. 'The gel darkens it just that little bit, darling. Wicked. Makes you look brooding. Scott Fitzgeraldish.'

Pleased, he kissed her, his mouth hard and ungiving on her cheek.

'Here, you come back here and lend a hand with clearing up

your mess,' she shouted as he blew another kiss and shimmied out of her flat.

He had cheered her up, was even vainer than Luvvie. With that, Melissa made up her mind and turned to the telephone on her wall.

'Hang on,' said a harassed voice. 'I'll go and see if he can take a call.'

As she hung on while the girl went to fetch Luvvie to the telephone, she could hear a piano playing in the distance and the sound of voices off, somewhere that echoed slightly, in heated argument. She seemed to wait for ages, heard Luvvie's footsteps coming rapidly across uncarpeted, hollow sounding wooden boards. They held rehearsals in the most godforsaken places.

'Melissa? You know I dislike being interrupted,' he said irritably. 'What do you want?'

'To extend an invitation.'

'Extend it quickly, then.'

She ignored his tone. 'They're having a barbecue next door but one, on Saturday. Josephine's invited us to help her mourn her fortieth. I thought I'd give you a quick call and let you know, because I just wondered,' she said, trying to sound casual to the point of near indifference, 'if you'd like to come. It's the neighbours, and you are, as it were, one of us. Eight o'clock onwards, completely casual. Something to fall in the pool in. I know she'd love to see you,' she finished anxiously, spoiling the effect.

'The point,' answered Luvvie, undeceived by all the blather, 'is whether *you* would love to see me.'

'Why am I calling you?'

'Exactly what I'm asking.'

'Depends, doesn't it?' Melissa said airily.

'On what does it depend, precisely?' he inquired in his best, heavy, John-Gielgud-like Shakespearian enunciation.

She eyed the litter left by Babe, a sinkful of crumpled silver foil, scissors, plastic bottles of shampoo and conditioner, two glasses on the draining board, coated with a film of bleached hair clippings, her own hairdryer, tongs, gel, spray and a machine load of used towels, draped all over the kitchen. The narcissistic little monster should have been an actor.

'On whether *you* would love to see *me*,' she answered finally.

'How astonishing you should ask. As I watched my underwear disappearing out of your window, and the amused expressions of the people on the top of the bus going by at the time, and Hosannah gawping with that great mouth down in the courtyard, so it would be all round the whole of Barnes in a flash that we had had a row, I was conscious of never wishing to set eyes on you again.'

'And?' she said after a pause that dragged on too long. She heard more anxiety creep into her voice and overcompensated by snapping, 'Don't go all pompous on me, Luvvie. Don't do a Larry Olivier about it. Just give me a yes or a no.'

'No.'

'No?'

'No.'

'Oh. Well, that's that then.'

'Give Josephine my best wishes for her birthday.'

'Fuck *you*,' she answered, coughing to cover the dismay in her words.

'Indeed,' Luvvie said gravely, and put down the receiver.

'Just goes to show I was *right* to throw all your friggin' underwear out. I wish it was you that went under the bus.'

She fished out one of the glasses, rinsed off the hairs and poured herself what was left of the vermouth, to dull a bad suspicion that maybe she'd asked for it, hadn't handled him too well, and to ease a niggling, miserable little ache that wouldn't go away.

Josephine's kitchen was piled high with food.

'I didn't *want* caterers,' she snapped as Emma sloped in with her head in a towel, a skimpy towel round the rest of her, looking for something to eat. 'Why does everyone think it's odd to want a simple barbecue? Go and put some clothes on.'

'I haven't got any.'

Josephine's mouth fell open.

'*Please*, Mother, don't start.'

Josie slapped packets of steak one on top of another into a leaning tower of Pisa of prime Scottish sirloin.

'There's an awful lot of food,' Emma remarked helpfully, going through a fridge in search of cheese.

'Your father gave an order to Marks and Sparks last week and told them to deliver it. He was trying to be helpful. Hosannah was supposed to put all this away in the fridges, and I was looking forward to a shower and a glass of wine. *Why* can't that woman do the job she's paid for?' A headache lurked in the back of her skull, waiting, a dull, fretful pounding.

'Hosannah's in a state,' Emma said darkly, munching a torn chunk of Camembert and picking bits out of a split bag of St Michael Italian mixed salad.

'When isn't Hosannah in a state? And when,' Josephine's voice rose ominously, 'isn't she bunking off smoking when I need her?' She went to the back door and sniffed, yelled, 'Hosannah, come on out, I can smell the fags!'

'She watched the news,' Emma said casually. 'Which was bad. Then at lunchtime Irma rang up and told Hosannah to call her back reverse charge, and spent about three hours on our phone telling Hosannah she's got engaged to a social worker. She's hiding round the back of the garage, crying and smoking herself to death.'

'Well, that solves Irma's immigration problem. Why's she crying?'

'She's crying happy Irma's getting married and crying furious because he's a social worker, and crying scared because the Home Office will send her home and someone will shoot her and she'll never see her grandchildren because they'll be born in England.'

'What's she got against social workers?'

'They're bare-assed. She says in Croatia Irma would marry a bit more machismo. I think she means Irma's boyfriend is skint and weedy.'

'Reverse charge calls for three hours at peak rates to Manchester. Are there any more of Hosannah's troubles I should know about while I do this without any *help*?' Josephine shouted, hurling tomatoes into a colander, suddenly losing her temper.

'Can I do that for you, Mrs Goddard?' John Denver Jr stood in the lobby.

'Go and get *dressed*,' Josephine hissed.

Emma tightened her towel.

Anything to get in here, and in my daughter, Josephine thought hysterically.

Emma vanished. Josephine fished a packet of paracetamol out of a drawer at the side of the Aga and gestured at the chaos. 'Over to you, Junior. Any problems knowing where things go, follow the smoke signals and you'll find Hosannah who is supposed to be in charge but is blubbering behind the garage.'

Even Garcia's steak mountain looked manageable in his big, steak-fed American hands. Male hands with short clean nails, fine bronze hairs all over their backs.

Josephine grabbed a bottle of wine from her overfilled fridge.

Melissa was throwing boxer shorts, Irma was marrying a wimp, Hosannah was a basket case, Emmanuel was her dearest friend and her husband and Millie were in his house, plotting against her, and recently there had been a lot of peculiar, secretive telephone calls for Garcia from someone called Vivian. Emilia was sulking, banished to her annexe, threatening to go back to Spain. Emma was no longer a child, bursting with sex appeal and getting out of hand. No one, only days from being *forty*, was taking the least bit of notice of *her*.

'Mid-life crisis,' she said. 'Don't you think? After all, I'm hitting forty.'

She watched him weigh her up with his eyes, saw him see a middle-aged woman, mother to her daughter.

'Ron said when he—'

'*No*. On second thoughts, I don't want to know. Junior, thanks for helping.'

She picked up the bottle, found a corkscrew in a drawer and fled.

Chapter Nineteen

Hospital management had tried to make the delivery suites homely and customer friendly by hanging Laura Ashley striped fabric at the windows, painting the walls pastel pink and putting an easy chair by the bed for fathers to sit in. Tom sat on one of its arms, watching the backs of two women doctors at the far side of the room, bent over his three-week premature baby, half an hour old. The doctors were murmuring to each other.

'Isobel,' he said with satisfaction, as though he had given birth to her himself. 'Isobel Morrissey. Very pretty.' He sounded pleased and happy.

Janey turned on her side, stitched up and exhausted. 'Are you sure you didn't want a boy? I hope so, because I don't want to go through this ever again.'

'No. So long as she's got all her fingers and toes.'

Janey lay back again. 'Fancy thinking you can make women pretend they've had a home delivery just by putting little homespun touches on a place as institutional as this. At home, you'd have the baby in bed with you.'

Changed into a nightdress, long hair combed and tied back, she felt packaged like a parcel ready for delivery to the post-natal ward, then home in a couple of hours. Where *was* home? A building site, once they moved and the renovating began. It had taken ages to sell the flat. To time a move with a new baby was grim.

'I'll take the children to my parents,' she said. 'When we move.' She lifted her head to look at the doctors. 'I don't remember them going over Francesca like that,' she said suddenly. 'I counted her fingers and toes before they took her over there. What are they doing?'

'Giving her the third degree.' Tom looked over, saw one of the doctors lift the baby's arms and legs, gently let them drop.

'Floppy,' she murmured to her colleague, stroking the tiny red, wizened face.

'Why isn't she crying, with all that poking and prodding about?' Janey felt the first painful stirrings of acute anxiety.

The senior of the two doctors looked round and asked, 'Where have we put your notes?'

'She was taking Valium,' Tom blurted before he even knew he was going to say it.

The younger doctor wrapped a white blanket round the baby and placed her beside Janey. 'A beautiful little girl,' she said. 'What are you going to call her?'

'Isobel,' Janey said suspiciously, not taking the baby. 'What's wrong with her?'

The doctor sat down on the edge of the bed, looked at Tom with kind, knowing eyes.

'We'll do more tests but I'm afraid, Mrs Morrissey, Mr Morrissey, you have a Down's baby.'

Isobel stirred in her white blanket and bleated, screwing up her face.

'My wife was taking Valium while she was pregnant,' Tom persisted, thinking, oh God, Janey looks as if she's drowning.

'Valium isn't relevant, Mr Morrissey. Down's syndrome is a chromosomal abnormality,' began the doctor, hurrying to explain.

'Isobel has an extra . . . Mr Morrissey?'

'She wouldn't even take anything for being sick. She was sick as a *dog*,' he shouted. 'She doesn't believe in taking pills.'

The two doctors eyed him warily.

'Mr Morrissey, you really must not blame your wife for taking Valium. This is nothing to do with Valium, this is to do with chromosomes. It happens more to older women, but not always. It's always a shock but I promise you, Down's babies can be the most affectionate and rewarding of children.'

'You don't understand. I'm not talking about blaming my wife,' he cried bitterly. 'I blame *myself*.'

He pushed out of the room, marched down the corridor and to the astonishment and consternation of an Indian sitting placidly smoking aromatic reefers in a corner, shouted, 'Damn, damn, damn!' and slammed his fist into the expectant fathers' waiting room wall.

* * *

The weather got hotter and hotter as the week wore on. Driving back from Wigmore Street where she had spent an hour inspecting bathrooms with Samantha's house in mind, Josephine mentally reviewed her wardrobe, her birthday rushing towards her at high speed, unstoppable, needing to be recognised in however half-hearted a manner.

She limped forwards in second gear, along roads jammed with home-going commuters. They shimmered with mirage, softened by the sun, smelling of tar and overheated rubber. Stale city air rushed past as she picked up speed down Park Lane, drying the sweat on the back of her casual linen suit.

Trust the fashion industry to shove linen upon us in the hottest summer this century, she thought. It crumpled and creased, it was uncontrollable and unwashable, and it was the *only* fabric in the shops.

She felt like a potato sack with a 'dry clean only' label, had had a good look at herself in the mirror that morning. You needed to be five feet ten tall and anorexic to wear linen frocks that bagged all round the bottom. She suspected buyers in the fashion trade delighted in making women's lives a misery. It was partly Garcia's fault, his forecasting: telling the fashion industry what women could be bullied into buying.

Sophia had started on HRT, said it was brilliant. Sophia was also on alcohol, nicotine and Prozac. The GP had finally given in to pressure.

Sophia and Ron on Prozac had become infuriating as born-again Christians, unnaturally happy, maddeningly full of smiles and goodwill instead of just plain maddening.

With Theo not very long in his grave, Josephine felt, the GP was wrong. They had no business being happy. Instead of whistling 'Bring me sunshine' all the time in an infuriating way, Ron should be miserable.

Sophia said the doctor said they were depressed.

Josephine swung out into the outside lane to overtake a Jag and wrenched the wheel crossly. They weren't depressed. They were bereaved. They ought to be unhappy.

She wondered about John Denver Jr, whether he was playing Graduate to Sophia's Mrs Robinson.

Sophia said HRT did wonders for your skin.

The point of HRT was that one's middle-aged Robin Reliant of a libido took off again like a Lotus Elan.

I bet it's more than skin, she thought, amused, as the Jag hooted, riding up her bumper, pushing her out of the way. It was sex, more like. Everyone knew hormones made you horny. She visualised Sophia's immaculate little face, a monument to Estée Lauder, peeping out of a froth of carefully arranged peroxide curls, bright red lips, just yearning for a toyboy.

Josephine smiled and cheered up. It wasn't all doom and gloom in looming middle age. I wouldn't mind worrying so much, she thought wistfully, passing a convoy of buses. If only it made me thin.

Yesterday evening she and Garcia had met in the garden. He had come out with a glass of wine, sat on the end of her lounger by the pool and asked her what she really wanted to do on her birthday.

'You can't go cooking and organising barbecues on your birthday. I'm here,' he said. 'At home. Do you want me to book a restaurant? Would you like to take a party to Quaglino's? I can beg Terence's table.'

Josephine shook her head, watching the still blue water. 'I've already settled on the barbecue. It's too late, too hot, too crowded and too noisy in Quaglino's. I don't feel celebratory about reaching forty. In any case, it's obvious you are frantically busy.' She waited for him to insist, say, 'I'm not too busy to spend time with you.'

The portable telephone he always kept by him rang.

'Yes? Vivian.'

Again.

'Garcia, who is Vivian?'

He patted her leg. 'A barbecue it is, then.'

He got off the lounger, walked away, talking to Vivian, but not before she had seen his expression when she insisted on the barbecue, turned down the invitation to take a party to Quaglino's. His look, she recognised with a shock, was one of profound relief.

Janey didn't like being in hospital and didn't want to leave Francesca, but the doctors wanted her to stay in overnight.

She asked if she could go home the following day.

'It might be better to stay a while. You're in shock,' they said gently. 'Having a baby with problems is always a shock.'

'If I'm shocked, I'll get over it better at home,' she answered. 'I'd rather be there. I need to be there for my other child. She's hardly more than a baby.'

After a certain amount of persuasion, and promises to report to her own doctor, attend clincs and see the midwife and health visitor, they let her go.

When she called home, the telephone rang and rang and Tom did not answer. She went to the sister's office and asked them to call her a cab.

At the house, she asked the cabbie to wait a minute. 'I have to go upstairs and get some money,' she said, getting out with Isobel and her overnight case.

He nodded, turned his meter off and climbed out. 'I'll give you a hand.'

The flat was strewn with Francesca's clothes and toys, remains of two TV suppers and the morning's breakfast.

'One night away and they reduce it to a pigsty,' she said cheerfully, rummaging in Tom's desk for money.

She opened the little drawer where he kept a few pounds, emergency money. There were two ten pound notes, some pound coins and a bundle of Guernsey bank statements. Garcia Goddard had bank accounts in Guernsey. Why would Tom have his bank statements? They themselves banked with Lloyd's.

When the cabbie had gone, she put Isobel in her Moses basket on the floor, cleared away the TV dinners, made herself a cup of tea and, curious to see how much Garcia Goddard's bank accounts were worth, went through the paperwork.

When Tom and Francesca came home from picking Francesca up from Janey's mother, she was sitting by a window, looking out over the rooftops, quite still and lost in thought.

'What are you doing here?' Tom cried, taking his key from the door.

'They said I could come home. I couldn't get hold of you, so I got a cab.'

'What's the matter? Is *she* all right?'

He looked warily into the Moses basket. Isobel looked all right, no different from, and just as ugly as, any other newborn baby. The idea of Isobel had kept him awake half the night, but now she was here she didn't look any more alarming than Francesca had. He was not deceived. Problems, for all of them, would come, sooner rather than later; a terrible burden of guilt.

'What are these?' She turned in her chair and he saw her lap was full of paper. 'Where did you get all this money,' she asked steadily, 'to put in offshore bank accounts with your name on them?'

Isobel stirred and began to whimper.

Janey held the statements out. 'This is why we can afford a house and have it done up, isn't it? Why you're suddenly a bit flush with bonuses and share options. I asked Daddy about share options and he said it sounded very odd to him, that you would get shares just when you're leaving the company.'

He took his glasses off, had gone paper white.

Francesca peeped inquisitively into the Moses basket, didn't much like what she saw, climbed into Janey's lap, clung round her neck and sucked her thumb.

Over the child, Janey confronted him. 'What exactly have you been doing?'

Chapter Twenty

Saturday dawned, a milky sky clearing early in the morning as the sun burned off the mist. Josephine woke thinking, as she did every year, that she and Ron ought to join forces, since they shared a birthday. She had that thought every single year but always knew, with a twinge of conscience for Sophia's sake, no way, I couldn't bear it.

While she had disloyal thoughts about her neighbours, the neighbours themselves were suffering and suffocating in their cramped and comfortless roof space.

Ron was trying to ignore his wife by being hard at work. Sophia was preventing him by hovering, sitting perched on the edge of his desk with her legs crossed and getting in his way. Her cigarette sent smoke drifting down his neck while she nagged, which irritated him intensely.

She leaned back against the cold water tank and began to hum 'Happy birthday to you,' smiled at him, eyes half closed against the spiral of smoke in the way he knew she thought made her look saucy.

'If those hormones you keep swallowing are going to make you skittish and think you look like Marylin Monroe, you should throw them away,' he said. 'You look ridiculous.'

But his wife was pleased with herself. What was more, she was waiting for praise. 'I have chilled the champagne, iced your cake, set the table, done the flowers and folded the napkins,' she announced, blowing a smoke ring with a small, full, scarlet mouth.

'Serviettes,' he countered, purely to aggravate her.

When Sophia gave a luncheon party, which she hadn't done since Uncle Harry, she was picky about etiquette. Had a thing about it. She knew more useless detail about protocol and how-to-eat-your-way-through-fifteen-different-settings-of-knives-and-forks than the staff of Buckingham Palace. She had books about it, dotted along the shelves downstairs, alongside Danielle Steeles and Mills and Boons.

'If you like. I had enough of napkins with Harry. The rest is down to Marks, Sparks and the microwave,' she said agreeably, refusing to rise to the bait. 'Thank God for ready meals. Drinks and nibbles at one, lunch at one forty-five and they will leave at six sharp. You'll need to drop hints like bricks to get rid of them because they aren't good at going and we've got Josephine's do at eight.'

'Perish the thought that our friends like us enough to want to *stay,*' Ron growled sarcastically.

'I have allowed for two glasses of champagne each, two bottles of white and two of red,' she persisted. '*Do not* go running down to the cellar fetching more. I do not want to have to fish the whole lot of us out from under the table.'

'How the devil do you expect to make that stretch with Benjie and Sandra? They drink like fish.' Benjie and Sandra were perfectly capable of going down into his cellar and getting more for themselves. And no doubt would.

'They'll come with supplies,' Sophia pointed out.

'In any case, it's my birthday and I *want* to be under the table,' Ron muttered mulishly. 'I don't doubt Benjie does, too.' A thought struck him. 'How old is he?'

'Benjie?' Her voice was elaborately casual. 'Fifty.'

It was Benjie's birthday too. Hence the double celebration.

She puckered her pointed little elflike face, looked more than usually as though she belonged cross-legged on top of a toadstool with a bobble hat over her forest of green Velcro curlers. 'We have the Goddards' party tonight. Once we are there, you can slide under Garcia's table and no one will care because they'll all be ratted too. But if you are in a coma under the table here *chez nous,* we won't be going anywhere. Will we?'

He refused to look up.

Her voice hardened. 'Ron, please don't get horribly drunk.'

'Damn,' Ron shouted. He had begun to write with a Biro on a pad of A4 but nothing happened. He opened his desk drawer and began a noisy search for a pen that worked, ran a short and stubby finger round his sweating neck, stretched his knitted

Aertex collar, cursed the heat, his receding hairline furrowed with discomfort.

Ron's long-suffering, martyred, face-screwed-up, just-sucked-a-lemon look, Sophia considered, bore great resemblance to Prince Charles's in tragic, sensitive mode, complaining about carbuncles, the state of the nation, the state of the monarchy, the state of his soul, the deplorable state of his fantasy life. The deplorable state of his wife. Or Camilla. Or lack of Camilla. All in all, it struck her, he seemed to complain a lot.

'Did you know that Camilla Parker Bowles's husband is the Armed Forces Chief Veterinary Officer?' she asked, following the sudden twist in her own train of thought. 'He runs a Dud Dog Division near Melton Mowbray. Fancy being famous for pork pies, dud dogs and being married to the Prince of Wales's mistress.'

Ron found a Biro with ink in it and was trying to concentrate.

'Dud doggies can't tell the difference between candyfloss and cocaine. Not being able to sort Semtex from Smarties is not a lot of use to the army.'

Ron fingered his left ear, breathed deeply and made an effort to keep his temper. 'I don't believe half the things you say. So why *are* you hanging around half dressed and getting in my way?' he inquired, throwing a fistful of expired Biros into the wastepaper basket.

Her face was framed by a spotted scarlet scarf holding back the Velcro curlers. The rest of her was dressed in Coco Chanel eau de parfum, duty free from Josephine after a trip to New York, and a short pink satin dressing gown that barely covered the remorseless advance of cellulite down her rather short, slightly bowed legs.

Sophia spent what little of her PG money was left over each month on glossy magazines promoting cures for cellulite and ageing. Her part of a cramped avocado bathroom, fashionable in the seventies, now stained and dingy, was littered with half-used anti-cellulite creams, body brushes, Japanese flannels, plastic massage doohdahs from Boots, wooden massage doohdahs from the Body Shop, loofahs and a row of coloured bottles of aromatherapy oils with fluff and talcum powder stuck all over them. An unused exercise bike drooped rusting in a corner.

'They never give you enough to last long enough to make a

difference,' she would complain, squeezing the last drop out of a free plastic sachet sample of anti-ageing preparation.

'My mother swore by Vaseline,' he answered every time.

And look at his mother.

'It's all liposomes and micromolecules. How do you know which one *works*?'

'You don't *need* any of them.'

'Don't I?' For a moment, he had made her radiantly happy.

About to explain that he meant there were better ways of spending what little money they had to spare, for once he held his tongue. Ron could not understand why cellulite, wrinkles and the effect of gravity should cause such a tremendous amount of grief.

Sophia remembered what she had come up to tell him in the first place, cleared her throat.

'What?' he asked irritably, his hand hovering over the telephone. 'I have calls to make, Soph, and if you've got nothing better to do than sit there with no knickers on and hum, there are still the CVs to run off.'

'I'm not sure we should eat in the dining room, but I've gone and laid it ready.'

The Biro stopped jabbing at the A4 and hovered. 'Oh, Lord, not that again,' he groaned.

'We can't keep eating in the kitchen for ever,' she said unhappily. 'It's full of PGs grabbing food. They leave it looking like a pigsty.'

'You've been running a boarding house long enough to know people behave like pigs.'

'I don't want Benjie and Sandra to know we run a boarding house,' she said sadly.

Ron continued writing.

'Did you know John Denver found a kitten on the common, on his way from the station? He has put it in the bottom of the Aga in a blanket in the simmering oven, because it's very new and it's got no mother,' she went on desperately. 'He hasn't noticed it's a hundred in the shade outside and that a kitten is not a sheep. The Aga is off, of course, otherwise the poor little thing would simmer to death. Do you think the oven will get fleas?' She chewed her chipped thumb and looked embarrassed. 'I'm scared.'

Ron put down his pen and put his head in his hands.

'He's there, I know he is,' she whimpered. 'Behind the curtains. I know he's going to think we're dancing on his grave. He'll *hate* us having a nice time while he's too dead to come and spoil it.'

'I cannot credit you believe that.'

'He *said* he would,' she moaned. 'He told me. He used to threaten to come and haunt me. Your uncle was such a cantankerous, mean, miserable, spiteful old bugger, I believe him. He'd refuse to go in the pearly gates out of sheer spite if he thought he could come and make us miserable instead. I have a feeling, Ron . . .'

'If my uncle is ass enough to want to spend eternity lurking behind my dining room curtains, let him. I hate birthdays and I hate being made to share other people's birthdays and being told I'm being haunted and I can't get drunk.'

Put like that, he sounded as if he had a point.

'The only conceivable compensation for getting older is getting plastered,' he added sourly. 'All this spending a fortune and impressing people. I can't imagine why you bother.'

'I'm bothering about *you*,' she retorted, rallying. 'That *sweet* boy John Denver is going to help me put balloons on the gate and a banner over the front door.'

Ron muttered to himself incredulously. 'Dear God.'

'Hosannah is sitting outside sunning herself smoking, so she can tell Josephine what Benjie and Sandra are like.'

'Oh, *God*,' he yelled. 'It's just like Peyton Place.' He picked up his pen again. 'And while you're up here tormenting me, there's another thing. Lloyd's Bank,' he said heavily, 'have pointed out that we are over our limit and until we clear it they've closed my overdraft facility.'

'At least we've got no mortgage.'

'Your damned stepmother and my spiteful uncle . . .' His voice tailed away. 'How many men are dependent on a couple of *stiffs*?'

'There you are. My stepmother, your uncle. You *do* believe Harry's there.' She picked up his empty coffee mug, went round and opened one of the drawers in his desk, took out a chemist's paper bag and put it down in front of him. 'I bet this is why you're so grumpy. You haven't taken your Prozac.'

* * *

Garcia went into overdrive, said he had to go into the office.

'You aren't going to do this,' Josephine answered. 'Not today. You can't.'

'I'll be here, this evening, darling.'

'This evening won't be enough.'

He leaned over their bed, kissed her in a way that reminded her of something, and then she could hear him calling Millie, yelling, 'Hurry up, we're late.'

Josephine got up and watched them run out of the wrought-iron gate, get into the grey BMW and drive away. Millie looked as though she had spent the night crying, Josephine thought, from what she could see of her face as she got into the car.

Serve her right if she had.

Since they had left her alone, she would enjoy herself alone. She wrote out a list of jobs for Hosannah, like making sure the barbecue was clean, and put it on the table. Then she went out to buy herself a present, since no one else had given her one. She spent lunchtime eating the best Italian food, with some of the best company, in London. She spent the afternoon in Riva.

Hosannah ran her eye down her list, sniffed derisively, threw it in the bin underneath the sink and ambled into the dining room to flick a duster over the furniture.

'By gum, how about I look at that,' she told herself in her best colloquial English as she leaned out of the window to shake the duster.

Sophia stood outside in the sun, shading her eyes, dressed in a very short pink linen summer suit and high white heels, and holding a hammer.

'What are you doing?'

Sophia's round, rosily painted little mouth was open with admiration at her own handiwork. A banner over her front door proclaimed 'Happy Birthday Ron and Benjie', blazoned in red and white lettering, flanked by a phallic display of round and sausage-shaped red, white and blue balloons.

'Putting up decorations. Doesn't that look jolly for the birthday boys?'

'Boys?'

As Hosannah leaned right out of the window to take in the full splendour of the arrangement, two stout, mousy girls with big, frizzy hair bounded out of Sophia's front door, backed across the courtyard and inspected the bunting.

'Look as though they've been in the tumble dryer, don't they?' Sophia remarked kindly. 'All that fuzz. Would you want to look like that?'

'Can't get Lycra bicycle shorts, T-shirts and Reeboks in charity shop,' Hosannah remarked sourly, sensitive about appearances. She and Irma wore other people's hand-me-downs, other people's shoes.

The two French girls chirped excitedly, '*Bonne anniversaire, Madame.*'

'You have a nice day too,' Sophia said graciously and remarked to Hosannah, 'Doing English so they can be bilingual secretaries. They look like the Dulux dog, poor things, though the big feet are more the Andrex puppy. No doubt one day they'll turn into some French executive's dream in the Pas-de-Calais. Good luck to them. Hideous place. Full of military graveyards and small, rather unattractive people.'

'Like Balkan peasants, huh?' Hosannah craned her ragged head round, fingered her blunt nose with a fingernail bitten down to the quick and looked baleful.

'Oh, for heavens sake, I was joking,' Sophia snapped. 'Stop feeling so sorry for yourself.'

Hosannah withdrew into the shade of the window like a tortoise into its shell and scowled.

'I've thrown everyone out for the day,' Sophia went on. 'Except John Denver because he's useful and helped me tack this lot up. Josephine's invited him this evening.'

'Emma invite him,' Hosannah muttered from the shadows.

'I got them all together at breakfast and I said, I know you're all paying to stay here but for once I need the house to myself. My neighbour's forty today and my husband's fifty-two, I said, and we've got this friend as well. Three birthdays, and I'm giving a lunch. So you will kindly take your sandwiches and make yourselves scarce until tonight. Go to McDonalds. Half of their English is hardly up to it, but they got the gist.' Sophia contemplated her hammer. 'You'd never guess Benjie's fifty. He's a bit of a dish.'

Hosannah reappeared, drawn by curiosity. 'Deesh?'

'Attractive. Heart-throb,' Sophia explained, needing to talk about Benjie to someone.

Hosannah gazed down at her thoughtfully. Josephine said Sophia was on HRT and it made you randy.

'Honeybun. Dreamboat,' Sophia rattled on heedlessly. 'Emma would say hunk. Slang. Not proper English. Don't bother looking in the dictionary. It'll say dishy Benjie is a cooking utensil.'

Hosannah frowned, storing the deliberately confusing, old-fashioned words away in her head.

Sophia put the hammer down on the steps, readjusted two of the balloons that had already begun to wilt and shrivel at the ends. She tried to tuck them one behind the other so that they looked less like condoms with grossly enlarged teats.

'General Rose,' she heard Hosannah mutter with feeling, from above. 'By gum, he is deesh. I don't have to look in him.'

'You mean in *it*. The dictionary is an *it*. Bad luck, though, there's a Mrs Rose.'

Hosannah sneered. 'Sure.'

'But I could carry a candle for him,' Sophia agreed. General Rose, from the papers, was an outstandingly good-looking and intelligent man battling a genocidal Mafia of criminals and psychopaths. Hosannah, notwithstanding a moustache, beetling brows, hair that looked as though it had been through a sheep dip and being a foreigner, had just earned feminine Brownie points for excellent taste in men.

'Carry candle?' Hosannah demanded, then sniggered and made a very filthy gesture.

Sophia threw discretion to the winds. 'This lunch is half birthday, half holiday reunion.' Who are you kidding? demanded a little voice in her head. The birthday is just an excuse.

Sophia put the hammer down and perched her pink linen bottom on the bench underneath the window. 'It was one of those holidays where you pay up front. We could have what we wanted, when we wanted, and do what we liked when we liked.'

'Booze,' remarked Hosannah critically, fishing a packet of Marlboro out of her pocket and lighting up.

'Garcia'll give you the sack if he catches you smoking indoors. And before you get self-righteous, it's worse for you than booze.'

'I am not indoors, and they are out.' Hosannah stuck her head right out of the window and blew smoke from the side of her mouth, like a navvy. 'So . . .'

'Ron nearly got deported, and we were all down in the bar that night until two in the morning. We clicked, you know? Ended up spending all our time together.'

Hosannah pushed the window up as far as it would go and settled herself on the sill. With the sun on her face, she puffed contentedly and listened with half an ear.

Sophia droned, bees droned through the tatters of honeysuckle over the railings, Melissa's cleaning lady's Hoover droned at the top of the flats, scales from Gordon's piano droned up and down, up and down, and traffic droned past as several thousand cars piled nose to tail down Castelnau, jamming side streets in every direction as they waited to cross the Hammersmith Bridge, shimmering in the morning heat. Walking down towards the Tube station, Josephine saw what was happening and burst out laughing.

'Gonna wet meself,' threatened the young driver sitting in the cab of a United Dairies truck.

He was stuck fast between the concrete posts that controlled the flow of traffic across the bridge. One of several traffic police standing on the road beside him looked up and grinned. The youth sweated, fidgeted wretchedly and went to wind his window up. The grin vanished smartly.

'Leave it,' the officer snarled. 'So you can listen properly to what all these nice people have to say about you.'

Two police officers leaned against their motorbikes, leather-clad in the heat. Arms folded and poker-faced, they listened impassively to the steady stream of invective pouring from the open windows of sweltering, frustrated, furious drivers creeping past. The youth moaned.

'Shouldn'a have tried it, sunshine, should you?' The copper leaned an elbow on the van door in a confiding, fatherly sort of way.

The young man shuddered and reluctantly studied the metal traffic-calming tracks and lumps of concrete embedded in the side of his bonnet, dragged out of the road by his drunken determination to go through with a truck precisely two and one half inches wider than the gap.

'If you don't let me go, I'll *go* in me pants,' he threatened.

An enraged driver in a dark blue Volvo estate crawled level and stopped to stare. The youth, shock-headed, a row of steel rings in one ear, stared back with haggard, bloodshot blue eyes.

'Stupid bastard.'

The youth's expression didn't change.

'So many times over the limit, it doesn't register.' The officer glanced at his watch, leaned down and spoke confidentially into the Volvo driver's window. 'A stag night, he says. Comes out of a club at six in the morning and thinks he can take Hammersmith Bridge home in his milk truck. Feeling a bit poorly now. He's been two hours waiting for a winch. I wouldn't like having that many spiked pints in *my* bladder and nowhere to go.'

The United Dairies driver ignored the burst of laughter, slumped in his seat, crossed his legs and tried to ignore the pain.

'Siddup, so we can all see whose traffic jam this is,' snarled the officer, letting go of the Volvo.

He dragged himself upright and sank into morose contemplation of losing his licence, losing his job, of what his mother was going to say, of what his girlfriend was going to say, of what he'd like to do to his mates who had put vodka and brandies in everyone's beer.

Thinking was worse than being yelled at, so he took to staring back at the furious faces moving slowly past him, their windows wound down, the better to abuse him. Losing the battle with his bladder, he sat on display until they got tired of it, winched him free and took him in to charge him, in a puddle of urine and humiliation.

Josephine went into Hammersmith Tube, heading for Harvey Nichols, and Sophia finished her description of debauchery on holiday, gazed out of the courtyard and wondered why there were so many more cars than usual.

'I put it down to fate,' she concluded.

Hosannah grinned evilly and breathed two thin streams of smoke from her nostrils. 'Sure. You know how they say what is fate in Sarajevo?'

'No.' Sophia visualised recent newspaper pictures of children lying in Sarajevo gutters with their limbs blown off.

'If I walk, bullet hit me. If I run, I hit bullet. That's Balkan peasant fate. Huh?' She lit a cigarette from the butt of the last one and threw the filter into the dust underneath the honeysuckle.

'I wish you'd stop trying to make out you're a peasant, Hosannah,' Sophia said irritably, relieved her definition of Bosnian fate wasn't worse. 'You've got more education than me or Josephine. And you could offer me one of those.'

'Josephine got a diploma for doing houses,' Hosannah retorted, putting the Marlboro pack back in her pocket.

'More education than *me*, then,' yelped Sophia.

'Yeah. She does curtains and I can do real writing *and* Cyrillic script,' Hosannah sneered sarcastically. 'Wrong education in wrong place for Balkan peasant fate in Surbiton. Communist economics and locomotive systems – *pah*. No good here.' She made a gesture in very poor taste, muttered something in Croatian that ended with the words 'Home Office', looked out across the common, black eyes glinting in the sun, unreadable, hard as nails and wholly indifferent to PGs, bank managers, birthdays and Benjie.

Sophia fell silent, having given away more than she intended.

Bea Beamish hurried past, from her house round the corner, a friend of Jospehine's, in a torn tracksuit caked with dirt, a smudge of pink paint on her hollow cheek, cement dust whitening bundled grey hair.

'Can't stop. Got a skip coming,' she called over the gate. 'Someone's taken the chairs away and parked in front of the gates. Don't know how we'll get it into the drive. *So* thoughtless. See you later, at Josephine's do.'

'That woman is quite mad,' Sophia said matter-of-factly. 'She has four dogs and I can't remember a time when they didn't have at least one room in the house stripped back to the bricks. Cement mixers and skips. They turn the street into a Gypsy site.'

The balloons bobbed gently on their streamers, red, white and blue. Hosannah's coarse and secretive features darkened, lined and cynical, full of a deadly ennui. She eyed Sophia coldly and rested her duster on the edge of the window, meticulously folding it into a tiny square.

'Terrible,' she answered eventually, unimaginable sarcasm packed into one short word.

'Do you know,' Sophia said suddenly, 'there are people who

cross the road when they see me coming, in case I'm bad luck? Is that fate? I keep wondering if we did something to deserve the things that happen.'

'Sure.'

'I wish you'd stop saying *sure*. I thought you'd understand,' Sophia burst out, 'because you're a refugee and awful things have happened to you, too.'

'Sure.'

'You don't, though. People don't. Our doctor sent a bereavement counsellor round but Ron sent her away with a flea in her ear and we went on holiday and Prozac instead.'

'Flea in her ear?'

'Oh, for God's sake,' Sophia screeched. 'Go look it up.'

'Ah. *Les puces*.'

'What does it *matter*?' Sophia raged. 'All I'm trying to ask you is, how do *you* cope?'

The dark face withdrew from the window, a cigarette glowed for a moment, then disappeared.

'Hosannah, *tell me*.'

'I get peesed off,' drifted in Hosannah's gritty voice from Josephine's dining room, followed by a butt sailing into the honeysuckle. 'I get tired, tired, *bloody tired*.'

The fading words were followed by the abrupt blare of Radio One. Madonna sang something lewd, the traffic jam on the bridge cleared, Gordon opened his window, leaned out, stretched, began singing 'Oh, what a beautiful morning, oh, what a beautiful day . . .'

His next pupil, the boy with a crew cut and cheeky Nigel Kennedy grin who had let Caroline Quinlan into the house, opened the wrought-iron gate, came in and padlocked his bike to the railings.

Minutes later a Mozart étude came from the window. Barney Darling yapped from Josephine's ruined back garden. Humiliated and frustrated, Sophia threw herself on to the bench between her front door and Josephine's, beneath the balloons. As 'Happy Birthday Ron and Benjie' hung limp in the blazing sun, she fumbled in the pocket of her short pink skirt, found a pack she didn't know she'd had and with shaking hands lit herself a cigarette.

* * *

Sophia, Hosannah decided, breathing smoke through the gap in her front teeth like the Listerine dragon, had a romantic view of suffering. Believed it had a point. Fate, huh.

In Hosannah's experience, people who were being shot at and starved alternately raged helplessly – fools, idiots, imbeciles, shook their fists at the surrounding hills where gunners trained their sights on bread queues – and sank into withdrawn, wordless despair.

Once humans stopped being human, all constraint was gone.

Goran had had an erection underneath his sweaty, stained fatigues when he thrust the bloody ears in his handkerchief into her face and demanded her flat. Her colleague perverted into an animal. Sophia could learn a thing or two, that cruelty was *random*.

Prozac. Hah. Hosannah sniffed contemptuously and went to get steel wool and detergent, to clean Josephine's barbecue. As she got down to work, she could hear Ron whistling in next door's garden. 'Bring me sunshine . . .'

Sophia stood over her ancient Aga and tried to coax John Denver's tiny kitten out with a bowl of milk.

'Come on, before my guests get here,' she murmured into the cold oven. 'Out you come.'

Feet clattered and thumped down the passage and into the kitchen.

'Are you still here?'

She called them her four French hens, four girls from Paris schools over on holiday, reeking of kiwi fruit soap and banana hair putty from the Body Shop. They went through the fridge like sniffer dogs through luggage at Heathrow.

'You already had breakfast,' Sophia protested. 'Eggs, bacon, tomato, sausage, mushrooms, toast and marmalade. I'm going to tell your parents I'm putting your rates up.'

From the garden, Ron's voice carried as he stopped whistling 'Bring me sunshine' and answered a call on the portable telephone. The plumbing banged as John Denver took a shower in the first-floor bathroom.

'Out, out, out. I have guests. This house is a zoo.'

The French girls fled.

* * *

Hosannah found Emilia in Josephine's kitchen, making herself lunch – tomato sandwiches and white wine.

'There is a man in my annexe, mending the boiler,' she said stoutly, backing out of Josephine's fridge with a bottle in her hand. 'He is clattering about and making a mess and he does not seem in a hurry to finish, and since you were out . . .'

'I don't care if you drink wine,' Hosannah said.

'I intend to talk to my son about you,' Emilia snapped. 'In my day, hired help didn't answer back.'

Flooded with sunlight, Sophia's dining room table sparkled with silver, crystal, her real mother's good and faded china. Harry seemed banished, his presence nowhere to be felt, reduced at last by the sheer brilliance of the day to a bad dream. The room had the sweet smell of stocks, bought with a couple of roses by John Denver Jr from the flower stall on the corner.

Ron had put two open bottles of Australian Cabernet Sauvignon to breathe on the sideboard. He had stopped skulking in the garden and was taking his turn in the shower, about to get dressed for lunch.

Half drawing a curtain against the sun, she noticed Andrew Quinlan's curtains were also closed, his windows tightly shut.

'*He's* about to get woken up by people shouting happy birthday and popping balloons,' she told a thrush hunting for snails in the empty dry crevices underneath the ruin of the honeysuckle. 'And about time too. Lazy creature.'

As the thrush flew away, she could faintly hear a telephone ringing and ringing in Andrew Quinlan's flat, echoed by the strident ring of her own. Taking one last, satisfied look at the table, she went to answer it.

'Now what's the matter?' Ron came bustling down the stairs, freshly showered and shaved and in a very good mood, to find her sitting on the bottom one with the receiver dangling loosely from her hand. He eased past her. 'Who was that?'

'Sandra.' She sounded distant, quite vacant.

'Held up?'

'You could say that.'

He sidled into the dining room and picked up the whisky decanter next to the warming red wine.

'Time for a Scotch,' he said jocularly. 'It is, after all, my birthday. Bring me sunshine . . .' He bent down and got a whisky glass out of the cupboard.

'Ron.'

'Bring me sunshine . . .'

'Sandra rang to say they wouldn't be coming, and to wish you happy birthday.' She made little burping, hicupping sounds that grew and grew until she was laughing hysterically. 'Happy birthday. She rang up to wish you *happy birthday* when Benjie was . . .'

Screaming with laughter, she flew into the dining room.

'Have a *wee dram*,' she shrieked, grabbing the wine from the sideboard. 'Have the whole bloody bottle because Benjie's had a stroke and is *dead*.'

She ran round the table, out of his reach, snatched at the wine.

'I never want to be sober again,' she screamed. 'You hear that, Uncle Harry?'

Sweeping a glass from the table, she ran upstairs as the first tears spurted from her eyes.

Chapter Twenty-One

Josephine emerged from Riva late in the afternoon in a mellow frame of mind, a coffee-coloured silk jacket and palazzo pants in a Harvey Nichols bag, and walked home slowly.

The courtyard was quiet, no one about. Sophia's bunting hung limp in the hot, still air, the balloons half shrivelled against her closed door. Josephine had expected open windows and riotous laughter from Sophia's dining-room window but it was almost closed, no sign of anyone inside. Probably all in the garden.

In her own ravaged garden, Hosannah, Emma and John Denver were busy setting out the party with the air of people who have things under control and are enjoying themselves, so she left them to it. No sign of Garcia or Millie.

Upstairs, she could hear two grey doves cooing softly, strutting on Melissa's roof. A lawn mower went up and down, up and down, up and down in someone else's garden, summer sounds bringing memories of Garcia playing cricket, and rainy days crammed in the pavilion drinking Pimms, tepid beer or tea.

In Garcia's study the fax, which had been burbling, went quiet, stuffed with paper. His business line rang and answered itself a dozen times, took messages, which meant, although she had looked to check, he wasn't there.

The year they were married they had celebrated her birthday by drinking champagne in bed. The following year they went to the Victoria and Albert Museum because Garcia wanted to look at a textiles exhibition. He sang happy birthday to her over tea and carrot cake in the cafeteria. The third year she was pregnant, and by the fourth Garcia was spending half his time building business in Japan, had just taken Millie on as an assistant. By the fifth he was discovering the extent of his entrepreneurial genius and was starting to make money. After that began the frenetic globetrotting.

He bought exquisite, sometimes quirky, increasingly expensive gifts, enjoyed grooming her, as she enjoyed grooming their home, into a showcase of good taste. This time, she wanted something different – nondescript – to make passing forty feel like a non-event, not the first half her life already over.

'You make it sound as though life is a half-empty glass,' Garcia had remarked when she had insisted on the neighbours only.

If my glass is half full of poison, I'd rather it was empty. It's *my* birthday and if I'm going to get maudlin and depressed, I'd rather do it with half a dozen friends who won't expect me to play hostess. But recalling the relief in his eyes when she had refused his invitation to Terence Conran's brash and noisy restaurant, she had kept her answer to herself. Coming from Garcia, whose motto in life was 'Any excuse for a party, the bigger and flasher the better', that look was so out of character, its meaning could only be dire.

He hadn't spent the day with her, hadn't even called.

Telephone out of order.

She snatched up the receiver on his side of the bed. Working.

She stood, dangling the receiver in her fingers, lost in thought.

Who?

For Garcia to have an affair, it had to be with someone who could travel, who would see more of him than his wife did. No mistress would put up with it.

Millie.

It was unthinkable; that stormy partnership would never survive romance. There was too much excitement already. Workaholics were essentially absorbed in themselves; two together wouldn't last five minutes. Anyway, Millie already had a partner, a trader in Manhattan working Tokyo hours from New York. And Millie more in Tokyo than Connecticut. They were perfect together.

Had to be someone else. One of his clients? Never. Staff? Risky and unprofessional.

But who else had any opportunity? He and Millie shared hotel suites around the world, which sometimes puzzled maids and receptionists. He could hardly bring women back and introduce them to Millie when they all bumped into one another at four thirty in the morning, the telephone going, Millie in her dressing gown, sleepless with jet lag and picking a sea of overnight faxes off the floor.

Garcia never anchored long enough in any port to go whoring like a travelling salesman, go finding girls. There were too many ports, too much pressure, too many business dinners that finished drunkenly at two in the morning, none of the privacy and time necessary for clandestine liaisons.

All the hype and stress and loneliness, the mania and exhaustion of Garcia's business schedules left no room for mistresses, not even masochists or airline stewardesses.

Except one who shared it.

Josephine replaced the receiver and began to believe the unbelievable. It all kept coming back to Millie.

I've been damn well putting up with it, she thought, trembling with rage.

Her heart pounded. She flew down the stairs and into his study. Feverishly, she rifled through the drawers of his desk, his in-tray, out-tray, a small amount of opened correspondence. The telephone displayed the date and time, was in answering mode. It held a stack of messages.

About to press *play*, she heard the fax hum. She hadn't thought to look in the fax. Josephine scrabbled the paper from the out-tray and began to rifle through it.

Reports on a project for Isetan. A letter from Marks and Spencer in Hong Kong. Reams and reams and reams of densely typed figures with notes written in the cramped and tiny handwriting of the new financial director who had taken over from Tom Morrissey. Then she came to what she was looking for. Two sheets of paper were headed 'Private and Confidential'. The first was headed, in bold capitals, 'GARCIA GODDARD: PERSONAL ASSETS'. Three British bank accounts, totalling about one hundred thousand pounds, lists of shares that meant nothing to her, no value given, little Roeban, abandoned for the past few months in his Biggin Hill hangar, and that was all.

None of the property was listed, nor the real bank accounts. All the properties were unmortgaged, were held in trust and did not legally belong to Garcia. The banks were offshore. Money was paid into accounts with Julius Baer in Guernsey, then transferred elsewhere, probably to the Bank of Butterfield in Bermuda. Or somewhere. Only Garcia knew. The arrangements were legal, convoluted, the money, if he wished, virtually untraceable. The second sheet was a short covering note to Vivian, enclosing the list.

The fax hummed again. She read the page slowly as it came through. A brief letter acknowledged receipt of the original of the list she was holding and that they had an appointment at GGIL for eight o'clock in the morning, the coming Monday. It was signed 'Vivian'. Under the letterhead, it was a routine note from an accountant, nothing more. Naive idiot. Her relief short-lived, her thoughts raced into overdrive. The fax proved nothing except that Vivian turned out to be an accountant and Garcia and he were working on something together, and that Garcia was hiding things.

What makes men act strangely, look haggard, avoid their wives like the plague and make lists of assets that hide how wealthy they really are?

Her mind raced on.

Garcia paid Emmanuel and his accountant in Bermuda to make sure he had no assets. They were all owned by the company or parked in trusts where they could not be touched or taxed or seized or made the subject of . . . *divorce proceedings*.

Her and Garcia's possessions were *untouchable*.

Her mind gagged on the word as the answer became blindingly clear. Of those possessions, only the few declared on the list could be the substance of an enforced divorce settlement.

She crumpled the fax as if she was wringing Garcia's neck, jumped guiltily as the door flew open behind her, squeaked in fright.

'They want to know, do you want Emma to open champagne and bring you a glass in your bath?'

Hosannah, in yellow leggings from the Oxfam shop and a vast yellow apron with little red balloons all over it, looked like a duck with chickenpox. Red-eyed, red-nosed and adenoidal from crying, smoking and being forced by Junior and Emma to peel onions, she stomped into the room and looked accusing.

Shattered, Josephine stood speechless.

'You aren't in a bath,' said Hosannah.

'I will be in a minute.'

Hosannah brightened momentarily. 'By gum, we got a lot of food. Junior got *black pudding*. Found it in the fridge.'

'Then you will be able to pig out,' Josephine said distantly. 'Go away, Hosannah.'

Hosannah's voice turned to a whine. 'No. I got a big carton of Slimfast.'

'I don't care right now if you got a big carton of rat poison, Hosannah. I have things on my mind.'

'I look like a fat pig and Irma acting like a turkey. She got a social worker, bare-ass social . . .' Hosannah's voice trembled. 'She never coming home with my grandchildren.'

'Go away. I don't want to hear about social workers' bottoms, black pudding, Serbs, Irma, or nothing. Not now. Go and tell them I don't want champagne and I'm going upstairs to have a nervous breakdown.'

Affronted, Hosannah muttered in her own language, sniffed nastily and sidled off.

'Josephine got a headache,' Josephine heard her bawling as she went outside again. Hosannah had divined the truth: Josephine had a deadly headache.

The bank accounts that mattered held a lot of money. The property was worth three million at least, even with the housing market in terminal recession. All tied up, ring-fenced, protected and watertight against divorce lawyers trying to get at it on her behalf. The lawyer who had ring-fenced them would be the same one Garcia would ask to act against her.

Emmanuel.

The horror of having Emmanuel become her enemy struck her like a blow. No *wonder* they were skulking in meetings with him, avoiding her, too scared to face her.

She leaned on Garcia's untidy desk and felt sick as acid burned at the back of her throat, corrosive as betrayal, and as bitter. When it passed, she hurried upstairs, afraid he'd walk in any minute and find her holding incriminating faxes.

With a sense of being disconnected from it all, she could hear them busy down below. She looked out, eyes like lead. The garden, so much smaller than it had been, from this angle was nothing but a swimming pool surrounded by paving and shrubs. The big brick barbecue was piled with covered dishes, waiting to be cooked. Over the wall, she could see Ron slumped on a stone seat in the far corner of his garden, morosely drinking whisky, which seemed a funny way to end his birthday lunch and augured badly for his behaviour later on.

Babe had the French windows wide open to his garden, was sitting on his patio, painstakingly varnishing his nails. Andrew looked down from his flat above.

Platinum-haired, Babe was ready for a party, got up like the dog's dinner in skin-tight silver tank top, silver arm bangles, bondage trousers and brown, bare, beautiful feet.

'What?' Babe's blue ice-chip eyes looked up.

'I said, I gave in my resignation yesterday,' Andrew said in his precise, pedantic voice.

Babe flicked his bangles up his arm, admired his tan and Rouge Noir fingernails.

'Whaffor?'

'I am tired of my ex-wife demanding all my money.'

A thought struck Babe. He put the varnish brush back in the little bottle. 'Was that your ex-wife coming downstairs crying the other day? Skinny. Tall woman. Orange looking.'

'She is tall and skinny and she may well have been crying,' Andrew said grimly.

'Wondered who she was. What's she want?'

'Money. She came to threaten me with some photographs that could be professionally embarrassing. I came to to find her *taking* shots.'

Babe looked up, alert with interest. 'Came to?'

Andrew met his stare unwinkingly.

'Where'd your wife get embarrassing shots?'

'A club,' Andrew said briefly, adding, 'she had me followed. He got shots of a cling-film session and a bit of beating.' He watched carefully to see how Babe reacted. 'He managed to tape an argument.'

Babe eyes were glowing. 'What was you arguing about?'

'Barbed-wire whipping.'

The blue eyes were opaque, imagining.

'They wouldn't. Said they couldn't control the damage. I said, I'm a surgeon, let me take care of that. Still wouldn't.'

'*Jesus.*'

'I shall go into private practice in Casablanca, then she can show it to anyone she likes. The Arabs won't care. If she's lucky they'll buy it off her and resell my cling-film entombed body to the tourists as dirty postcards. I'll probably be able to buy myself in Soho eventually.'

'Oh, *man.*' Babe's vicious grin spread wide.

'Do you want to come with me?' Andrew asked abruptly.

Babe flicked his bangles. 'Thought you'd never ask. Your place or mine? Better make it yours. He gets jealous.'

'I'm asking you to come with me to Egypt.'

Babe's mouth fell open. 'You're kiddin'.'

'Not at all.'

'Whaffor?'

'You have the right kind of depravity,' Andrew answered gravely. 'You have the morals of a sewer rat and physical perfection. I have been in love with you for months.'

'Don't know I could live with your mouth,' Babe answered offhandedly, rubbing his nose. 'You know, like, you talk too fuckin' much. Long words.'

Andrew smiled beatifically, soft pink cheeks bunched like apricots. 'Exactly. We will drive each other to distraction, which should suit both of us extremely well. I think you'd find if you needed something more than I can offer, the Arabs are pretty relaxed.'

'Might not like it,' Babe drawled. 'Might come back.'

Andrew shrugged. 'You'll find me very tolerant.'

'Your place,' Babe said, getting up.

Josephine showered, dried her hair, took the coffee-coloured silk palazzo pants and their loose jacket from the tissue in the Harvey Nichols bag.

Chic, casual, cool. Perfect for the career woman arrived at a certain age, carving out her destiny. And, she thought grimly, about to carve up her husband and didn't care who knew it.

Chapter Twenty-Two

People were drifting into the garden from the rest of the terrace. Of everyone invited, only Bea Beamish, her daughter Abigail, Emmanuel and Samantha came from further away; Bea and Abigail from round the corner, Samantha and Emmanuel from across the common.

'Oddballs and maladjusted, the whole lot,' was Garcia's well-known verdict on his neighbours. He gave the Beamishes, in particular, a wide berth.

Abigail and Emma had brought their mothers together one wet afternoon by being sent home unwell on the same day from nursery school.

Bea Beamish had thick, coarse, prematurely grey hair. At first Josephine, having seen her many times at the school gates, thought she'd gone white overnight. But it was merely cement dust coating her from head to foot, chapping her lips. Bea had rough and callused hands, broken and blackened fingernails and chisels clanking in the bib of her dirty denim overalls as she heaved her grizzling, blotchy small daughter into the front seat of a dented, rented, dirty white pick-up.

'My other car's a Porsche,' she called, seeing Jospehine stare. 'Don't worry. The working classes haven't moved in.'

'I didn't mean . . .'

'Abigail's got chickenpox,' Emma said, bright-cheeked herself. 'She's got spots all over her tummy.'

'DIY,' explained Bea, resettling her chisels. 'Putting in a new kitchen.' She wound down her window, switched on the ignition and ground the pick-up's gears horribly. It lurched and stalled. 'Damn. Why pay someone else to do what you can do yourself? Anyway, Abby's probably given Emma the pox. Sorry.' She started the pick-up. 'Two weeks of itching and whingeing when the kitchen's rubble, the water's off and Molly's due at the weekend. Having six. Brilliant timing, innit?'

'Sextuplets?' Josephine stopped half in, half out of her Volvo, astounded.

'Puppies. Guinea pig's pregnant as well, though you can never be sure with rodents until one day you go to clean them out and find mum smirking on a nest of what look like maggots. I always think their babies are much to the credit of guinea pigs. Do you think we'd take to our children if they started out looking that revolting?'

'If they're both spotty, why don't we let them play together? They can itch and whinge at each other and we can take it in turns to put up with it.'

Bea rummaged in her bib, underneath the chisels, and produced filthy tissues, builder's merchant's receipts and a grubby bit of card. 'Harry's business card. Our number's the bottom one. Got to go and organise some bricks and pick up some sacks of plaster. I'll be back around three. Give me a ring.' She handed the card through the pick-up window as the exhaust belched smoke. The pick-up jerked forwards, she spun the tires and screeched away.

Garcia, much the worse for wear, called that evening from his hotel in Taiwan.

'Emma has chickenpox and I met a rather peculiar mother,' Josephine told him.

'I've been with peculiar people all evening,' he complained. 'Shifty. Full of deceit and spittle. You wouldn't think you'd get bad Chinese food in Taiwan, but you can. Dinner was lousy.'

'Dinner was liquid, by the sound of you.'

'Believe me,' he answered heavily. 'You'd be bouncing off the walls too, were you here.' He had staggered to bed at two in the morning, couldn't sleep, got up and was calling home in a paroxysm of homesickness, to be comforted. 'Business is wretched. I am lying in bed with the phone on the pillow, missing you. I hate it here. It is hideously hot and humid and I have the runs and the people are roaringly nasty.' He waited for sympathy.

'The Japanese think we're disgusting for blowing our noses. I wouldn't know what habits would offend a Chinese but I'm sure we have some.'

'That thought is a great comfort to me in my . . .' He lost his thread for a moment, fell asleep, woke up, remembered why he was calling. 'My desperate loneliness.'

'Maybe you should stay at home sometimes.'

That met a heavy, offended silence.

'Beatrice Beamish, whose child gave Emma chickenpox, pulls her house around and collects brick stacks. She goes to evening classes for wiring and plumbing. I've been thinking we could go into partnership. I could do her interiors.'

Garcia's grasp of technology was stretched by changing a light bulb.

'Why don't you?' he answered sulkily.

'Her husband's depressed. She does all the work.'

Garcia, whose idea of self-help was looking in Yellow Pages, snapped, 'I'm not surprised. This call is costing a huge amount of dough.' And from the point of view of comfort, a poor investment. Already asleep, he put down the telephone.

It's not her father who's the loser in that family, Josephine thought afterwards, visualising little Abigail Beamish sitting miserable and spotty in the greasy pick-up, jolted and jerked by her mother's driving, filmed with plaster spilling from a pile of sacks in the back. Plaster, dogs and guinea pig hairs and straw didn't go well with chickenpox. Abigail would come to her, where there was hygiene, comfort and everything in order.

Poor Abigail. Fancy bursting into tears at the age of six because being banned from school and having to stay at home for at least two weeks was practically the worst thing that could happen to you in your very short life.

Recently, Bea had torn down her original work to build an extension, pulled her kitchen out again. The house was once more almost as demolished, someone remarked brutally the previous week while looking at Abigail, as her daughter.

In Josephine's garden, John Denver Jr had lit the barbecue and was also looking at Abigail.

'Jeez,' he whistled.

Abigail drifted listlessly past, to sit down behind her mother.

'She's *way* too skinny,' Emma muttered.

'No more than Kate Moss.'

Shrouded from head to toe in loose layers of black from Monsoon, it was hard to tell how emaciated Abigail was until her sleeve fell away from her wrist and it poked out, thin as a twig.

Abigail was fleshless, her face full of delicate, jutting bones, huge green eyes. Shoulder-length, luxuriant, tightly curling copper hair was pulled back into a snood. Doc Martens underneath the long skirts looked like bovver boots on a shining, fragile angel.

'Rubbish. Abigail's anorexic,' Emma snapped. 'It's obvious. She hasn't had her periods for *years* and she only eats laxatives and apples. They'll soon have to put her in the hospital. Stop staring.'

'She's your friend. Can't you help her?'

'How? She hides in that horrible house and cuddles their horrible old dog. She hasn't got any friends.' She stalked into the house.

'What's getting up your nostril?' Hosannah demanded, stacking bottles in the freezer to cool white wine quickly.

'Boys,' Emma snapped, with deliberate insult to John Denver Jr 'With no manners. Don't know it's rude to stare.'

'Ho, you're jealous.'

Emma shot an evil look, poured orange juice into a glass and went to search for her mother. After looking in her parents' empty bedroom, she went outside again, to find people clustered around John Denver Jr, fetching food, and her mother in some new clothes she hadn't seen before. When food was around, Abigail silently retreated and disappeared.

'Happy birthday!' everyone cried, raising their glasses to Josephine.

'Your presents are in the kitchen,' Emilia said.

'So you're not going to bottle out after all,' Bea called. 'Happy fortieth. Come and sit with us. When's Garcia coming out?'

'Garcia isn't here,' Josephine answered.

'Oh, he is. I saw him when I arrived.'

Can't even bring himself to say hello, the treacherous rat. 'Birthdays, weddings and funerals,' Josephine said. 'One should always attend them. Most especially funerals.'

'Merry birthday, darling.' Melissa blew affectionate kisses in the air on either side of Josephine's cheeks. Over Melissa's shoulder, Josephine could see Barry parked by himself at the end of the pool, nursing a bottle and a glass. Gordon wandered over with a beer in his hand, sat down beside him.

'Love,' pronounced Barry, refilling his glass, 'is a crocka shit.'

'Trouble with Babe?'

'What a whore,' Barry said flatly.

Gordon coloured, carefully took off his shoes and socks and stuck his legs into the pool.

'I don't know much about love, or whores, myself. Wish I did.'

'Shouldn't bother.'

'It's nice and cool,' Gordon sighed, feeling fussy and fusty and out of touch with life, out of his depth and inadequate confronted with real-life anguish. He touched the letter he carried around in his pocket, against the moment when he might actually post it to *The Times*. 'I might go in, later. Why don't you cool off?'

'Yeah. To drown myself. Babe's been shagging Andrew Quinlan.'

'I didn't know Andrew was inclined in that direction.'

'Better off ignorant about Quinlan's inclinations. Unless you're that way inclined yourself. Which that little bastard is. I knew all along, but I hoped . . .'

Gordon worried he was going to cry.

Instead, Barry took his sandals off. Gazing into the depths, they sat side by side with their feet dangling in the water, sharing the bottle of whisky and a sympathetic, if deeply uncomfortable, silence.

'The wounded are on the whisky already. Barry is going to get *extremely* drunk,' Melissa observed. 'And who can blame him, poor soul?'

'Move over,' Emilia said to her dogs who lay on their sides, panting, at her feet. 'Let Melissa sit down. What an interesting outfit, Melissa.' She picked at her food with a fork. 'Why is Barry getting extremely drunk?'

Melissa pulled a palest green silk Chinese shirt straight over skin-tight sparkly scarlet trousers and sat down with grave, ungainly dignity. 'Borrowed from Wardrobe at work. I shall probably split 'em and end up indecent. Dr Quinlan's pinched his Babe, is why Barry's getting paralytic.'

Emilia peered at the pair at the end of the swimming pool and inquired, 'Where's Luvvie?'

'No idea,' Melissa said curtly.

Someone told a joke and a gale of laughter shook the little crowd around the barbecue, huge, tipsy, belly-tickling, raucous laughter. John Denver Jr shovelled steaks, chicken, sausages on to plates piled high with salad, tiny new potatoes and mustard. Beneath a pink and white awning, Hosannah had arranged salad, fruit, cheeses, French bread, lemon tarts, chocolate mousse, sorbet in an ice bowl and cream. A birthday cake, square and decorated with sugar roses, sprouted forty white candles, ten each side.

Melissa smiled brightly, as if into the fierce lights of the cameras, got up and headed for the barbecue, delivered her lines over her shoulder like the pro she was. 'To hell with darling Luvvie.' Then she followed Emilia's gaze.

Josephine, on her way indoors to find Garcia in his study, met Samantha and Emmanuel coming out of the kitchen door.

'Jo, happy birthday.' Emmanuel, holding a silver-wrapped box, moved to hug her.

For a moment she stopped, held his eyes, then ducked her head, avoided him and went on inside without a word. Samantha stared after her.

'*Well*,' she exclaimed.

'Did you see that?' Emilia said to Melissa.

The party stood riveted by the monumental snub.

Into the sudden silence Sherrine rode round from the annexe on Emma's bike. Discovering that everyone was in the garden when she had arrived unannounced at the open front door, she had scoured the house from top to bottom until she found the bike in the basement.

'What's she doing on my bike?' Emma cried, interrupted by a long scream that split the evening air.

Everyone turned to stare at the house next door. All they could hear as the howl splintered and broke off was a lawnmower and beyond that the distant roar, like blood in the ears, of London's weekend traffic.

Chapter Twenty-Three

Josephine heard the scream, standing with her ear pressed to Garcia's study door. Taut with rage, fuelled by shame, she hesitated. The thing that held her in check was Millie's being on the other side, deepening her turmoil.

Millie had become, as years went past, the secret enemy. Millie was worse than secretary turned office wife who knows her boss better than his real wife. Millie was no secretary but a full and equal partner. Free, independent, wealthy, clever, sarcastic, pretty Millie with her long legs, gym-honed, narrow waist, Armani suits, Gucci loafers, New York chic and New York banker had more access to Josephine's husband, more claim upon him, knew more of his secrets than Josephine ever did.

Garcia scared most people. Millie scared Garcia. The fights were appalling. Screaming matches. While everyone else was still shaking, they had their heads together, in cahoots again. They plotted deals, outfaced the Japanese, hired, fired, travelled the globe. Millie knew Garcia's salary, was on his life insurance. Key-person life insurance. Each was vital to the other.

They shared ups and downs. Literally when it came to the frequent Japanese earthquakes. Airline strikes, Taiwan typhoons, Hong Kong hurricanes. Were even reported dead together. Josephine had answered the telephone one day to find Millie's mother screaming down it.

'Dead,' she shrieked. 'They called me up to say she's on the manifest.'

Josephine asked her what she was talking about.

'Haven't you seen the news?' Millie's mother yelled.

Josephine's mouth went dry.

'Blown up. A bomb. Scottish town. Haven't they called you?

They must have called you. They call everyone. The whole plane is dead.' She wanted Josephine to say something, deny it, but Josephine trembled, left the phone dangling and went to put the television on.

The telephone rang and rang. The airline rang. Millie and Garcia were on the aircraft manifest.

Somehow, people found out. Shocked, horrified, they began calling, call after call after call. Garcia had friends *everywhere*. Josephine, unable to tell Emma, felt she'd die herself.

Bored, stuck waiting for a flight, Garcia had eventually called home to complain, mellow with first-class lounge brandy and all unaware. She slammed the receiver down, appalled, thinking it a hoax.

He called straight back. 'What are you playing at, Josephine?'

'You're dead,' Josephine shrieked. 'Why aren't you dead?'

'Sorry,' Garcia snapped, taken aback. 'I do my best but some things I can't manage, like resurrection. What the hell are you talking about?'

She had stared at the telephone, wide-eyed and speechless with fright. 'Is this a hoax?'

'What?'

'You're not a hoax?' she had quavered. 'Or am I finally going off my head?'

When eventually he understood what had happened, he was abruptly, brutally, sobered. Negotiations with the client had dragged on. At the last minute they had changed their flight, too late to alter the Lockerbie manifest.

Every trip a drama. Outrageous stories. Millie-and-Garcia stories. Starting an interior design business, her bid for independence, a life of her own, unplagued by Emilia's baleful presence, now seemed like small defiances, sadly insufficient.

Garcia's door was a stone wall because confronting him, ackowledging their failure, in front of Millie was unthinkable. And Millie was sticking like glue, her American drawl clearly audible from the other side, strained and shrill.

There was a pause.

She's on the telephone, Josephine thought frantically. Here I have my life falling apart around me while outside the neighbours are getting drunk and disorderly and having a good time and inside those two are acting for all the world as if I do not exist.

Josephine began to know what it was to want to kill.

A male American voice growled nasally through the door.

Puzzled, she crouched down and peered through the keyhole, could just see Garcia's back as he sat at his desk, his chair tipped back, no receiver in his hand, talking into thin air. The American lawyer began arguing with Millie and Garcia butted in. New York property laws. Disposal of New York leases. Company law. A company registered in Britain had no recourse to Chapter Eleven and would be fully liable for the terms of the lease.

They had a lease on the New York apartment. It must be to do with the personal assets fax.

The conference call ended.

'I *told* you we couldn't go for Chapter Eleven,' Millie yelled immediately. 'I told you and *told* you. We're registered in Britain. How many times do you need to hear it?'

'British law is *stupid*,' he yelled back.

'And calling lawyers about what we already know is stupid,' Millie shouted. 'We can't afford it.'

'I wanted to be *certain*.'

There was silence. Garcia's fulminating about Britain's shortcomings was familiar.

Now the call was over, they might be coming out. Retreating hastily, Josephine thought, Millie's in the know, worrying about money. That must mean Millie *was* part of the breakdown.

As long as she was here, there were no answers. Her presence made Garcia impregnable.

Hearing Garcia's door opening, Josephine backed into the drawing room and closed the door gently. Hosannah had recently had a brief affair with Brasso and the gleaming fire dogs caught her eye.

'Do I think,' she muttered to herself, 'twenty years in jail would be worth the absolute and total satisfaction of battering them both to death?'

Not really.

Slumped on the sofa facing away from her, its tall back hiding them, interrupted in the middle of an intense conversation about kicking parents out of your head, which was cool, and dying a nasty, lingering, boring, naff kind of death, which was uncool and stupid, Abigail and John Denver Jr froze. He put his finger to his lips and shook his head.

For a moment, the room was very still, hushed. They could hear Josephine's distraught breathing. Then a 747 descended towards Heathrow, followed by a Quantas jet, passing right over the roof, very low. Beneath the rising scream of its four engines, Abigail whispered, right in his ear.

'What's she doing?'

I don't know, said his shrug.

They stared at each other in consternation as Josephine's rage collapsed and she began to weep.

Abigail pulled a face and they had to sit quite still, trapped.

'Uncle Harry,' Sophia moaned. She had come down after a brief sleep, while the worst of the bottle of wine she had drunk wore off. Her head was heavy, ached, her eyes felt raw with crying.

In the dining room, cupboard doors and drawers stood wide, their contents strewn across the floor.

'What do you want?' Ron, padding up soundlessly, spoke right behind her, made her jump with fright.

'He said he would.'

'What are you talking about?'

'Uncle Harry,' she muttered wretchedly. 'Poltergeists make a mess like this.'

'Worse upstairs,' Ron said. 'You'd better come and look.'

'You're drunk.'

'*You* said you never wanted to be sober again.'

She collapsed at the unused table, still set for formal luncheon for four, its silver neatly set, John Denver's flowers wilted by the heat, tried to get her thoughts together. One huge thought buried all the others.

Benjie.

She gazed at the chaos. Then a thought did form itself. Obvious. She'd been asleep, he'd been drunk, and the front door open. Burglars.

'Did you call the police?'

'To report a *ghost*, Sophia?' His words were only a little slurred, his tone withering. 'Come on, look upstairs.'

'Oh, God.' Sophia surveyed the chaos of their bedroom where

somone had gone through every drawer, every cupboard, every shelf. 'I was in here,' she cried, the hair suddenly standing up on her neck.

'Passed out,' Ron said grimly.

'How could they do it? They've cut them up,' she said stupidly, picking up and fingering underwear slashed to ribbons. 'And used my scissors.' Her dressmaking scissors lay on the top of the chest of drawers in which he kept his sweaters, at the far side of the room.

'Left you a message,' he pointed out.

The ugly word was scrawled in lipstick on her mirror, blood-red.

'I'll go and call the police,' she whispered.

'And there's something else I noticed.'

'It was you, wasn't it?' she said hoarsely, her throat closed up with fear.

The photographs she had hidden carefully right behind the back of one of the drawers slid all over the carpet as he threw them at her. Benjie, sunburned and naked, looked up at her.

'There was only one day you got to stay in on your own,' Ron said matter-of-factly.

It had been too hot for the beach, too hot for the pool. She had pleaded a headache and, after an argument, Ron and Sandra had taken the hotel trip, souvenir shopping, together.

Sophia brushed the back of her hand across her eyes.

They had had three hours.

In the photographs they were laughing, lobster-faced, swimwear etched in white on their burned bodies.

'Knew you'd be naff enough to take photos.'

Benjie wanted something to remember her by.

'Fast worker,' Ron remarked distantly.

Falling in love was not what they meant, that time in the sea. A week, a long time on holiday, changed that, made them desperate.

Benjie had a fancy Japanese camera, set it on auto at the end of the enormous American bed. Some pictures were blurred because they were laughing so much. Some of them were not blurred at all. She glanced down with dread.

'Slut,' Ron said.

'I'm not a slut. I loved him, and now it's over.'

'Lies,' he went on, as if marvelling, swivelling his eyes to the ceiling as if begging God for understanding. 'All this time, lies, lies, lies.'

'No.'

'You miss him.' He stopped rolling his eyes around and said it kindly, as a statement of fact. 'Don't you?'

'Don't look at me like that.'

'How am I looking at you, Sophia?'

Sophia began to cry with terror, tears running and rolling down her face. 'As if you are sorry for me, patronising me.'

He seemed confused. 'Sophy, I'm trying to be reasonable. I understand. You want to be with Benjie.'

Sophia began to shake.

'Mr Nice and Solid Stockbroker with the ghastly wife. With *me*, it's another matter, isn't it?' he went on, rambling to himself. 'Boarding school at five. Buggered by the housemaster at ten. The odd divorce or two. No money. Wife has a sadist for a stepmother who taunts me in her bloody will. Harry in my front room for months, then leaves with bugger all of a handshake.' Ron's eyes were glassy. 'My son is an idiot who jumps off a cliff.' He frowned, seemed lost, but his maunderings were now completely sober.

She followed his every move as he wandered back and forth. 'Theo was an accident. He *loved* you. You were his dad.'

Ron pinched his mouth and considered. 'And my wife. You planning to go running to Benjie?'

Sophia's nerves snapped. 'He's *dead*,' she howled. 'They're all *dead*, Ron.'

He was exaggeratedly patient, talking to a foolish child, his eyes shining. She found herself staring past him, at the bottle of Prozac on the mantelpiece behind him, fear blooming in her stomach. The scissors he used to slash her clothes while she lay in a drunken sleep lay across the room.

Ron caught her easily as she ran for the door, stood barring her way. She opened her mouth and tried to scream but no sound came out.

'Poor Sophy.' He sounded full of sorrow. 'They're all dead. That's exactly what I *mean*.'

He reached for her. Sophia backed and backed, reached behind her and, as he came at her, brought the scissors down with all the strength she had.

He screamed.

In Josephine's garden, the birthday party froze, open-mouthed with horror.

Chapter Twenty-Four

For a moment all they could hear was water slapping the sides of the pool. Barney Darling barked uneasily, was nudged sharply by Emilia.

'That came from Sophia's house.' Bea Beamish's saying what they all knew brought them scrambling to their feet.

'That was a *real* scream. Not someone playing.' Millie, opening Garcia's door, turned back and listened. 'Did you hear it?'

Garcia, talking urgently on the telephone to Vivian, was holding the receiver with his shoulder. 'Couldn't not. Where'd it come from?'

'Excuse me?' said Vivian.

'Where did it come from?' Garcia repeated.

'Over there,' said Millie.

'There was an alarming noise from a neighbour's house,' Garcia told Vivian. 'I think we'd better go and have a look. I'll call you back.'

As he rang off, Millie ran into the hall, found Josephine by the front door, scared.

'Someone needs to go and look,' she said anxiously.

Hosannah appeared from the kitchen.

'Put that away,' Garcia snapped.

Hosannah looked straight through him and tightened her grip on the cleaver.

'For God's *sake*, Hosannah.'

'I think we should have a look before we call the police.' Emmanuel said calmly, coming in from the garden. He glanced round. 'No cleavers, Hosannah. Put it away.'

Abigail and John Denver Jr appeared in the sitting-room doorway.

'We should call nine eleven?' he asked.

'Nine nine nine,' Abigail said.

'I'll call,' said Melissa, running into the kitchen where the portable was on its hook.

'Stay here and we'll go,' Emmanuel said quietly to everyone else. 'Just me and Garcia.'

Hosannah growled and muttered.

'*Not* you, Hosannah.'

'Where's Emma?' Josephine asked Abigail who looked scared, shrank into her black robes, and shook her head.

Garcia and Emmanuel reached the landing on the first floor, where PGs' rooms, cluttered with disordered clothes and suitcases, stood empty. Across the landing's threadbare carpet, Ron and Sophia's bedroom door was partly open.

'Ron?' Emmanuel sniffed. '*Blood,*' he whispered. 'Ron must've flipped his lid.'

Garcia pushed the door cautiously. Blood, on the walls, the bed, seeping across the carpet, smelling strong and hot, sour and coppery.

For a moment, no one breathed.

'He can't be alive,' Emmanuel muttered. 'But check while I talk to her. Don't touch Ron except to see if he's got a pulse. Oh, *shit*.'

'Put him down,' Hosannah growled, creeping up the stairs behind them, pushing past.

Garcia grabbed her. 'Get out. You'll make things worse.'

Her eyes went to Ron, raised themselves to Sophia, gleaming with surprise. 'How? What's she goin' to do? Cut my ears off?' she jeered. 'This time, *I* got a knife.' She wrenched free from Garcia and leaped, straight past Emmanuel, into the room.

Sophia raised bloody scissors. Emmanuel shot out a long arm and jerked Hosannah's arm high in the air.

'*Drop* it,' he shouted. 'It's all right, Sophia. Sophy, it's OK, I've got her. You can put them down. No one is going to hurt you.'

As Garcia quietly crossed the room under cover of the scuffle and felt Ron's neck, praying for a pulse and finding none, Barry's voice called from downstairs. The police were on their way.

One car was in Sheen, one in Mortlake when the call went out from Twickenham. The two police Rovers picked up speed, nosing through late-evening traffic, weaving in and out, on both sides of the road. Skidding through a red light, the Sheen car got stuck behind an elderly woman who panicked, stalled and blocked the road. Because of that small delay, the Mortlake car was first on the scene, followed a minute later by an ambulance howling like a banshee, flashing every blue light it possessed.

'Where's the casualty?' yelled the eager young paramedic with crew-cut hair, poised for action like SAS about to storm an embassy, freshly trained and keen as mustard. He came bounding out, overdosed on adrenaline from screaming around South London on the wrong side of the road, creating mayhem. On the far side of a small courtyard he could see the open front doors to three large houses.

'Peculiar things going on here,' he cried, and for the first time felt a twinge of fear.

Inside Ron and Sophia's house, the tension was palpable.

'It's awfully quiet up there,' Gordon muttered.

Led by Babe, padding on silent bare feet and flexing his muscles like Arnold Schwarzenegger, the birthday party, hearing help howling to a halt outside, was creeping doubtfully up the stairs, consumed by curiosity, terror, and fascination disguised as needing to see if anyone wanted rescuing.

The women stood at the foot of the stairs, staring up.

'Garcia? Emmanuel?'

John Denver Jr looked fearfully up the stairs and whispered to Gordon that he had a nasty premonition about what might lie up there.

Melissa hustled her way through the little crowd and began to climb, followed by Barry. As they reached the landing, they hung back, peered around.

'Which room?' Gordon whispered.

'In front of you,' Barry whispered back.

Babe pushed the door wide.

'Oh my God.'

So much blood. Garcia kneeling by Ron, lying on the floor. Hosannah, relieved of her cleaver, standing guard stubbornly with her arms folded, watching Sophia like a scruffy alley cat eyeing a rat. Emmanuel talking quietly to Sophia as she sat on the end of her bed with bloodied hands, not looking at him.

Melissa edged forward, peered past Babe.

'Poor woman,' she said softly from the safety of the doorway.

Then Bea came up behind her, took one look and brought welcome distraction from the horrors by keeling over, fainting dead away, having to be taken carefully down the stairs as the paramedic and the police came running through the front door.

From the entrance hall, all the duty officer could see at first was a crowd, some fancily dressed, others in wet bathing suits, towels hastily thrown round shoulders, bare legs and feet.

'They're up there,' Samantha pointed, called. 'If you'd all get out of the way, the police need to get past.' She hauled at Bea Beamish who was coming round, and added, 'My husband's up there.'

'What the *hell's* going on?' demanded a familiar, beautifully articulated voice, projecting itself with professional ease over all the clatter and urgent voices.

'Bloody murder,' Barry answered weakly over the banisters as the police officer squeezed his way towards him.

'Will you get this lot *out*,' the duty officer yelled.

The newcomer gazed up, astounded.

'*Luvvie.*' Melissa breathed a long, expiring breath. 'Oh, Luvvie.'

The officer from the second car galvanised himself into action. 'Out, out, all downstairs. Come on, now. Downstairs and out, but no one leave. *No one leave.*'

'Get out but don't leave,' Millie said plaintively. 'What *do* you want us to do?'

'We will go back to my house,' Josephine said.

'Next door, officer,' called Gordon, suddenly in charge. 'Come on, all of us next door. Let the police deal with it.'

The birthday party, traumatised, sheepish, obeyed and began to shuffle back where it had come from. They went into Josephine's big kitchen, began giving names and addresses and shocked, hushed accounts of what they had seen to two police officers.

'I think,' said one officer to Sherrine, 'what we could all do with, my love, is a hot sweet cup of tea.'

Next door, as the grey-haired duty officer hesitated on the threshold of the bedroom and surveyed the scene, the other man began sealing the front door behind the departed party with scene-of-crime tape.

The duty officer walked gingerly between the bloodstains on the carpet, squatted and felt for Ron's pulse.

'Nothing, is there?' said Garcia.

'Who is this gentleman?'

Sophia looked across. 'My husband.'

'What happened?'

Garcia stood up. 'We got here too late,' he said sadly.

'He was going to kill me,' Sophia said in a small-girl voice.

'You stabbed him to death?' the officer asked.

Sophia looked down at Ron expressionlessly and nodded slowly.

Hosannah muttered angrily in Croat.

'And who are you?' the officer demanded.

'Balkan peasant,' Hosannah snapped.

The young paramedic, bright-eyed with excitement and tension, arrived in the doorway on the heels of his partner.

'Don't go in,' the older paramedic said quickly.

One look and he swayed on his feet. 'Life extinct?' he croaked, as he had been taught.

'They sent me a rookie?' asked the policeman sarcastically, then added more gently, 'There's nothing you can do for this poor gentleman.' He turned to Sophia. 'I am arresting you for serious assault and you will come with us to the police station.'

'I'm a lawyer,' Emmanuel said. 'I'll come with her.'

'Everyone leave the room and the house. Don't touch or take anything and be careful where you put your feet,' the officer added tetchily. 'Don't go treading in blood and wrecking the scene.'

A small group of the curious stood around outside, waiting to see what was going on. The sky was a deepening blue and in the warm dusky light streetlamps began to flicker on.

When Sophia, bundled into a third car between two officers, was on her way to Twickenham, the duty officer walked carefully out of the room the way he'd walked in, made sure the house was secured and all witnesses except Emmanuel coralled next door. Then he called the Force Medical Examiner who would pronounce Ron dead and remove the body. Finally he called his detective superintendent, who would bring in the CID.

* * *

Detective Superintendent Jock Wilson was also enjoying a barbecue in his back garden when his bleeper went off. His wife listened to the conversation that followed and pulled a face.

'Couldn't you finish your supper, at least?'

Before she'd finished protesting, he was gone.

Jock Wilson was a big man, tall and broad and stocky, whose bulk filled doorways and whose head bumped lintels when he forgot to duck. He rubbed his forehead where he had banged it on Sophia's bedroom doorway. 'AMIT on their way?'

The duty officer nodded. It was his duty to assign an officer to log the area major investigation team's arrivals and departures, along with the doctor's, the photographers', the forensic scientists' and everyone else who had reason to attend the scene of crime.

'Witnesses?' the detective inspector asked.

'Next door,' the duty officer explained. 'They were in the middle of a party in the garden, heard a scream and came round to see what was going on.'

'Did anyone see her do it?'

'We're taking statements.'

'Mr Goddard and Mr Gilmour say he was dead when they got here.'

The Force Medical Examiner arrived and pronounced Ron dead.

Jock Wilson pointed without touching it to a packet on the bedroom mantelpiece. 'Looks like they were both on Prozac.'

'Must have been suffering from depression,' said the police doctor.

'I've read that stuff can make you flip your lid.'

'It has a mixed reputation,' answered the doctor. 'In the USA recently one chap ran amok with a shotgun. He'd been taking Prozac for two or three years and one day he just broke out and I don't recall offhand how many he killed.'

'Looks like we've got a Prozac victim here.'

The doctor got to his feet. 'Difficult to prove. When you're ready, you can take him away.'

A police photographer arrived and began unpacking his equipment.

'Trouble is,' went on the doctor, 'people take that stuff for depression and they say it works. But sometimes people are depressed for a very good reason and *should* be miserable. If you go suppressing something, say bereavement, you're damming up powerful feelings.'

'Makes people feel good when they shouldn't?'

'Precisely,' the doctor agreed. 'Whatever happened to good old-fashioned guilt and grief and getting over things?'

'Instant sunshine,' the duty officer ruminated, gazing at Ron. 'Fine and good until something upsets the apple cart. *Then* look what happens.'

The doctor peeled off his gloves fastidiously. 'If you think that's the case here, you'd better get a psychiatrist to see her before you interview her.'

Jock Wilson took himself off to do exactly that.

'You can make a statement now or come down to the station later. We've got forms with us, if you'd rather do it here,' one of the officers in Josephine's kitchen said. At the thought of going over what she'd seen and writing it down, Melissa began to cry.

'I'll bring her to the station,' Luvvie pronounced in his best Rumpole of the Bailey voice.

Melissa wept harder than ever, because he was back.

'Where are Garcia and Josephine?' John Denver Jr asked, looking round all their shocked faces.

'Mr Goddard was in the bedroom,' one of the officers said, busy taking Babe's name, address and account of events with an expression of ill-disguised wonder at the tousled bleached hair, brightly painted nails and pouting lips.

'It was my daughter-in-law's birthday party we were at,' Emilia said, putting the remains of Barry's whisky into her tea with a shaky hand.

Suddenly, in the face of tears running down Melissa's face, the shocked trance broke.

Gordon, gentle but showing unexpected qualities of leadership, handed out tissues, made extra strong tea, comforted Sherrine who did not understand anything at all.

Emma, though, crept over, put her head in Hosannah's lap and cried and cried and cried.

'I feel like hell.' Josephine rinsed her face and leaned on the white marble edge of the basins in their bathroom, peered in the mirror. Pinched and haggard, her eyes looked as if she hadn't slept in weeks and the coffee silk jacket looked as though it *had* been slept in for weeks.

'We all do,' Garcia answered wearily. 'We have to go down and talk to the police.' He took off his shirt, which had blood on it, splashed cold water over his face.

'Garcia.'

He shook drops from his hair and grunted.

'I can't bear any more.'

'I doubt any of us could,' he said shortly.

Josephine sat down on the top of the lavatory. 'Are you having an affair with Millie?'

She held his stunned gaze.

'If not Millie, someone.'

He turned away, leaned over the basin on his hands and stared down the plughole.

'I'm so confused and muddled and miserable, I don't even think it matters who it is. I've had enough, and I want a divorce. I don't want a lot of haggling. I don't want your money, just somewhere to live, then I'll look after myself.'

'You may well have to look after all of us.'

'That doesn't make sense.'

'Why?' he asked into the plughole. 'Why, right now?' The bathroom lights drew black rings round his exhausted eyes.

'Soph used to adore Ron.' Josephine's voice trembled. 'I used to adore you. I can't see any point—'

'You *are* the point.'

'I've heard you. I've sunk to listening outside doors and I've heard you plotting and planning with Emmanuel and Millie. Chapter Eleven and all that. What are you doing? Selling the apartment and hiding money so you don't have to pay me if we split up?'

'You've been spying?' He spoke to himself. 'How odd.'

'Who's Vivian? Why are you sending lists of assets to Vivian?'

'Vivian,' he answered woodenly, 'is the receiver. He takes GGIL over on Monday morning. We were obliged to give him a list of our personal assets that could be involved in the liquidation. Until now, he's been advising us on our duties as directors, to make sure we complied with the law. From Monday, he works on behalf of our creditors.'

Josephine said nothing.

'We are bankrupt,' Garcia broke the silence eventually. 'Chapter Eleven is American company law. It allows companies who are potentially viable to trade their way out of insolvency if the judge agrees.' He rubbed his eyes until they were red. 'I have to go and talk to the police, then we still have work to do. We've lost more than three million sterling in the last month, Jo.'

'Ron is lying dead,' she said evenly, 'and you're thinking about *money.*'

'Tom Morrissey bled us dry,' he cried angrily. 'I'm not *only* thinking about money. I'm sad and angry and confused, like you. Sophia deserves to go to prison, and will. Tom Morrissey kills a twenty-eight-year-old company and there's not a thing we can do. What I'm worried about is you and me and Emma.'

She stood up. 'I don't think so. You've never worried about Emma and me. You worry about making money. Deals. Catching planes. Rushing about like a whirlwind. You've never had your feet on the ground long enough to *know* Emma. I'm sorry the company's in trouble, but you worry about money, Garcia. Nothing else comes close.'

There was a heavy knock on the door. She opened it to find the duty officer outside, his fist raised to bang again. He lowered it.

'Mrs Goddard?'

'Unfortunately.'

He looked taken aback. 'Would you and your husband come down before we go? We want to arrange for you to give statements.'

'Certainly.'

Without looking at Garcia, Josephine left the room.

Lights blazed as the area major investigation team did its work in Ron and Sophia's house. Slowly, the birthday party began to drift back to the other houses.

Babe hesitated at their front door.

'Sorry,' he said.

'I doubt it.' Barry opened the door to their flat. 'When do you want to clear out?'

Babe jigged his legs, looked uncertain.

Barry marched inside, grabbed a huge, battered suitcase from under the bed and threw it open.

'Then you can bloody well go *now.* Take your stuff and get out.'

It said it all, he thought, when Babe was gone. Four years living together, and everything he possessed went into a single case.

'Of course,' Luvvie said, when Melissa asked anxiously.

'You'll stay?'

'I'll stay.'

'Luvvie?'

'What?'

'I am *truly* sorry about the underclothes and the bus. I *swear* never to do it again.'

'You want to bore me rigid by behaving yourself?'

'You can overstep the line,' Melissa said grimly. 'I learned that tonight. And how much I need you.'

They went to bed and clung to each other like they used to when they first met.

'They can use Emilia's old rooms. They'll have to sleep on the floor and do the best they can. At least it isn't cold,' Josephine said.

John Denver Jr shepherded the bewildered group of PGs into their new quarters. Obediently back late from McDonalds, they had gathered in the courtyard, finding police tape all over their front door and nowhere to sleep.

When John Denver Jr had explained to them what had happened, he left them, scared and muted, sorting out blankets, to walk Bea and Abigail home.

Gordon put Sherrine, who had meant to barter for the bike and forgotten all about it, into a cab, to go home to her sheik.

Emmanuel came back from the police station where he said Sophia would see a psychiatrist in the morning, before being interviewed. He and Samantha went home.

Millie, exhausted, was found asleep with her head on the kitchen table, surrounded by a sea of mugs and milk bottles.

'We are all shattered,' Josephine said sadly, waking Millie up. 'You'd be better off in bed. It's already Sunday morning.

Garcia has told me what is happening tomorrow. Go get some sleep.'

Everyone seemed to have gone. She turned lights off, went leaden-footed up the stairs.

'You wouldn't think you'd sleep after a night like this, but I'm dead,' she said, going into their bedroom.

Garcia didn't answer. He sat downstairs in his study, going over what she had said, until a bit before dawn he fell asleep on his sofa.

Hosannah shook Emma gently, sitting on the step at the back of the garage, in the warm, dark night. Emma burrowed into her big squashy breasts and cried harder.

'You got to go to bed.'

She felt Emma shake her head.

'Look,' Hosannah drawled, more than usually Lancashire because of her extreme distress. 'You a big baby, or what? You think Irma behave like a turkey? She's seen a whole heap a dead body. *And* friends.'

'It was *Soph*,' Emma screamed, muffled, beating at Hosannah with her hands. 'It was Soph, it was Soph, it was *Soph*. Why did she do it? Do you know why?'

'Aye, aye. You big, big baby. It was Soph and she don't deserve it. Innocence and Experience, remember? You want a fag?'

As Emma wept hysterically, Hosannah held her firmly, rocked her to and fro, to and fro. The unshed tears, dammed up since leaving friends to die, her home to vandals and strangers, her life in ruins, to become an uneasy visitor in a foreign land, streamed in an unending torrent down her face as she, too, wept for Ron and Sophia.

Chapter Twenty-Five

Sunday, they were survivors. Dazed, disorientated, the world a new, changed, unfamiliar place with Ron no longer in it.

The YMCA and YWCA claimed, in mid-August, to be full, but Josephine persuaded them to take the PGs as emergencies. Hosannah, unnaturally subdued, looked wrung out and spent a lot of time, when the PGs had gone, cleaning what had been Emilia's rooms much more thoroughly than usual. Garcia spent a lot of time alone in his study. Millie called home, cried, then ate a large pile of peanut butter and jelly sandwiches.

'Comfort food,' she told Emma wanly. 'Help yourself.'

'Not hungry,' Emma said, puffy in the face. Listlessly, she picked one up, peered at its filling, sniffed at it, pulled a face and bit a tiny corner off.

Ten minutes later, they made another plateful.

'You know,' Emma said sincerely, 'I'm not ready for all this.'

'Peanut butter?'

'Grown up. Relationships and stuff.'

'No,' Millie answered. 'But don't think it's always like that.'

Emma helped herself to another sandwich. 'I'm quite glad I'm a virgin.'

Millie nodded and didn't seem at all surprised.

Sunday night, Millie got up and wandered the dark house and garden, unable to sleep. She met Garcia downstairs in the kitchen, boiling the kettle and watching Sky television at four in the morning.

'Can't sleep either,' he muttered. 'Tea?'

'At least you guys have each other,' she said. 'It's not so bad for you. Yes, it is. I didn't mean that.'

He filled the teapot and set it on the table. Dawn turned the sky milky, the first birds cheeping.

'Well, that's something else you and I have to talk about,' he told her reluctantly, feeling empty as a husk. 'It might not only be GGIL that just went under.' He explained, briefly.

'How can she do this *now*?' Millie demanded, furious.

Garcia said all he knew was it was Monday morning and time to get dressed.

At nine o'clock, they called all their staff together and announced that GGIL had ceased trading and their jobs no longer existed. Vivian had taken over, GGIL was no longer in Garcia and Millie's jurisdiction.

Why?

One of the bitterest pills was knowing they could never openly say who had done the damage, not even what had happened; they would have to let gossip and speculation run as it would.

'Can't even defend ourselves to the trade,' Garcia said bitterly, coming out of the meeting where, eventually, everyone had cried.

Vivian was efficient. The removal vans were at the door by eleven and by four that afternoon two teams of men had stripped the building like locusts.

In his shirt sleeves, Garcia reviewed his empty office, all the pictures gone from the walls, books from shelves, only dusty marks showing where things had been that morning.

In the next room, Tom Morrissey's replacement and a new assistant had worked through the weekend and, haggard, were still at their desks. Three Australian secretaries, kept on as a skeleton staff, chattered cheerfully over the kettle, making coffee as if nothing had happened.

Vivian would sell the building's contents, from computers to Bic Biros, from the boardroom table to the company's archive of fashion magazines. The small amount that second-hand office furniture would raise would go towards paying their debts. Garcia began making a list of what he could buy from himself to keep going for the moment and help furnish future offices.

'Cannibalism,' Millie observed, reading it.

'The estate agent values the building at three-quarters of a million and we borrow against the sale,' Garcia muttered.

They needed seed money, for starting again, which the property sale would give them. Starting again was bleak, neither of them young any longer or full of zest. Starting again was finding a way through a maze of decisions: which contracts could be saved, which licences renegotiated, which parts of the business merged with others. A lot depended on other people; they would draw deeply on their reputation in the trade. More than half the paths would lead to dead ends, requiring daily new directions.

Decisions, decisions, decisions.

Late in the afternoon, banging and shouting outside on the pavement became audible even at the top of the house where they sat.

'Press and disgruntled creditors,' one of the Australians said, going past to the loo. 'They've been shoving abuse through the letter box.'

The telephone rang incessantly. It took time for the news to get round. Clients rang expecting service as usual, freelance staff rang and were told they were not needed, furious creditors wanted to know about their money and the press wanted a statement. A reporter slid in behind Vivian's assistant as he came in with sandwiches, the front door unlocked for a moment.

The man ranted up and down the echoing reception hall, shouting for the story.

'Get the police,' cried one of the Australian girls, scared.

'Let's get rid of him,' Garcia said, tired of the fuss.

The two accountants and he hustled the reporter out of the building. Garcia peered down at the group on the pavement. 'They're out for blood,' he observed. 'Yours and mine.'

'Other people will go under because of us.'

'I don't know how I can say it after this weekend, but I could strangle Tom Morrissey and enjoy it.'

'You can count on one thing,' Millie said with a strained grin. 'The creditors' meeting will be worse. Tomatoes and rotten eggs. Look at it as a learning curve, Garcia, honey.'

Garcia turned away from the window.

'For once in your life,' she grinned, 'you'll have stay mum and keep your temper.'

Vivian had drummed it into them: 'The creditors will go for you like wolves. Answer direct questions with short answers. If in doubt, say you don't know and refer the questioner to me. On no account react or lose your temper.'

'We're *supposed* to be registering a new company, planning strategy, rescuing a licensing business, cataloguing what we can salvage from here, finding a buyer for our premises and falling over ourselves to be helpful to Vivian who will submit a detailed report to the DTI on our performance as directors,' Garcia snarled. 'How about making a start?'

'Sure. I was only going to say, duck when you see a hand go up, and whatever you do, don't turn up in your very best suit.'

Their new financial director stuck his head round the door, beaming. 'Want to know the good news?' He sounded as though he could hug himself.

'Is there any?' Garcia demanded rudely.

'The staff went off thinking they wouldn't get paid this month, isn't that right?'

'They won't,' Millie said. 'They'll gripe all over the place about it to people who matter and who will think we deliberately fixed it so they didn't get their wages. It'll all help sink us.'

The accountant, a tall, cadaverously thin young man with light blue eyes, laughed a laugh of sheer joy. 'I wrote to the bank to give them notice that we couldn't cover this month's payroll.'

'Get on with it,' Garcia growled.

'I used a second-class stamp.'

Millie's head shot up in instant understanding. 'It went through?'

'They got the letter today,' he said smugly. 'There's nothing they can do.'

'There is a God after all,' Millie said reverently.

'Everyone's paid. The bank was even rather nice about it and showed a sense of humour.'

'A second-class stamp,' Garcia howled. 'You fucking genius.'

The three of them rolled around the bare little office, shrieking and crying with laughter.

One of the Australian girls put Emmanuel through to Garcia's extension. He was still breathless with laughter.

'Thought you'd want to know. Sophia's fit to plead,' Emmanuel said.

Garcia's laughter died away. 'I'm surprised. How long will she get?'

'Ten to fifteen, for unpremeditated murder. If they can argue she flipped on Prozac, probably less.'

'And Tom Morrissey walks free.'

Later, during the evening, Emmanuel called again.

'Vivian can pursue Tom in the courts.'

'He won't. His job is to maximise his firm's fees and collect for the creditors, not get vengeance for Millie's and my failures.'

Millie didn't accept that it was a joint failure. That, too, was a source of grief.

'You know, this may not be the disaster you take it to be. You have a thriving second company that has been propping GGIL up. Without that incubus in Islington and the upkeep of a broom cupboard of the most expensive real estate in the world in Tokyo, you and Millie can cut free, concentrate on consultancy, at which you are outstandingly brilliant.'

'Cheers,' Garcia said ironically.

'It's one of your businesses that's gone under, not your whole lives.'

'I like your choice of words,' Garcia observed bitterly. 'It seems Jo wants to cut free.'

The lack of response told him Emmanuel already knew.

'What with your fees for this, and your matrimonial department's fees, you'll put in some awesome billing. I shouldn't be surprised if I'm not personally responsible for half your yearly profits.'

'Do you think Jo knows her mind?'

'You tell me, since she seems to confide in you,' Garcia answered grimly. 'We've talked. She admits it's lousy timing. She's fed up being left alone and now she's got this idea that if Sophia had seen the light and left, she wouldn't be sitting where she is. Jo reads that as telling her to act. So far as being on her own is concerned,' Garcia admitted, 'for the immediate future, while we get back on our feet, it can only get worse.'

'Thought about going to Relate?' Emmanuel asked with maddening cheerfulness.

Garcia shuddered. '*You* never went to Relate.'

'I'm a serial monogamist. You are monogamous. Different style altogether.'

'I never saw this coming,' Garcia pleaded. 'I couldn't, could I? Like Tom Morrissey's black hole.'

Silence told him louder than words that Emmanuel was not at all sure, on either count, that he unreservedly agreed.

Relate, indeed. For the tenth time that evening, Garcia rejected it. The idea was preposterous. When they got home, both shattered, Millie said she would go straight up to bed.

Garcia went to his study, threw his briefcase into a corner and slumped in his chair. Facing the sleeping, darkly shadowed garden, he could just make out the pool, a gleam of water beyond the yellow light spilling from the house. He stared into the dark at where he knew the gap in the wall was. Sophia's garden would soon look uncared for and it would be no time at all before the Australian stepbrother wanted to sell it. Garcia wondered briefly what the legal situation was if Sophia went to prison for a long stretch.

The fax hummed passively among a chaos of personal papers and piles of old *Vogue*s and *Harper's Bazaar*s hastily stolen from the office archives. They went back many years, and he took them for sentimental reasons, not seeing why Vivian should impound them.

Ron had died in a mess of blood; GGIL died in a mess of confusion, disorder, clutter, rooms abruptly torn apart, their carpets scuffed and worn where desks had stood. He was about to give in to the longing to weep that had overtaken him when he had dismissed his staff, when he froze, turned to find Josephine watching him.

'Have you eaten anything?'

'Yes. Thanks.'

The tears would have eased him, but they dried, from shame, at the sound of her voice. In fact, he had eaten nothing, was nauseous. The brandy bottle, he thought longingly. Or sleeping pills. Better still, both.

'I keep hearing Millie crying in the night.'

'Sorry she disturbs you.'

'I don't mean it like that. If I'm asleep, do you get up and cry with her?' She meant it compassionately.

Wordlessly, he shook his head, fumbling for enough energy to get angry, so much easier, more businesslike, than grief.

'I'm *really* sorry about the company.'

Yes, she was, but he sensed clearly that that was not what she had waited up to say.

'Garcia, there's never going to be a right time for us to talk. You'll be away more than ever now, putting it all back together again.'

He had admitted to Emmanuel that she was right. Vivian's demands were consuming and urgent. Millie swung from rage to tearful hysteria to intensely focused strategic planning; her volatile moods disrupted his. Business survival was now or never. Like an exhausted swimmer racing for a distant shore pursued by a school of sharks, he felt threatened by distraction, by having to drag his thoughts into domestic effort; he couldn't face exhausting, emotionally negotiated conciliations.

'It's late,' he said, getting up to fetch the brandy. 'I've got to be out by five. We've got a frantic schedule tomorrow.'

'Garcia, I don't want to talk about your schedule. I need to know what *you* think we're going to do.'

She would no longer be deflected. As the clouds that had brought late-afternoon rain cleared, he could see the fine sliver of a crescent moon hanging in the midnight sky. Seven in the evening, said the international clock on his desk, displaying New York time. A *ping* from the telephone told him that Millie had been talking to someone on an extension upstairs. Probably her banker who was giving them advice.

'I'm not thinking rationally. Too tired,' he tried. 'Let's go to bed.'

'No.'

'OK.' He attempted heartiness. 'Want a brandy?'

'Uhuh.'

'I do.' He fetched the bottle and a glass, planted them on his desk and in the green-shaded light confronted her cautiously.

'I want you to put it on your *schedule* that we are getting a divorce.'

Garcia swallowed his brandy in one gulp, coughed until his eyes watered. 'My schedule's full,' he gasped. He patted himself on the chest, breathed normally, helped himself to another. 'Answer's *no.* I don't want to do anything so hasty.'

'Divorce by consent takes two years. Living apart. That's not hasty. Will you move out, or shall I?'

'No one's moving anywhere. You can have a temporary separation while I go to the Far East grovelling and leave it that,' Garcia roared, brandy hitting his over-exhausted brain like a sledgehammer. 'I haven't got time for all this nonsense.'

'Being married to you is one long temporary separation,' she cried.

'It's how I pay the bills,' Garcia snapped.

'It's how you avoid being close to me.'

He clutched his head and tried to remember what it felt like to have a good night's sleep and wake up rested, feeling sane.

'What grounds do you imagine you have?'

'If we wait two years, we don't need grounds. Anyway, I tried to tell you when Ron died.'

He turned on her, appalled. Her mind was made up to wreck what remained of his life with a terrible, stubborn naivety.

'I can't afford divorce,' he shouted. 'I can't afford a fucking *taxi*, Josephine, never mind alimony.'

'I don't want alimony.'

'My mother, if you must know, thinks you're going mad.'

'Really?'

She didn't care what his mother thought. She didn't care what anyone thought and she didn't want taking care of. Deepening self-doubt wormed and squirmed in his gut. To quell the sickness, show some small defiance, he poured himself another brandy.

Chapter Twenty-Six

'They are going,' Josephine had said firmly. 'It will do them good to get out of here.'

The buzz of the alarm woke him at four, while it was still dark, and for a moment he panicked, thinking, I have to catch a plane.

Emilia and Emma had to catch a plane. To Seville. For two weeks, for the holiday Emma felt deprived of when all her friends were away.

They didn't leave for *hours* and he was only going to the office.

He realised the bed beside him was empty and lay, eyes closed, trying to focus his half-awake thoughts, still very drunk.

Millie stood in front of him, contorted with rage, accusing, accusing . . . *you're so dumb* . . . and he was dumb . . . lips wouldn't move as her eyes became Vivian's, sharp as lasers, probing for weakness and guilt. Vivian submitted a report on him to the Department of Trade and Industry where suddenly, vividly, his father appeared, sitting behind a huge desk, sipping whisky for breakfast.

'Let Papa drink his tea in peace,' Emilia said in Spanish, turning her back at the far end of the long room.

Garcia tried to read the report, written in Japanese, but a column of ants crawled over it and got in the way. Papa, indifferent, stared into his glass, morose, swirling the dark amber liquid round and round. Funny-smelling tea, funny look in Papa's eyes. Moist. Grown-ups don't drink tea in a *glass*. Even a child smelled a rat in that one. He could smell it now, lying in the empty, rumpled bed.

The dream dissolved. It was his own brandy breath he could smell.

Josephine last night, as she watched him drink his way steadily through much of the bottle, had a look he recognised, after years of blotting it out.

His own. Watching his father.

The painful image formed.

Papa. Clever, gifted, successful, uneducated Papa, a self-made man whom nobody taught to look after his money, drinking away the agony of failure and bankruptcy, who sank to the bottom of the whisky bottle, out of control, and died an angry, defeated death. All he left his only child was indolent, frivolous, feckless Emilia, lifelong obligations and a frightening mountain of debt.

'Look after your mother,' his father had ordered, his voice a breathy whisper, suddenly rallying behind the green hospital screens to meet his heir's eye with a last, exhausted appeal in his own. 'Look after everything for me, won't you?'

Garcia nodded a deathbed promise, which he faithfully kept.

Control freak. Emma's favourite insult. What did she know? He was eighteen when Papa died. By the time the debts were paid and he began to have a little money in the bank, working an eighteen-hour day to pay bills and look after people had become normal, being in control an unbreakable habit. Josephine *asked* him to look after her. That was how they met.

Manhattan. Seventy-four.

Garcia had been covertly inspecting the ladies wear displays in Bloomingdale's (with a view to suggesting to them how they could do them one hell of a lot better).

August, the city streets so hot and humid, he could have wrung out his shirt. Ruminating on Bloomingdale's, he sat in a bar where heavy rock fought with air conditioning, each trying to make the more horrible noise, idly watching puddles forming underneath the air-conditioning units as they struggled with sluggish, unbreathable air. Ninety-eight per cent humidity. He felt like a turtle in a tepid tank, nursing Jack Daniels with melting ice floating in it, wondering why he had ordered a drink he didn't really like.

'For heaven's sake, pretend you know me.' A voice, an unmistakable, cut-glass English voice hissed sibilantly through all the noise and babble. A girl grabbed at his arm. 'Please.'

A needle-sharp observer of places and people, after one first sidelong glance he could have described her as precisely as a photograph. About five foot five, narrow shoulders, thin arms, fine wrists. Slim. Plain cotton shift with no bra and very small breasts. Dark blonde, thick, straight hair in a pony tail. Eyes hidden behind dark glasses, in a bar so pretentiously ill lit you could read the wine prices only if you held the list right up to your nose. Poseur.

As he turned away, a stocky man with the build of a bouncer and the face of a frog came after her, fought his way through the crowd, sidled up, clamped his mouth to her neck, breathing, 'C'mon, baby, loosen up,' while fumbling through the thin cotton of her dress for those child-like breasts.

Garcia looked round. No one else took any notice. The frog raised a bulging eye over her shoulder and met Garcia's face leaning menacingly into his.

'That's my *wife*.'

The frog let go.

Garcia glared at her, raised his wristwatch. 'I have been waiting for *hours*.'

'Sorry I'm late.' She swatted at her persecutor with an overstuffed shoulder bag. 'Stop *following* me. Pig.'

'Where've you been?' he demanded in the tones of a man who had a right to know.

'Waiting for the babysitter,' Josephine shot back, parking herself on the stool next to his. 'She was late.'

Bemused, the frog looked from one to the other, shook his big head, backed off disappointed and cruised away in search of other prey.

'You are lucky, though through no fault of your own. He could just as easily have shot you or stuck you with a knife,' Garcia said pointedly. 'New York is a very dangerous place and you are being extraordinarily careless and British. How do you know *I* won't rape you?'

She shoved the dark glasses on to the top of the pony tail. Deep Welsh grey. Greenish grey. Thick lashes. Defensive. Young, pretty, very English with rosy skin. Defensive and foolish in New York.

Garcia sighed. She was *asking* for trouble.

'You're English, and you don't look at all like a rapist. That disgusting *creep*,' she snapped, 'who was harassing me, did. Anyhow. Thanks.'

Garcia slid his Jack Daniels down the bar to get the bartender's attention.

'It's tattooed on our foreheads, is it?'

'What do you mean?'

'You couldn't have known I was English until I opened my mouth. My mother is Spanish. Half New York is Hispanic. I look like everyone else.'

She shrugged.

'You shouldn't be let out of the nursery alone.' He stuck out a hand. 'Garcia Goddard, from London, over on business.'

Her hand was fine-boned with very long fingers and slightly large knuckles, her palm damp from the inferno on the streets.

'Josephine Crathorne, from London. Architect's assistant. Over on holiday. Looking at museums and art galleries and buildings.'

'What do you like?'

'The Chrysler Building,' she began eagerly.

'To drink.'

'Oh. Wine.'

'My wife,' Garcia said, as the man came up, 'would like to drink some good red Californian wine.'

New Year's Eve, eighteen months later, he took her back.

They had dinner downtown and emerged late, into winds off the water so cold, their sinuses froze.

'Drinks,' he gasped, his face numb, flagging a cab.

Past a few bare trees bending with the fierce wind, leafless branches dancing, braided with a myriad tiny lights, they swung by St Mark's Square and stopped in the Village.

'Oh, *here*! I was being chased, and you were drinking . . .' she paused, knowing him well, now. 'Why were you drinking Jack Daniels? You hate it.'

Inside, he ordered champagne.

'Last time we came here, we were play-acting. This time it's for real. Will you marry me, Jo?'

She'd known for a long time that she'd say yes.

Garcia took the diamond out of its jeweller's box, sparking and flashing fire in the blue light from the bar.

'With you, and a million in the bank, I shall be secure,' he joked as the clock stood at a quarter to twelve.

'No wonder you haven't got a million,' she said, turning the glittering ring. 'I should think you just spent it.'

'The million comes next, now I've got you. Which finger do I put this on?'

The hands on the clock jerked towards midnight and she held out her left hand.

'*Total* security,' he went on nervously, trying to wrench the diamond on to her middle finger, 'would be two million. We could live off the interest.'

Happy New Year.

'*This* finger, idiot.'

Happy New Year.

They were delirious with joy.

Afterwards, she realised, when it came to money, he really didn't know how to joke.

'He works too hard, like his father did,' Emilia told her when Garcia brought her home with the diamond on her hand. She peered at it closely. 'He has excellent taste.' Being my son. 'As he should.' Emilia gave a tiny, charming shrug as if to say, you and I, we understand each other . . .

'I lost a husband whom I *adored,*' Emilia persisted when Josephine, wondering what exactly she was supposed to understand, didn't answer. 'To ambition and overwork.' A tear swelled in the corner of her dark Spanish-Inquisition eye. 'A stroke. Shockingly sudden.'

'I thought Garcia's father . . .' Josephine, surprised and puzzled, was restrained by good manners from asking any questions.

'You'll find my mother has an infallible technique for dealing with unpleasantness or guilt,' Garcia told her later, when she asked about his father. 'Denial. You'll find if she doesn't like something, it simply never happened.'

Remembering his own words woke him to a crashing hangover. He stared at the ornate Victorian plasterwork on the bedroom ceiling that Josephine had restored with a toothbrush, a water spray and extraordinary patience, tried to ignore the exhaustion and alcohol burning in his eyes, to force himself to *think*.

They were all stressed out past breaking point. Quite apart from the business with Sophia, Josephine was stuck on the sidelines in the bankruptcy, unable to do anything except keep her own little business going and watch the real mayhem helplessly. Being able to do nothing must be worse than what Millie and he had to endure. At least they were involved, were in the thick of the action, making and taking decisions, already rebuilding a future.

Garcia got out of bed, steadied himself.

She didn't mean it about divorce. It would blow over when things calmed down.

He took a tepid shower, found Josephine asleep in the room next to Emma's, covered with only a sheet, her window wide open to the pearly dawn. She had done nothing more than go off to find somewhere to sleep that was fresh and cool. He tiptoed out and left her there, to wake Millie, dress and prepare for the daily round of frenzied work.

Chapter Twenty-Seven

His head throbbed like a pile-driver. Four hours of uncertain, nightmare-ridden sleep had left both of them looking like ghosts. Millie's mascara was smudged, he noticed, sitting across from her on the rattling, sparking Tube train. Signs of the times: trim, fastidious Millie already frayed, a clown at half past five in the morning.

Garcia's brain felt too big for his skull, the outlines of things dancing and flickering in front of his eyes. Brandy-and-Temazepam-dazzled, he wondered how addicts managed. Eighteen hours to face in the office, sweltering more from tension than from the continuing heatwave.

Walking from The Angel via the back streets, past closed and shuttered antique shops, along alleyways still cool and sweet from overnight showers, they let themselves in at half past five to find the alarm, lights, air conditioning and the few remaining computers all dead.

'*Well?*' Garcia demanded in frustration four hours later, snapping light switches at the bottom of the stairs on and off. 'How long are we going to let this go on?'

Millie, down in the lobby, paused in her transient watching of the removal of the few remaining fixtures and fittings, ensuring no one removed the desks, chairs, photocopier, fax and other necessities that they had bought second-hand from themselves through Vivian, so they could continue to work.

The half-filled removal van with its casual, indifferent men outraged her. The value of office furnishings here, in New York, in Tokyo – anywhere – lay almost entirely in the fact that they were *there*; to parcel them into random lots for auction merely satisfied the scorched-earth rules of liquidation, raised some meaningless sum of money to disappear into Vivian's pocket in the guise of professional fees.

'*We* have to get a new account.' She came up the stairs towards him, still watching the removal men below, so they couldn't hear her. 'GGIL is entirely Vivian's responsibility now.' She gestured at the almost empty building, spoke with the strained patience of a mother whose teenager baulked at his chores. 'This, until we move out, is us. NewCo.'

One of the men dropped the drawers of a metal filing cabinet on to the marble lobby floor with a teeth-grating crash.

Millie raised her voice in strident despair. 'NewCo. New start, honeychile. So when are you going to damn well fix the billings?'

Preoccupied by the complexities of international company law fizzing around his tired mind like firecrackers in an overload of intentions, facts, figures and a dozen combinations of ways forward out of all the mess, Garcia was simply and momentarily astonished.

NewCo, barely born, a Bermuda baby recently christened. Intercontinental Consultants.

The new baby needed an electricity account. It already had two first-class accountants wasting time sitting upstairs with no computers, three secretaries with no keyboards, gossiping and writing things by hand, their travel agent, to whom they owed money but who with true, New York Jewish mordant humour took it in his stride and was fixing Garcia's Sorry Trip to the Far East, and the Japanese trainee with the exquisite face, who had to keep looking up the word 'bankruptcy' in the dictionary. They were still without a cleaner.

No one to delegate the practical stuff to, no one with a metaphorical screwdriver sticking out of their pocket for the fixing of trivia. Seventy staff to seven; Chairman to Mr Fixit. Just like that.

'OK.'

It took a lot of arm-twisting bluster over the phone to get the electricity board to hurry itself, but after lunch the power came back on. Pleased with themselves, they settled down with a pile of notes to make overseas conference calls.

'I don't bloody believe this,' he yelled, hearing the line go dead.

'Why doesn't this work?' Millie demanded.

'I've a nasty feeling in my water that I know,' Garcia said, and called Vivian.

'Oh, you can make *local* calls,' Vivian explained with horrible cheerfulness. 'BT's one of your creditors. I can't authorise GGIL to run up any further bills.'

Vivian had *power*, would report to the Department of Trade and Industry on their performance as directors. Tantrums would look bad. Garcia gagged on the rage that rose to choke him, swallowed it, and said, 'I think I'd better come across and see you.'

Vivian was sitting in his own comfortable office, confronted by a row of telephones, and even more dapper than usual in a suit sharp enough to cut your finger.

'How can I help?' he asked, a busy man, collecting other people's money.

'You can reconnect my telephones to the international lines. And my fax,' Garcia suggested politely. 'Please.'

Vivian played with his pen. 'I already explained,' he pointed out.

'I run a global business,' Garcia argued, bloodshot, haggard, blinded by his headache. 'Excuse me.' He popped aspirins from a foil pack and chewed them briefly. 'We are working our butts off helping you collect money. I want to collect my creditors' money and pay our debts. How the . . . how am I supposed to do that when nine-tenths of my business is overseas and I haven't got a fax and phone?'

'Well.' Vivian inspected his pen carefully, not unsympathetic. 'I can't help you. Could you work from your home?'

It was unjust to hate someone for doing their job. Reminding himself that only last week he had been a fair and decent man, Garcia suppressed a frighteningly illuminating insight into how Sophia might have gone over the edge.

Then promptly had a brainwave.

'By the way,' Vivian called after him in that clipped, public school voice that ate through Garcia's brain. 'Bit of advice?'

Garcia turned at the door, ready to kill.

'Aspirins make ulcers. Want a recipe for hangovers? Never fails.'

Couldn't imagine the precious boy needing a hangover recipe but anything to humour those with power, especially when you knew they didn't know you were one up on them, could afford to be gracious. Garcia put on a grateful face.

Clutching a bit of paper detailing a mess of egg, milk, Tabasco sauce and other nastiness, he raced up his office stairs.

'Idiots,' he yelled, pulling the desk he had saved from Vivian away from the wall. Behind it, flush with the wall, were the jacks for his personal direct lines, unlisted and billed separately from the rest of the office. He plugged in a telephone; the dialling tone purred loud and clear. He whooped for joy and thrust it at Millie's ear. 'Isn't that the most *beautiful* sound in the world?'

'Right,' she said briskly. 'All you have to do to make it kosher is tell BT to bill us as Intercontinental Consultants.'

A lot of small victories win wars.

Garcia threw the aspirins and Vivian's hangover recipe in the bin, sent one of the Australian secretaries out for cheese and ham sandwiches, and told her to make a pot of coffee when she got back. He sat for fifteen minutes, writing and drawing 'Intercontinental Consultants' on a pad, doodling logos, trying for a brand-new image.

By the time he had eaten his sandwiches he had thrown his efforts on top of the aspirins, arranged for a design consultant to present ideas and half a dozen different styles for logos and new company stationery, and written a pile of faxes. Sitting in the desert of his empty floor, the fax whirred, flying electronic darts around the world. Depending on time differences and how much people already knew, how many rumours they had heard, responses were already coming in.

Millie, working head to head with Vivian over in his office ever since they had retrieved the secret jacks, arrived back early in the evening, stuck her head round the door and said her brain was fried, how was his?

Garcia looked up. 'Better since I gave up aspirin. The good news is the Swiss confirmed the bridging loan and we've had a bite at this place before the estate agent put it on the market. Lower offer than the valuation, but no commission. We can be in and out of debt in short order.'

She came in, picked at the remainder of his sandwiches and wandered off eating crusts. One of the Australian secretaries' quick footsteps crossed the creaking floor above his head, amplified by emptiness. The girl could have left already, as could his financial staff. Instead, most nights the staff worked as late as they did, still willing to believe in them, even though Bloody Beau Brummel over the way, and the creditors, would hound them and persecute them, hang them out to dry.

Which was only right and proper. But it was going to be bloody, *bloody* tough.

Islington was back from its summer holidays, back to work and school. It roared and sweated and hurried along its choked roads and grimy pavements, Upper Street a river of traffic until late in the evening when finally the sun sank, the air cooled and a delicate purple dusk settled over the city.

'Want a beer?' Garcia asked at half past nine, his hangover at last subsided into a ferocious thirst.

'If you go out and get it.'

He felt in his pocket for change. 'Ah.'

'There's a cash point round the corner,' Millie said, absorbed in the computer screen in front of her.

'All that's in our cash point, right now,' Garcia observed, 'is an overdraft.'

'We have to be able to afford a beer.'

'Holes in walls don't cough up on overdrafts. The cupboard is bare.'

Then she did look up.

They were forced to stop work earlier than they wanted, to catch the last Tube to Hammersmith and a late-night bus up Castelnau, having emptied their pockets on to the desk and discovered that between them they had not enough money – and no means of getting more – to stay on in the office and go home by taxi. Taxis weren't something, as Janey Morrissey had once discovered, you could get on credit.

Chapter Twenty-Eight

A couple of days after Emma and Emilia went to Spain, Abigail appeared, asking for Emma's address.

'Are you writing to her about something special?' Josephine inquired, not prying but interested, writing it out.

'I'm going to boarding school.'

Josephine's pen stopped. 'Where?'

'Same one as Emma. I'm going into the sixth form. I had an interview last week, and they accepted me, so long as I'm seven stone by half term.'

'Did they now?'

Abigail flushed painfully. 'John came round and saw our house, and he just stood there, saying, "Jeez, how can you live in this . . . *DUMP*?" I wanted to die, I was so ashamed.'

Josephine regarded her carefully. 'But?'

'Mum didn't say anything for *ages*, and I thought she'd never speak to me again for bringing him there.'

'He walked both of you home after . . . that evening.'

'Not then. He came back to talk about Sophia, and he saw our house in the day, with Dad sitting there looking miserable and all the . . . *mess*. And the dogs running around. *You* know.'

Yes, Josephine thought guiltily. But like everyone else, I never said anything.

'Then Mum said she suddenly saw it through his eyes, and he was right. She'd never realised how awful it was. She cried,' Abigail ended miserably. 'Really cried. Said it had all been to get away.'

'From what?' Whom?

Abigail looked at the ground and her face suffused. 'Dad, I think.'

Unseen, Josephine nodded. 'And they're sending you away?'

'*No.*' Abigail was fierce, the mouse quite disappeared. 'I *want* to go away. Going to boarding school was John's idea. He's been *brilliant*.'

You want to *live*, Josephine thought. Hooray for John Denver. She gave Abigail the address. 'Write to Emma and tell her.'

'You don't think she'll mind, do you?' Abigail asked humbly.

'Absolutely not,' said Josephine with conviction. 'Emma's much too nice for that.'

The morning Abigail's air letter reached Emma, she read it lying on a lounger by the pool in a bikini.

'Abby's coming to my school,' she called. 'And she's eating. Wow.'

'Good.'

Emilia had been subdued this holiday, distracted, had taken to examining the impersonality of her house, rented out to other people all summer except for the two weeks she spent here. 'Can't leave anything private. They don't look after things,' she grumbled.

Emma thought her grandmother seemed a bit depressed. So was she, and inclined to bad dreams, though lying in the sun, reading and swimming all day, shopping in the market, talking Spanish to the old gardener who had known her since she was a baby made her feel a little better.

It'll be all right, she thought, to have Abby at school. The thought cheered her up. She could talk to Abby about Sophia; no one else would understand.

While Emma read her letter again, Emilia went up to her bedroom at the top of the villa and dressed with very particular care.

The shaded house set on a hillside among orange orchards was shuttered, its face expressionless, as she got out of the taxi. She waited for it to drive away, then tapped with her fist on the closed front door. When it opened, she saw with a catch in her heart how greatly he had changed.

'I have looked forward to this so much, so much,' he said, gentle and loving, so full of joy her heart squeezed with hope. 'Come in, come in.'

'I was overjoyed to get your letter asking me to come,' she said, following him into the big, cool living room, its shutters half open. They drank small cups of bitter coffee with sweet, wafer-thin almond biscuits.

'How are you?' she asked. He had the walk of an old man, it was hard to watch, though he wasn't so very old at all. He smiled, went to his bookshelves, took down some heavy volumes.

'I wanted to show her to you as she was,' he said, putting them down before her, opening the photograph albums, full to bursting with pictures of his wife. 'I so wanted you to come, to show you these.'

Photographs. So many photographs. Emilia picked one up and examined it; his wife had had a sweet, serene, a *lovely* face.

'I loved her so,' he said. 'It hits hard, when they go, doesn't it? I wish I'd understood, a long time ago, and I could perhaps have been of more comfort to you when . . . Look how beautiful she was.' He had passed a trembling hand across his eyes.

Well, she thought, as the taxi bumped and lurched down the hillside, down the bad roads to the main road at the bottom, beside herself with shame, you silly, deluded old fool, you got what you wanted. You went there to hear a declaration of love.

And she had.

[illegible]

[illegible]

[illegible]

[illegible]

[illegible]

[illegible]

Chapter Twenty-Nine

The courtyard was very empty, so many people gone. Ron was buried in the small town he came from, Sophia was in prison, pleading diminished responsibility and self-defence, her story the subject of renewed outbursts on the effect of domestic violence on women. Andrew and Babe had gone, no one quite knew where, and Andrew's flat was up for sale. Melissa and Luvvie were both presently working in the North. Emma was back at school and Garcia was in New York. Five of them left, spread thin in the three big houses. Josephine, Emilia, Gordon and Barry. And Hosannah.

'It seems strange,' Barry observed, bumping into Josephine one damp evening as Concorde thundered over the Barnes reservoirs, arriving from New York. 'Garcia was on that so often, it seems funny not to see him coming through the gate with half a dozen cases, and Millie in tow, a couple of hours later.'

'Yes.'

'How's he doing?'

'OK. They work so hard, I don't think they have time for anything else. In that sense, it hardly matters to Garcia where he is. They'll be back on their feet and making money in no time – people like them always do.'

'People like what?'

She didn't answer.

It was strange, though. Garcia had never been here, at home, in a normal sense, but even in his absence he filled the house. Now he wasn't coming home at all, she often lay awake listening to the first planes coming over, unable to shake off the feeling that at any moment he would walk through the door.

'Do you miss him?'

She didn't want to ask herself that question.

Barry missed no-good, two-timing, vicious little Babe, was

grieving, desolate at losing him, despite what everyone said and thought: you're better off without him. Barry, more almost than anyone else she knew, understood love wasn't rational, that its meaning was reconciliation.

'You know,' he remarked. 'Some people are frightfully *married*. I always thought you and Garcia were, even though . . . I wonder if you realise how married you are?'

Even with Barry, it was too raw a question, and she retreated inside her house. With Ron and Sophia's house empty next door, while the stepbrother applied for permission to sell, through the courts, the terrace felt eerie, still and silent, brimming over with *absences*.

I don't like it here any more Josephine acknowledged to herself. The emptiness made her nervous, the beautiful, perfect Victorian house she had loved was no longer the home it once was, though, oddly enough, since her holiday, Emilia had been remarkably pleasant. Positively friendly.

'This feels very peculiar,' Garcia growled, waiting for the carousel to start and deliver him his luggage, on his way through JFK into Manhattan and his apartment, instead of flying like a homing pigeon for Heathrow.

Their second, all-important, month-long Far East Sorry Trip had gone extremely well, less confidence, less face lost than he and Millie had dared to hope. Things were tougher even than he had feared but there was no reason why, in the coming year, they shouldn't start looking up.

Vivian no longer needed them. When Emma went back to school and they could stop pretending everything was carrying on as normal, he and Josephine had agreed he would move to the apartment in New York, reverse-commute as necessary.

When he had agreed to that, she had agreed to a six-month stand-off before they talked about divorce.

Consigned to the wilderness, Garcia worked, hoped and waited.

The shops had put up their Christmas decorations. Saks, Tiffany's and FA Schwartz had bouncers working the entrances, controlling lines of people stretching half a dozen blocks queuing to get in. Christmas Day was just over a week away.

He had faxed Josephine. 'Emma and my mother will expect me home at Christmas. I will have to start right now making plausible excuses for being over here, unless I come—' His pen paused. He wanted to write 'home'. '—to Barnes.'

She had faxed back, on her office paper. 'Why don't you bring them to NY? I'll say, for once, I have too much work to go away and your bankruptcy means you must be over there. They'll be disappointed, but they'll believe it. Emma keeps telling me I'm getting more and more like you. My present to her is a new pair of skates, so you can take her to the Lincoln Center. If you were to invite Abigail, I think she'd be thrilled and that Bea would pay for the ticket. They'd both like to meet up again with John Denver who is not far away. New Canaan, Connecticut.'

They had agreed to keep their uncertainties from Emma, just explained that, his business being in difficulties, he had to go to America.

'She's used to it, after all,' Josephine had said pointedly.

In brand-new, very pretty offices smelling of fresh paint and new furniture, Garcia reviewed Josephine's fax, answered it with one agreeing to bring Emilia, Emma and Abigail over for Christmas and lie his head off about why.

All afternoon he dithered, an unaccustomed and uncomfortable state of mind. Abruptly, he decided he would do it. He found an envelope and put a British Airways return ticket, London to New York, inside. An open ticket, no card, no letter, no appeals, no ranting and raving, no *pressure*. Just an open, heartfelt invitation, and she would make her own decision.

He sealed it and had it couriered across.

'What are you going to do for Christmas?' Barry asked.

She knew he wanted to invite her round, for drinks and present opening and turkey. He had taken to having little dinner parties, inviting his straight friends for her to meet. They either wanted to go to bed with her or tell her all about their wives, generally both.

'Go to bed, I think, and sleep.'

Work mounted up and the weather was vile. Site visits were generally freezing, shopping a seasonal nightmare. Josephine hurried past Harrods where the traditional display of Christmas trees on the façade of the building swayed in a raw, biting wind, shoppers fighting to get in and out of the store. Knightsbridge Tube was crammed to its gills.

She sometimes felt overwhelmed by the commitments of work, had trouble with builders on a particularly important site in Fulham, was behind with a couple of quotes. There would be no time before Christmas to go and sort everything out.

An *Evening Standard* flyer, flapping on its board, shouted 'West Confessed to Twenty More Says Lay Visitor'.

Sophia, she thought, could still get life, like Rosemary West. The Prozac was her best defence. The thought that Sophia and Rosemary West might one day meet in prison was deeply disturbing, but unlikely. She would more likely spend most of her sentence in an open jail and be out in eight to ten years of a fifteen-year sentence.

Josephine wrote to her regularly, had no reply and guessed it would be a long time, if ever, before Sophia came out of her paralysing shame.

It turned colder and colder, winds flecked with tiny, icy snowflakes flayed the skin. Blizzards in the North, the Home Counties and London shortened the odds against a white Christmas. Even in central London there were frosts, hard, lasting all day, whitening gardens like a thin fall of snow.

Two mild days broke the cold spell, a dreary drizzle soaked the pavements. Leaves, slimy and treacherous, slicked the pavement outside Josephine's courtyard gate until the council street sweeper, in bright yellow oils and scabby gloves, dragged his shovel and cart along to scrape them up beneath the familiar roar of jets descending towards Heathrow. He glanced up as one screamed right over his head, unusually low, hidden by cloud.

At the very moment the incoming 747 released its wheels for landing, Hosannah's outgoing aeroplane lifted from the runway, hung for a moment straining for height, then vanished into the low cloud obscuring her last sight of England. President Clinton, brokering doubtful peace in the Balkans just in time for Christmas, gave the Home Office its chance to deliver her expulsion notice, along with a pile of Christmas cards for Garcia from people who did not know he had gone away. She was allowed two days to get ready.

The afternoon of the day she left, the telephone rang.

'Willy Flynn for you,' Josephine called.

Hosannah had sent Willy Flynn her rent book, fully paid to the last day, and the key to her little-used bed-sitting room, with a stilted, badly spelled note of thanks.

Josephine heard her end of a short conversation.

'No. Yes. Tomorrow. No. No. Willy Flynn, thank you. You a real gentleman.'

'What did he want?'

'He ask me to marry him so I can stay.'

Josephine had a surge of hope. 'That would keep you safe!'

Hosannah had looked scornful. 'Safe? More than one kinda prison,' she muttered darkly and went to finish packing.

You are a mean, self-centred, unkind and nasty person, Josephine scolded herself, but she couldn't help it. Her first thought when Hosannah had opened her deportation order was, how can they? Now I'll have to find a new housekeeper. She had become dependent on Hosannah, as she had on them, and finding a replacement would not be easy.

No one else was around. Emmanuel and Samantha would have made Christmas bearable but had flown off to their house in the Bahamas because Samantha was pregnant and wanted to lie in the sun while she could still wear a bikini.

Face it, Josephine told herself. By your own choice you have an empty house and are faced with nothing more festive for company that Rambo and Barney Darling, and a large pile of work.

Even the larder was empty.

Chiswick Sainsbury's was a zoo.

Josephine circled round and round the car park until a Rover pulled out in front of her. She reversed to let it pass, and a rusty Renault darted the wrong way round the system and shot into what should have been her space. Josephine leaned on the horn and two young men with crew cuts and earrings grinned triumphantly through the Renault's filthy windows.

'I have out-of-date bacon, rindy cheese, a bag of muesli a horse wouldn't thank me for, and a pile of Hosannah's revolting polenta,' she shouted.

Their faces mocked her.

No turkey, no parsnips, no plum pudding, no mince pies, no cream, no . . .

Pigs.

She cruised away.

Checkout queues stretched right to the back of the shop, every trolley piled to its limit with food.

'Mine,' she hissed, diving for the last of the small free-range turkeys, snatching it from under the nose of a young woman with acne and an infant bawling in a babycot.

A bored and cross-looking shelf filler in blue overalls shovelled diced venison into the chill cabinet to disguise the turkey shortage. The baby's howling drowned out the short, pithily explicit suggestion its teenage mother spat as she trundled her trolley angrily off towards frozen poultry and cheap Christmas crackers.

'Happy Christmas,' Josephine muttered.

Redcurrant jelly, cranberry sauce, bread sauce, bacon, pork stuffing, flour, bread, butter, cheese, a mini Christmas pudding, brandy butter, cream, mince pies, a bottle of sherry, fresh fruit, vegetables, eggs, biscuits, a small Christmas cake . . . At the end of the queue leading down the hardware aisle, she gazed at her shopping doubtfully. It was an awful lot of food for one person, but she couldn't put any of it back.

Leaning on her trolley, she tried to pass the time by meditating; a good mantra under these circumstances would be 'Profit, profit, profit'.

A small child in a pale blue anorak played in the crowded space, squatting on the floor, rearranging plastic jugs on the bottom shelf. The two youths from the Renault came round the corner and caught her, not badly, with their trolley wheel. Startled, she clambered off the floor, ran backwards and clutched at Josephine's coat, looked up expecting to see her mother.

'Hello,' Josephine said. 'Who are you?'

A slight woman with dark hair and eyes turned from the trolley in front and came to take her.

'Sorry,' she told Josephine. 'She will mess about. Chessie, come here and *stay* with me.'

A baby, maybe six months old, lolled in a babycot on top of her shopping, a moon-faced, passive little thing, staring up at the shop lights with vacant blue eyes. The child sat down on the floor in the shelter of her mother's legs and began sucking her thumb. The queue inched forwards, customers jammed together by people still doing their shopping, trying to get past. The mother opened her bag and took out a brown envelope from which she drew a new cheque book, ready for the till. The blue Barclay's cheques had a name and address printed on the tear-off label on the front: 'Mr and Mrs T. Morrissey, Morgan's Cottage, Morgan's Lane, Chiswick.'

Chessie. Francesca Morrissey. The child looked up and slid her thumb out of her mouth, her big brown eyes staring at Josephine staring at her. Janey Morrissey turned, half smiled, half apologetic.

'Janey Morrissey?'

Janey's smile wavered.

'Josephine Goddard.'

Stony-faced, Janey looked at the cheque book, understood what had happened and slowly put it back in her bag.

Josephine said slowly, 'We never met.'

Janey turned away, inched her trolley forwards and stood staring at its contents, trapped by needing her shopping, by the turmoil and overcrowding in the shop, her back signalling absolute rejection.

They shuffled closer to the checkout. A young man in a baker's white overalls was working it like a demon, hurling tins and packages down the belt, his scanner going *beep, beep, beep.*

Janey began to load her shopping on to the belt.

Josephine made one last effort. 'Would you have a coffee with me? In the coffee shop.'

Janey gathered her shopping and Francesca, went to walk away, involuntarily looked back, met Josephine's despairing eyes. 'Would you like a fizzy drink?' she asked Francesca abruptly.

Francesca skipped for joy as her mother turned her heavy trolley round and pushed it towards the coffee shop.

Chapter Thirty

The coffee shop was empty except for them, everyone else being desperate to get as far away from Sainsbury's as possible.

'What do you want?' Janey asked bluntly.

'You know what your husband did?'

Janey nodded almost imperceptibly, her baby passive in her lap.

'I need to know why.'

Janey's brown eyes were opaque, unreadable. 'We were stuck,' she said eventually. 'It was his way out.'

'Way out of *what*?' Their coffees lay between them, untouched and going cold.

'Our circumstances. I was pregnant without meaning to be, and we lived in a hopelessly unsuitable flat, with a negative mortgage and no hope of getting out.'

'He's a crook,' Josephine cried.

The woman behind the counter looked over curiously and Francesca slid off her chair and underneath the table.

'Don't think she's so young she doesn't understand anything. She does.'

Josephine bit her lip. 'But you stayed with him. He should have gone to prison.'

'Yes.'

The quiet admission took Josephine by surprise.

'And if he had, I'd have waited. It wouldn't have made any difference.' The baby fidgeted and began to whimper. 'He couldn't *earn* any more than he did.'

'Most people,' Josephine said bitterly, 'don't regard that as an excuse for crime.'

'I'm not making excuses for crime. You wanted me to explain. One thing I do know.' Janey took a bottle of baby milk out of her bag, pulled a face.

'Want that warmed up?' the woman called from over by her counter. She came over and took the bottle from Janey.

Francesca went with her, to watch her.

'What?'

'If your husband and Millie had made Tom feel he could say, look, I'm out of my depth, he'd never had begun fixing the books. It was a case of one thing leading to another. He didn't *want* to do it. How do you think he felt, yelled at and insulted when he was doing his best? It's as much their fault as his.'

Josephine stared, aghast.

'And the children need him,' Janey said. 'When I first found out, I went off to stay with my parents and told them Tom and I were having a bit of difficulty after Isobel was born.'

Their eyes travelled to the baby.

'Down's,' Janey said. 'Francesca never stopped crying for her daddy. I couldn't bear it.'

Josephine nodded. Emma had cried as a little girl every time Garcia went away, thought aeroplanes went up in the air for ever and ever and never came down again.

'If you're going to wish punishment on him, you should have a look at her,' Janey added, indicating her baby. 'I was in such a state when I was pregnant, the doctor gave me Valium. Tom knows it's nonsense, the doctor's told him time and time again, but he has this idea fixed in his head that it's the Valium that did something to damage her. Isobel is Tom's life sentence,' Janey said simply. 'Every time he looks at her, he remembers what he's guilty of. Didn't your husband ever do something you needed to forgive him for?'

Oh, God. Janey Morrissey was a better person than she would ever be.

The woman from the counter and Francesca brought the bottle back.

'Thank you,' Janey said.

I've got to get out of here. 'I think I understand. I needed to know.'

'Yes. You would,' Janey answered.

'I'm terribly, *terribly* sorry.'

Isobel sucked contentedly as Josephine pushed the flimsy table away and fled.

* * *

Fighting rush-hour traffic all the way took an hour and a half as far as Hammersmith Bridge. Crawling across the bridge, she looked out over the river, black and gleaming with lights, remembered the van driver who got stuck, and a young painter working on the side, who fell to his death that summer.

On the second try, she got through on her mobile to their lugubrious travel agent in New York.

'Can you get me a seat between now and Christmas Day? To JFK?' She could hear his breathing.

'It would be easier for you to grow wings yourself.'

'Can you try? Please?' If anyone could get a seat on a British Airways plane when it was impossible, he could.

The windscreen wipers thumped and swished as rain, turning to snow, swept across London. She turned them up to high speed as she sped down Castelnau. As she waited at the lights near Riva where she had had lunch so long ago, or so it seemed, the phone rang.

'I've called in every favour they ever owed me. Now *you* owe *me*,' he said. 'Tomorrow, eight forty-five flight.'

'Happy, happy, *happy* Christmas,' she cried, and accelerated away.

She threw the food in the freezer and Barry said he'd take the dogs, keep an eye on the house. When she called, Emma picked up the phone.

'Mum! Do you want me to get Dad?'

'Please.'

As she waited, Josephine eyed the clutter on her desk.

'Jo?'

'We'll *both* pay the bloody bills,' she said. 'And I'll get a cab from JFK. With three feet of snow, there's no reason for you to turn out.'

'I'll meet you,' he said.

After they cut the connection, she realised he didn't have her flight number, not even the date. He'd find out from the airline. Garcia was good at that.

The Lincoln Center was crowded with skaters and spectators, music whirling, like the snowflakes, through giant angels' mighty gilded trumpets.

Emma twirled, did a long, lazy figure of eight, then flew away and danced by herself to the music.

'Did you say your parents were splitting up?' John Denver Jr called, catching her up.

'Yeah. They think I don't know why Dad's over here all the time and Mum's looking miserable. They always think kids don't know anything,' Emma called back, swooping away, 'but they jolly well do,' she cried, swooping back, bright with cold and exercise. 'That's why I'm glad Mum came.'

Abigail flew over to join them.

'Well, have a look at that, know-all,' John Denver ordered, pointing to the railing where Garcia and Josephine were watching them.

Among the hustling, jostling crowds, Emma could see her parents, their arms round each other, lost in a long, long kiss. Joy bloomed and blossomed in Emma's chest, left her breathless, aching with relief.

'Oh, *yuk*,' she yelled, hurling herself against John Denver. 'I love you.'

Arms linked with Abigail in the middle, the three friends swept away, whirling and twirling, dancing and dancing and dancing to the cold sound of the music, dancing over the ice.